DEADLY FAUX PAS

AN AMERICAN IN PARIS MYSTERY BOOK 6

SUSAN KIERNAN-LEWIS

SAN MARCO PRESS

Murder Flambé

Ella Out of Time
Swept Away
Carried Away
Stolen Away

The French Women's Diet

1

The child's screams raced up and down my last nerve.

I steadied myself against the kitchen counter and turned toward the sound. But before I could speak, my sitter called from the bedroom.

"Don't worry, Missus B! I got him! C'mere you little monster!"

Piercing giggles followed, nearly as shrill as the screams just seconds before.

I took in a breath and let it out slowly.

I recognized that it wasn't little Robbie that was exacerbating my stress, although granted he wasn't helping. It was the impending arrival of my dearest and only child Catherine and my grandson that had me agitated. *Correction.* I'm pretty sure if it were just those two I wouldn't be in the state I now found myself in.

Todd was coming too.

I turned and glanced at the vintage ceramic clock in the kitchen of my Parisienne apartment. It wasn't quite five o'clock. They were due to arrive any moment.

I turned to look at the dining table. It was set with my best china and silver—vintage flea market finds—and with borrowed crystal from my downstairs neighbor Geneviève. I hadn't lit the candles yet but there were two small vases of peonies sitting at both ends of the table.

I'd last seen Catherine a year ago when she visited me here in Paris. When she left, the chasm of misunderstanding and reproach between us had taken nearly the whole year to even start to close up.

Thanks to Todd.

I knew that probably wasn't fair to Todd and I made an effort to scold myself for the thought. What had happened between me and Catherine was my fault for setting up an expectation that my dear girl couldn't help but try to meet. And when she failed—believing that she'd let me down—she had turned away from me.

All my fault.

I walked to the window in the living room and glanced out, half expecting to see the taxi pull up below where Catherine and her little family would disembark.

In my mind I saw Catherine look up, searching the windows that she knew belonged to my apartment, and smiling when she saw my face. I saw little Cameron, whom I hadn't seen in over a year, follow his mom's example, his little face erupting in barely contained excitement.

"Missus B?"

I turned to see my thirteen year old sitter Haley standing in the hallway, my rambunctious little ward—all two and a half years of him—grinning as she held him on her hip.

"Should I give the Robster his bath now? He's not gonna wanna miss all the fun."

I came over to give the toddler a kiss.

"Good idea," I said. "And thanks for staying this evening, Haley. I'll call you an Uber to send you home."

"No problem," she said before turning to disappear into my ensuite bathroom with Robbie.

I have no idea what I would do without that girl, I found myself thinking. Not only was she wonderful with Robbie, but he adored her.

Not to mention the fact that she'd actually protected him with her life one night last spring by single-handedly fighting off a murdering intruder. Thinking of all my loved ones whom Haley had in fact kept safe that night, I turned in search of my adorable and extremely precocious French bulldog Izzy. I found her where I should never be surprised to find her—sitting in her bed in the kitchen, waiting for something to fall from the counter.

"Dinner time?" I said to her which prompted her to jump up and begin running in tight little circles on the parquet floor in anticipation.

As I made her dinner, my thoughts drifted back to how this whole life-in-Paris thing had begun two years ago and how amazing it was that I was really here now.

Two years ago on my anniversary trip to Paris with my husband I was violently widowed, then placed under suspicion for his murder, and finally when the dust settled found myself living in this gorgeous two-million-euro apartment in the eighth arrondissement in Paris.

Yes, a lot had happened in the past two years, not the least of which was my becoming the legal guardian to my late husband's love child Robbie. I'd recently had his name legally changed to match my own: Baskerville. Someday I would tell him all about his mother and father, but in the meantime I intended to make sure he had as wonderful a childhood as I could give him.

Unfortunately it had been Robbie that had driven the wedge between me and Catherine.

I set Izzy's dinner bowl on the floor. With so many people

sitting at the dining table tonight—especially my eight-year-old grandson Cameron—I had no doubt Izzy would come in for her share of dropped tidbits.

The sounds of laughter and singing came to me from the bathroom as Haley gave Robbie his bath. I decided that five o'clock was plenty late enough to smooth the jangles out of my nerves and reached for the bottle of Pinot Noir to pour myself a glass.

The last time Catherine came to visit me she'd done it alone because Todd had refused to allow Cameron to accompany her. A part of me wished that Catherine could see what I saw, that Todd was controlling and self-serving. But you can't make someone see something if they don't want to see it and I often worried about what kind of a person that made *me*, wanting her to be dissatisfied in her marriage.

But knowing and feeling are two different things as I know well enough. Which was why I was presently crawling with agitation to see the three of them again.

I knew my acting skills would be put to the test as they'd never been before for the whole of their visit with me.

A knock at the door prompted Izzy to bark mid-gulp in her dinner which resulted in an unfortunate coughing attack. Haley called from the bathroom, "Is that them?"

I took a quick swig of my wine and glanced around my dining room before meeting Izzy at the door where she was anxiously waiting for me to open it.

I opened the door and found my downstairs neighbor Geneviève on my threshold.

Eighty-four years old Geneviève Rousseau lived one floor below me. Wise and calm—especially considering the turmoil I tend to bring to the apartment building on a fairly regular basis —she had become one of my dearest friends in Paris.

"*Chérie*, you look beautiful!" Geneviève said as she entered the apartment, stooping briefly to greet Izzy. "And it smells wonderful!"

She would have reason to take some pride herself in that since she was the one who'd helped me decide what to make for tonight's welcome dinner. She had also helped do half the prep work even though she had her own very special guests about to arrive this evening.

I moved back into the kitchen.

"Why am I so nervous?" I asked as I poured her a glass of the wine and topped off my own.

"It is always nerve-wracking to play a role that is not natural to you," she said as she took her wineglass from me.

"You are referring to the role of loving mother, I presume?" I said with an arched eyebrow.

She laughed.

"You know very well I am not. Family is not always decided by blood. I think family is who we say they are. What time are you expecting them?"

"I thought your knock might have been them. What about you? When is Noel due in?"

Geneviève had twin sons she had not seen in nearly ten years. Both were gay and there had been an unfortunate altercation with their father a decade ago for which Geneviève had sadly paid the price. To Geneviève's immense joy, her son Noel had reached out to her last Christmas and was bringing his American husband for a visit at the same time that Catherine and Todd would be staying with me.

She had told me many times that it wasn't the twins' fault for the breach. They'd been badly hurt by their father's rejection. But Geneviève's husband had been dead nearly six years and before last year, neither twin had attempted to reconnect with their mother.

I know Geneviève was beyond thrilled to be reunited with at least one of her sons, but I was still predisposed not to like him because of his lengthy disconnect from her. Many a night I'd seen the sadness in Geneviève's face and knew it was because she was thinking of her boys.

Haley came into the living room with Robbie in his pajamas. He instantly ran to Geneviève squealing *"Mamie!"* As I watched her kneel and throw her arms around the toddler, I found myself worrying yet again about the language confusion I was generating with Robbie.

While my French was adequate, I spoke mainly English to him. Plus, Haley, a rising junior at the American School in Paris, was practically anti-French and had learned only enough French to order a *pain au chocolat* at the local *boulangerie*.

Yet, Geneviève—who served as a grandmother for Robbie and likely the only one he would ever get if you don't count me —spoke to him in French. I get that. He reminded her of her own little lads from many years ago and, for Geneviève, the art of babytalk was definitely in French.

As a result, Robbie babbled in a fascinating mixture of French, English and Franglais. Adorable, yes, but I wondered how in the world his little brain was sorting it all out.

"Wow," Haley said as she stepped into the kitchen. "That smells great."

"If you can keep the little man occupied," I said to her, "I'll prepare a plate for the both of you. I'd like for Catherine to see Robbie so we'll need to keep him up a little later than usual."

"No problem," Haley said, holding her hand out to Robbie. The child swiveled away from Geneviève and charged after Haley. Izzy followed, wagging her stubby little tail in happy anticipation.

"Has Catherine said any more about taking Robbie?" Geneviève asked in a low voice as she sat in one of the dining room chairs.

Last summer Catherine and I had both come to the conviction that she should take her half-brother Robbie back to the States and raise him with her son Cameron. It would allow Robbie to have some semblance of a stable family life and it would also allow Catherine, who had not been able to conceive in the eight years since Cam, to expand her family.

But after the catastrophe last summer, Catherine had gone

home alone and nothing more had been said about the idea. Unfortunately the annihilation of our idea—and the unspoken acknowledgement that that demolition had been because of her husband Todd—had then proceeded to create the rift between us. Although ostensibly it was Todd's outright rejection of the plan that was the reason why Catherine didn't take Robbie, the chasm between us was created because Catherine thought I blamed her for not standing up to her husband.

Nothing could be further from the truth. Well, that was an exaggeration. At first I *had* prayed Catherine would stand up to him but, in the end, I saw that even if she succeeded in taking Robbie home with her, I didn't trust Todd not to mistreat him or at the very least make him feel unloved and unwanted every day of his life.

That, I could not allow.

And so in the end I was the reason she hadn't taken him.

"It's a subject we take pains not to broach," I said to Geneviève. "She always asks about Robbie so I know she still cares. But she tries not to care too much. Walking away from him last summer was just so painful."

"Of course," Geneviève said, clucking in that way that the French do to convey a myriad of different emotions or messages, none of which I've ever been able to accurately interpret. "And what about Jean-Marc? Have you heard from him?"

I nearly laughed out loud. If Geneviève was bent on making sure I stopped obsessing about Catherine and Todd's impending visit, she was doing a good job.

Jean-Marc was the American-hating French detective who'd initially tried to detain me for the murder of my own husband two years ago and who had become something altogether different as our acquaintance developed.

Just as our relationship had—amazingly—started to evolve into something I never would have imagined for myself in my sixties—*a romantic episode*—a calamity, triggered by me, shattered what had been started between us.

I take the blame for that because on the face of it there was no other way to look at it. I've had Geneviève and my good friend Adele Coté analyze what happened last summer a thousand different times and in their versions there was nothing else I could have done. Jean-Marc's wife had been on a collision course with catastrophe for years and my involvement in her life was irrelevant to that momentum.

On good days I believed them. On not so good days I saw it the way Jean-Marc saw it—that I had been the instrument of Chloe's death.

"I haven't heard from him," I said. "Not since he took that job in Nice last fall."

Technically I had talked to Jean-Marc since then. I called him last spring during a desperate moment. And while at that time he very quickly let me know he was no longer open to communication with me he did call back a few weeks later to ask how I was doing. Which was nice but nothing more.

The bottom line though, however, was no. Jean-Marc wasn't a part of the equation anymore.

Tant pis, as the French say.

Too bad.

3

After Geneviève left to go back downstairs to get ready for her own guests—they would come up later for dinner—I went to the kitchen to do last-minute touches on the *blanquet de veau*. I already felt more balanced and grounded after Geneviève's visit (I'm sure the two glasses of Pinot didn't hurt.)

I put some Ella Fitzgerald on the HomePod even though it conflicted terribly with the zany sounds of the children's show *Oggy and the Cockroaches* that Haley and Robbie were watching in the living room.

I took in a deep breath and then let it out. It had been weeks since I'd gone to my yoga class and I badly missed the meditative component of the practice. In my business, being able to step outside the clamor and chaos of my job was absolutely essential.

As a private investigator whose clients are nearly exclusively American or British expats, I make a decent living here in Paris.

And that was necessary since my husband Bob died leaving me financially high and dry with a city full of creditors, a foreclosed townhouse in Atlanta, and zeroed-out retirement funds.

Here in Paris I had a place to live—thanks to my adoptive father Claude Lapin who died and left me this apartment along with a little money. My work with the Paris expats helped fill in the gaps to pay the bills. Even with a paid-for apartment, Paris is an expensive place to live.

As a private investigator, I am basically a people-finder. I track down cheating spouses or runaways and perform any of the other mostly unsavory things the average private detective does—uncover credit card debt, dig up job histories and criminal records, track down people trying to skip out on their bills—and generally address the basic unpleasantries of life.

Back in the States I did skip tracing which was more computer-oriented than what I do here in Paris which is a whole lot of running around knocking on doors. But in the new version of my job here in Paris I find getting out on the streets, following people, watching them, questioning them and seeing how they live is infinitely more interesting.

I'm not sure what that says about me but I've learned not to examine those proclivities too closely.

As I got the salad compiled in its bowl ready for dressing, there was a hard knock at the door that I didn't recognize. Catherine's tap would've been more tentative—so was Geneviève's come to think of it. I forced myself not to think of how Jean-Marc's knock on my door once sounded.

This knock sounded like someone wanted to serve me with a subpoena.

It had to be Todd.

"I think they're here!" I sang out to Haley and Robbie as I dried my hands on a kitchen towel, checked my appearance one last time in the hall mirror and hurried to let them in.

"Darling!" I said as I opened the door on the three of them.

Instantly my grandson Cameron hurtled into my arms. I kissed his face and hugged him tightly before pulling back to get a good look at him. It had been so long and I was breathless with the realization of how much he'd changed.

At eight years old, he was taller than I expected. His brown hair hung in a shag mostly in his eyes—eyes that reminded me so much of my late husband Bob. And then he grinned and he was simply and only himself, my dearest grandson.

"Oh, my darling boy," I said, tears springing to my eyes. "I've missed you so much!"

"Me, too, Grammy!" Cam said and then peeked behind me at Haley and Robbie who stood, waiting.

I released him and turned to Catherine. I held out my arms and she walked into them.

"Mom," she said, giving my arms a squeeze before pulling back, her cue for me to now greet Todd.

I turned to him, the smile on my face already hurting in the effort.

"Todd," I said as he stepped in for a hug. "How good to see you!"

I noticed that Catherine was looking past me at Haley, Robbie and Cameron. It hadn't taken five seconds and the three children were already talking animatedly among each other.

I credited that mostly to Haley who tended to be very straightforward with her feelings or intentions. As I watched the children I suddenly saw Haley as Catherine and Todd must see her—with her heavy eyeliner, facial piercings, goth stud collar and dressed in all black down to her motorcycle boots. I don't know why I hadn't realized before how she must appear to them. I guess I'm so used to seeing her that I don't see the strange attire anymore.

Nothing to be done about it now.

"And this is Haley," I said too cheerfully as Todd and Catherine moved into the living room while I closed the front door. "And of course Robbie."

"Hello, munchkin," Catherine said, going to Robbie. She knelt in front of him. "Do you remember me?"

Robbie is not a shy child but I recognized immediately the moment that he became overwhelmed by the noise, the attention and the strangers in his house. He turned away from Catherine and buried his face in Haley's knee. I watched Catherine's shoulders stiffen at the rejection and I wanted to take her into my arms.

Do mothers ever stop caring about even the slightest injuries to their children?

"It's well past his bedtime," I said to Catherine as she got to her feet. "He's pretty tired."

Robbie lifted his arms to Haley in the age-old mime of *pick me up* and she obliged before turning to Cameron.

"Want to see his remote-control helicopter?" she asked.

"Heck, yeah!" Cameron said and followed her into my bedroom where we'd moved Robbie's bed while Catherine and her family were visiting.

"Which is our bedroom?" Todd asked as he picked up their suitcases and moved to the only other bedroom not filled with laughing children.

My face already ached from the frozen smile on it but before I could ask Catherine if she wanted a glass of something, Todd emerged from the guest room and went to the door of my bedroom.

"Cameron!" he called, careful not to enter the bedroom. "Come wash up for dinner."

He just wants to interrupt his fun, I thought before I could stop myself.

"I will in a minute, Dad," Cameron said.

"Now!" Todd said firmly.

That was the moment when I saw what was going on. In spite of Catherine's best efforts to make me believe otherwise, I saw the truth mapped out in living color across the walls of my apartment.

Todd had resented Catherine's attachment to Robbie last summer which he clearly saw as another version of my attempt to woo her away from him. And now he was watching his son fall under Robbie's spell too.

That was also the moment I began to wonder why they were here. Had Catherine begged him? Had his allowing Cam to come to Paris required that *he* come too? Or was Catherine hoping futilely to position Todd such that he would meet and fall in love with Robbie himself?

My heart ached for her. Because if that was her plan, I could've saved her the cost of the international flight. Not only was Todd never going to be open to taking Robbie, the time had passed when I was open to it too.

Robbie was a part of my life. A very big part. I was not letting him go.

It was Catherine my heart broke for. If she'd only told me what her plan was—but I mentally shook off that notion. Because even if we'd been in a place where we could honestly share with each other, she wouldn't have been open to hearing what I had to say. My poor darling girl was all alone in her desperate scheme to win Todd over to her side and bring Robbie home with her.

And the worst of it? From a mother's point of view?

I couldn't even comfort her without making it worse.

4

I knew getting Robbie to go down with the sounds of so many adult voices in the other room was going to be difficult, but Haley was a master at distracting the child with stories at bedtime. Cameron had begged to come too when she took Robbie into my room but Todd wouldn't hear of it.

"You'll just keep him awake," he said, pointing to Cam's place at the dinner table.

I stomped on my immediate impulse to say something to soften the rebuke to Cam but I knew better than to countermand an order from his father. I could think of few instances more tedious for an eight-year-old than being forced to sit at a dinner with adults. But Cameron sat, his head down in glum acceptance.

I turned my attention away from my unhappy grandson and reminded myself that this was exactly the sort of ongoing situation I'd been expecting during their visit and I couldn't react the very first night they were here.

I turned to my other two dinner guests, Geneviève's son Noel and his husband Bill. Both were lively and convivial conversationalists. Geneviève on the other hand was unusually quiet tonight as she watched the son she hadn't seen in so many years.

"It must be so exciting what you do," Bill said to me, his eyes bright with interest.

An American high school English teacher living in Nashville, Bill had met Noel when they were both at an educators' conference in Paris five years ago.

Out of the corner of my eyes I saw Catherine lean toward Cam and murmur in a low voice to him.

"Well, it has its moments," I said to Bill. "Has Geneviève told you any wild stories? Because you can't believe everything you hear."

Geneviève laughed and waved a dismissive hand in my direction.

"Everything I've told them is the truth!" she said. "It is never a dull moment since Claire Baskerville has moved into the building."

She turned a loving, doting eye on her son who sat to her left. Noel was a handsome man in his late forties. Like most French men he wasn't immediately forthcoming, but I'd caught several fond glances toward his mother during the course of the meal.

"Did you hear the news about the virus?" Todd asked, his voice at least several decibels above anyone else. I forced myself not to cringe. Not that he was the quintessential Ugly American, but he did tend to make himself heard as if he were afraid he might not be.

"Oh, it will stay in Germany," Geneviève assured him.

"Really?" Catherine asked as she rubbed Cam's back. "What makes you think so?"

"Our leaders are hypervigilant," she said.

Todd turned to Catherine.

"We better keep an eye on it," he said. "In case we have to reschedule our flight to leave early."

"Oh, Todd," Catherine said in a strained voice. "I'm sure it'll be fine."

"You *want* it to be fine," he corrected. "As usual with you, reality is a very different prospect."

"What do you think, Noel?" Bill asked. "Worried about getting trapped in Paris?"

Noel grinned and leaned toward him. "Can you think of a better place to be trapped?"

"Do you think they'll impose a lockdown?" Todd asked, his fingers drumming the table as he spoke.

"There is nothing to worry about!" Geneviève said. "Everything will be fine, *je suis sûr.*"

"More wine, anyone?" I said to general laughter. I noticed that Todd didn't laugh.

"I'm serious," he said, pulling out his phone. "I don't want to get stuck here. I have a major meeting in Tallahassee in two weeks."

"Mom?" Cam asked quietly. "Can I be excused from the table?"

Catherine nodded and Cam slipped away to my bedroom where I could hear Haley's voice as she read to Robbie.

It made me angry that Cam had to sneak away to spend time with Robbie but I reminded myself that this was the situation I was challenged to endure and getting angry was not going to help.

"They say the cases are mounting in Paris!" Todd said as he looked up from his phone.

"I really don't think it's anything to worry about," I said and was sorry as soon as I did.

"Of course, *you* don't think there's anything to worry about," Todd said, his lip curled in a sneer. "You would like nothing better than to have us trapped here."

Possibly not all of you, I thought as I busied myself with collecting everyone's dinner plates.

"Raspberry torte and coffee," I said. "Who needs decaf?"

"We'd better," Catherine said giving Todd an uncertain look. "Our sleep schedule is already so screwed up. Better not make it worse."

"You don't need coffee at all," Todd said as he frowned at his phone.

I knew I shouldn't look at her but I couldn't help it. Was she going to let him get away with that? But she wouldn't look at me and so the moment passed. I went to the kitchen and put on the kettle for the coffee and began cutting the torte.

Geneviève joined me in the kitchen.

"You are not really worried, *chérie*?" she asked.

"About the virus? No. It is what it is."

We could hear raised voices coming from the dinner table and I felt an urge to run to my bedroom and close the door so the children wouldn't hear.

"But we just got here!" Catherine said.

"I'm sure the president will let us know in time if they're going to impose a lockdown," Noel said calmly.

"How would *you* know?" Todd said. "You haven't lived in France in a decade."

I turned to Geneviève.

"I'm sorry Todd is being an ass," I said.

"Do not worry, *chérie*," she said, patting my arm. "Every family has one."

"I just can't see why she puts up with him."

"She does because of the boy," Geneviève said with a shrug.

I knew she was right but I still hated it. Divorce *would* be terrible for Cam and it wouldn't be great for Catherine either, especially financially.

Not to mention I wasn't entirely sure she wasn't still in love with Todd.

"How is he with Robbie?" she asked.

"Pretending he doesn't exist. Doing his best to keep Catherine and Cam away from him."

Geneviève nodded as if she wasn't surprised.

"It's only a few days," she said. "Try to enjoy being with your daughter and grandson."

"Todd's not making it easy."

"I know, *chérie*," she said with a smile. "But when have you ever done anything easy?"

5

Later that evening after Geneviève and Noel and Bill had gone downstairs to Geneviève's apartment, Todd took Cameron to settle him down for the night. Haley had gone home an hour earlier.

I was in the kitchen trying to decide if I should let the dishes soak or tackle them now when Izzy came and sat in the doorway emitting a low rumbling growl. It was not aggressive, in fact it was more of a whine than a growl. But it was still a communication that told me in no uncertain terms that it was time for her to be let out.

I dried my hands and reached for her leash by the front door when I noticed that Catherine was standing in the living room staring out the window.

"Catherine?"

She turned toward me.

"Are you okay?"

She nodded and walked over to me.

"Last call?" she asked, nodding at Izzy.

"I'll just take her downstairs to the courtyard," I said, lifting my voice up at the end as if to invite her to come.

We walked downstairs in silence, Izzy pulling on her leash the whole way while I gripped the railing. At sixty-three I didn't take even the simple act of walking downstairs for granted. I knew how easy it was to miss a step.

Once we reached the courtyard I found myself at a loss for words. I'd worked so hard not to react to what I'd seen tonight between Catherine and Todd—and between Cam and Todd—that it had pushed any natural responses I might have had with my daughter out of my head.

There were so many verbal land mines to step around.

"You must be exhausted," I said. "Feel free to sleep late tomorrow."

"Cam won't sleep late," she said wearily.

"No, but I'll be up so he'll be fine."

She nodded and didn't say more. I knew she was disappointed in how Todd had behaved around Robbie—which was to basically ignore him unless she or Cam got too close to the child. I knew her master plan to get her husband to accept Robbie had failed miserably, right out of the gate.

"Do you think you're ever coming home?" Catherine asked as we waited for Izzy to sniff at a geranium planter. It had been a hot day and the heat seemed to stay in the air, thick around us like a heavy shawl.

"You mean for a visit?"

"No, I mean permanently. Are you here for good?"

I needed to tread carefully here. I didn't want to indict her father by way of my explanation if I could help it.

"I have a good life here," I said. "A comfortable one."

"You couldn't have a comfortable life back in the States?"

"Not in the same way. Hurry up, Izzy!"

"Why not?"

I sighed. How to explain what I was almost positive she already knew?

I could fill out a lengthy list of all the reasons I couldn't go back: I had her father's creditors waiting for me back in the States, I had no place to live back in the States, I was too old, too irrelevant, and virtually unemployable back in the States.

Plus—not that it was a big reason to stay— but in the two years that I've lived in Paris I'd gotten used to the fact that men once more turn to look at me when I enter a room or walk by their café table.

It had been a long time since that happened in the US. It had taken a long time to get over the fact that it never happened anymore.

Who am I kidding? I don't think any woman once she hits fifty ever gets over their new status as invisible alien.

I'm not invisible in France. It would be hard to give that up.

"A lot of reasons," I said evasively.

"Have you heard from your father recently?" she asked abruptly.

Now that did take me by surprise. While I'd vaguely outlined the situation to Catherine about my biological father —a crazy crime lord living in Dubai who felt he was exhibiting fatherly concern by banishing anyone from my life who he felt had disrespected me—Catherine had never asked me about him until this moment.

I turned to look at her, perplexed about where the question was coming from.

"I was just wondering," she said with a shrug.

"He hasn't contacted me," I said. "Not since last summer."

That was the truth as far as it went. It was true I'd received no more mysterious text messages from my father Philippe Moreau and I'd not felt that incessant creeping sensation on the back of my neck that made me feel as if someone was watching or following me. But in the two years that the man had made himself known to me—and I chalk up at least two murders in his column, one of which I believed to be my husband—I knew not to trust that he was done with me yet.

"That's good, I guess," she said. She rubbed her bare arms as if she were cold which had to be impossible since even tonight the heat stayed trapped in the courtyard, hemmed in by four foot thick brick walls.

"Sometimes I wonder what Robbie will think about Dad, you know?" she said.

"I intend to tell him about your father."

Only the good things.

We started to move back toward the door to my apartment building.

"I hate that he won't have a father growing up," she said.

That sounded like capitulation to me and for a moment I felt relief when I heard her say the words. But I also knew she was fishing for me to argue with her, hoping that I had a different view of how things might go.

As much as I wanted to give her what she was looking for, I couldn't bear to do it. She deserved the truth. And the truth was that Robbie wasn't going to have a father or a family unless you counted two elderly women and a French bulldog.

"What about Jean-Marc?" she said as we entered the building. "Do you ever see or hear from him?"

"Nope," I said breezily. "That ship has sailed."

Sailed and then sunk to the bottom of the lowest level of the deepest ocean.

"Too bad. I liked him."

That surprised me since the one time Catherine had met Jean-Marc, she had behaved very aloof with him. I'd thought at the time that if she'd just give him a chance she would like him. But then things with Chloe blew up and Jean-Marc left town so that, as they say, was that.

As we mounted the slick stairs to the third floor I couldn't bear the distance between us any longer.

"Is there anything you want to tell me, darling?" I asked.

"Like what?"

I knew by her sudden sharp tone that she was about to answer me in full daughterly irritation. Combined with her jet lag, I wouldn't fault her for that but then she did something that surprised me.

She told me the truth.

"I thought he'd change his mind once he saw Robbie," she said.

"I'm so sorry, sweetheart."

"It's okay," she said, leaning on the bannister as if every step up the stairs was more laborious than the one before.

My heart went out to her. I knew she wanted Robbie in her life and I loved her to bits for wanting him.

But the fact was, it *was* okay.

Now I just had to get her to the point where she realized that.

Regardless of how we all got there.

6

The sun was so hot you could actually feel the heat drill up through your very soles from the famous stones of the Champs-Élysées.

The visit to the Arc de Triomphe had been my idea. It was close to my apartment—only about fifteen blocks away—and surrounded by dozens of cafés and bistros for us to enjoy along the way.

Unfortunately I'd forgotten I was dealing with Americans.

Not that I'm not American myself of course, but after two years of living here, I'd filed some of the sharper American edges off. I was now slower and more deliberate than when I first arrived. I saw the point in spending an hour at a café just to watch life go by. It had taken me a while and I'm by no means as insouciant as the French, but I'm working on it.

When I suggested that we go to the Arc de Triomphe today, I was seeing an opportunity for a lovely stroll, possibly a lengthy stop at Parc Monceau along the way and certainly at least two stops at cafés to hydrate, nibble on tasty things and people watch.

Catherine, but more particularly Todd, saw the outing as a

starkly underlined goal of *Going To the Arc de Triomphe.* Do not pass Go, do not dilly-dally, and once you've reached your destination, stop and analyze whether it had been actually worth the effort.

I've been in Paris long enough to know that every outing, every errand, even every walk in the park was really about the journey.

So, since I'd forgotten that key element of dealing with People-Who-Are-Not-French, the outing was ill-fated from the get-go.

Todd allowed Catherine to push Robbie in his stroller since I had my hands full with Izzy on her leash and there was no other option unless he wanted to appear even more of a jerk than he already had. At least he still cared about how he looked.

Cameron took over pushing the stroller from time to time and every time he did I could see Todd stiffen in annoyance. Fortunately, there was so much to see along the way—cafés, colorful stationery shops, dogs, beautiful women sauntering by in beautiful clothes—that we were all at least minimally distracted by the walk.

I'd made coffee this morning and had Pop Tarts and cereal for Cameron, but my primary plan was to stop at one of my favorite cafés along the way for espressos and pastries. While Catherine seemed to adapt well enough to what she clearly saw as a detour from the task at hand—which was getting to and then checking off seeing the Arc de Triomphe from her list— Todd only became more agitated.

I quickly realized that there was no way we were going to be able to enjoy a pleasant hour in a café watching skateboarders, bicyclists and pedestrians stroll by. Not with Todd drumming his fingers on the table and fanning himself as if he were a disgruntled southern belle being stood up at the plantation barbecue.

Robbie, long used to such stops, refrained from climbing out of his stroller and contented himself with making faces at Cameron and throwing bits of *pain au chocolat* at Izzy.

"Can you get him to stop doing that?" Todd said, frowning at Robbie. "He's making a mess."

I felt my blood pressure rise. Cameron immediately pulled back from Robbie and began to focus on his own *pain au chocolat*. I pretty much hated Todd at that moment but I swallowed down my irritation for the sake of family unity. Or something like that.

Todd of course knew that Catherine had wanted to bring Robbie back to the States with her last year. He was acting as if he was afraid he was still going to end up stuck with him.

How I wish I could reassure him without causing a major family eruption.

"Are we near?" Catherine asked as she pushed her espresso cup away and picked up her phone to look at her map.

"Oh, it's very close," I assured her. "You don't remember from last summer?"

"I don't think we ever did the tourist thing, did we?" she asked, squinting at her phone.

"Why are we sitting outside?" Todd asked petulantly. "Surely they have AC inside?"

He twisted in his seat to glare at the few patrons inside who, obviously in his mind, had been lucky enough to snag better seating.

"It's in order to people watch," I said, knowing that nothing I said would matter.

He snorted and wiped a sheen of sweat from his forehead.

"Relax, Todd," Catherine said, still looking at her phone.

"Don't tell me to relax," he snapped at her.

I saw Cameron's body brace and he turned to me.

"Tell me more about the Arch, Grammy," he said.

I instantly recognized the time-worn deportment of a child

trying to camouflage the unhappiness that was impossible to ignore between his parents. My heart went out to him and I wondered if Catherine was aware of the extra work she was forcing on her son by making him attempt to assuage or mitigate the friction between her and Todd.

"Well," I said to Cameron as I dunked my croissant in my café au lait, "the Arc de Triomphe was designed in the early eighteen hundreds. It was built to honor all those who fought and died for France in the French Revolutionary War and the Napoleonic Wars."

"Wow."

"If you want we can climb to the top," I said. "You get an incredible view of Paris from up there."

"If we have time," Todd warned.

I bit my tongue. *What kind of hurry were we in?*

"Right after World War I," I said, "a pilot flew his biplane through the arch."

"No way! I wish I could've seen that!"

"It was captured on a newsreel. I'll bet it's on YouTube."

"I'm not allowed to watch YouTube."

"Well, maybe your mom or dad could sit at the computer with you while you watched."

"He said he's not allowed," Todd said tightly.

"Todd," Catherine said in a warning voice.

"What? He just told her he's not allowed to watch YouTube!"

"Do we have to do this?" Catherine said. "He won't watch the damn YouTube. Happy?"

"That's not what this is about!" Todd said angrily. "It was about your *mother* trying once again to preempt our rules with him!"

I felt my muscles tightening and I swear my pulse sped up. I could literally see Cam shrinking under the ugly barrage between his parents. I felt an inexplicable foreboding descend on me. I didn't know if I was just reacting to the stress of having them here—each of them so clearly unhappy—or if I was picking up on an intuition that I should be paying attention to. I shook the premonition off as silliness. I had a tendency to make something out of nothing. Clearly I'd need to watch that impulse while they were staying with me.

"Okay, you two," I said brusquely. "*Enough.* Todd, I misspoke. Of course there's no question of my encouraging Cam to go against your rules. Forgive me. Catherine, did you see the map? I believe it's straight down this road. Is everyone ready?"

Cameron was on his feet before I finished speaking, checking to see that Robbie was belted in before grabbing the stroller handle.

I reached for Izzy's leash while Todd stood up and tossed down a handful of euros, most of which fell to the ground.

"And his name is *Cameron*," he said between gritted teeth. "Not *Cam.*"

7

With the day's heat, it seemed, came smells that the cooler weather always hid. Smells like garbage from the alley ways, dog mess, and diesel fuel from too many cars.

By the time we'd left the Champs-Élysées my head had started to throb.

I'd planned to treat us at a favorite bistro off one of the side streets but Todd wanted a burger and the familiarity of an American chain, so we'd ended up in the cafeteria-like ambience of the 5 *Guys* restaurant which had recently opened up on the famous boulevard.

I like a good hamburger as much as the next person. But I must have lived in Paris too long because I couldn't help but feel horrified that we were eating what is essentially a fast food American burger *on the Champs-Élysées*. And yet, that is what we did.

If I thought for a minute that eating a burger on the most famous avenue in the world would appease Todd, I was sadly mistaken. He complained about the "weird" taste to the meat, the flaccid fries and the flat Coca-Cola while the rest of us listened and picked at our lunch.

I was never so happy to walk away from a street that usually never fails to ignite excitement and enchantment in me. Robbie had fallen asleep as soon as we left the restaurant, for which I was glad. Todd and Catherine sniped back and forth at each other like a snarling tennis match with poor Cameron dodging every lobbed insult as if it were a grenade primed to explode on impact. Who knows? Perhaps he'd already experienced a few of those in his young life.

I hated seeing the discord between Todd and Catherine and I hated seeing what it was doing to Cam. I'd already noted two years ago when I saw last saw him that he seemed less free and easygoing than I'd remembered. At the time, I chalked it up to the fact that he was getting older. But now I think the daily relentless fusillade of his parents' unhappiness was changing him, restraining his natural buoyancy.

"I told Haley we'd meet her at the park," I said to Catherine as I pushed Robbie's stroller toward Parc Monceau.

I was well aware that the last time Catherine had been at Parc Monceau had to rank as one of the worst experiences of her life but I was also aware that I couldn't allow her to write off this amazing venue. I needed her to take charge of the memory and force her will upon it. And what better way to do it than with both Robbie and Cameron on hand?

I chattered on and on about the carousel, the ducks and the pond, all the amazing flowers and the two hundred and forty year-old Egyptian pyramid at the park until I could tell that Catherine was slowing her pace as if attempting to put off the inevitable.

"You know Robbie and I come here all the time," I said to her.

"Still?" she said doubtfully.

"I'm not going to let what happened spoil it for me," I said. "Or for Robbie. It's too magical a place to let that happen."

But I could tell she wasn't convinced.

"There are not enough magical places in the world," I said, pretending to be oblivious to her less-than-eager reaction.

But the closer we got to the park the more I started to think that coming was a mistake after all. It's all very well for me to force myself to forget what happened in the park with Robbie last summer but Catherine doesn't live here. She has no reason to put herself through that when she's just as likely to never come here again.

As we reached the park's dramatically scrolled and golden entrance gate, I spotted Haley leaning against the gate, looking at her phone, waiting for us.

"Whoa!" Cameron said. "Those gates are amazing!"

"They are, aren't they?" I said. "But you know what's nearly as amazing? The best macarons in the universe. Do you want to see them?"

"You mean we're not going to the park?" he said, crestfallen.

"Hi, Haley," I called.

She waved at me and grinned at Cam before checking on Robbie still asleep in his stroller and then taking Izzy's leash from me.

"We saw the Arc de Triomphe!" Cam said to her.

"Oh, yeah? That's cool," she said before turning to me. "Are we not going in?"

"You know what?" I said. "Change of plans."

I swear I saw Catherine's whole body relax.

"How about we go to Ladurée instead?" I said.

8

L adurée, the famous luxury Parisian bakery on the Champs-Élysées, usually tends to proclaim its wonderfulness by a block-long line of tourists snaking out the front door and around the corner. Today was no exception.

It was pretty clear that Todd had had his limit of stopping at cafés, famous or not. He balked at the door as if physically unable to enter.

"Holy crap," he said. "Is there really nothing else to do in this town but stuff your face with food?"

"It's Paris!" I said with forced gaiety. But I saw that Catherine was seething at his comment.

I get it. Paris wasn't Todd's cup of tea. Frankly it was hard to believe that there was anyone *not* enchanted with this city, but it seemed my son-in-law was one of that rare breed.

As we stood there looking into the window at the tiers of colorful macarons and tarts, Robbie woke up in one of his rare cranky moods. And since I couldn't bring Izzy into the restaurant—one of the few places in Paris she isn't welcome—I turned to Todd and asked if he'd mind staying outside with her.

I think he was surprised I trusted him with my dog and frankly I wasn't entirely comfortable with the idea. But he seemed to relax just a bit as he reached to take the leash from Haley.

"Sure," he said. "I've got some work calls to make anyway."

I caught Haley's eye as she frowned at the interaction. It made me love the girl all the more that she seemed to have a problem with the idea of Todd minding Izzy.

Once seated inside the famous sweets emporium, we ordered our macarons and coffee and I felt myself relax for the first time since we set out. And I wasn't the only one. Cam and Catherine teased Robbie back into a good humor and laughed and smiled more than they had all morning.

I hate to think that had something to do with the fact that Todd was not at the table but there you are.

Haley released Robbie from his stroller and pulled him onto her lap. I was always surprised at her limitless capacity to engage with him. Just when everyone else is praying he'll fall asleep, she's happy to read to him or play a game.

She really is worth her weight in macarons.

"Did you hear about the impending lockdown?" she asked.

To tell you the truth I'd completely forgotten about the possibility.

"Are you serious?" Catherine asked, her face suddenly twisted into a worried frown.

"Yeah, but Macron is thinking about only shutting down the major cities—Marseille, Lyon, Nice, and of course Paris."

"Why just the cities?" Catherine asked, her eyes going in the direction of Todd standing on the other side of the plate glass window. He was on his phone.

"My dad said if they can contain the virus in the higher population areas it'll help stem the flow to the rural areas," Haley said. "Or something like that."

"When is your flight out?" I asked Catherine.

"Not until next week."

I glanced out the window. I don't know who Todd was talking to, but whoever it was appeared to be agitating him. It was possible he was hearing about the imminent lockdown. I prayed that didn't mean he would cancel the rest of their visit. As tense as it was, it was still a balm to see Catherine and Cam again.

My phone rang from where I'd set it on the table and I saw the picture of my friend Adele Coté appear on the screen.

A forensic tech thirty years my junior, Adele and I met two summers ago when her brother and my husband were both brutally murdered. She helped me find the truth about Bob's death and I returned the favor by uncovering the culprit in her brother's murder.

Since the private DNA laboratory she worked for was often called in to relieve the workload in the forensics department of the Paris homicide division, Adele often had proprietary information on various criminal cases which made her an invaluable resource to me.

But aside from that, we were just really good friends.

"I'll take this outside," I said and stepped away from the table. As soon as I walked out of the shop I felt the heat slam into me like a wall of linebackers.

"Hey, Adele," I said.

"How is the visit going?" she asked.

"It's good. Can you come to dinner tonight?"

"I'll have to let you know. I'm just calling to see if you'd heard the news about Jean-Marc."

I felt a sudden tightening in my chest.

"What news?" I said, bracing myself and not really knowing why.

"I didn't know whether or not I should tell you," she said.

"Just tell me," I said wearily. "I'm not in high school anymore. I can probably handle it."

"I heard he was getting married."

9

After that the rest of the afternoon pretty much passed in a muffled cacophony of color, sound and sultry heat. We left Ladurée and went to Monoprix to pick up items for supper and I found myself going through the motions of selecting deli *au gratin* potatoes, a premade green salad and a rotisserie chicken while I responded to Catherine and Haley, who kept asking me if I was okay.

By the time we were finally heading back to the apartment —with Adele's news, the heat and the tension of the day pressing in on me like a clamp—I had to forcibly shake myself out of my dark mood.

I felt gut punched. Literally.

It was just so hard to believe! Jean-Marc had just been widowed! And while yes, it had been no kind of marriage for many, many years, still—the whole point of relocating to Nice was because he was overcome with guilt and shame—not to mention revulsion with Paris and with me over how Chloe died.

As I tried to shake myself out of my funk, I saw that Catherine was pushing Robbie's stroller while Haley was holding both Izzy's leash and Cameron's hand. I looked to see how Todd was handling that, but he seemed preoccupied with his phone and whatever he was reading on it.

"Are you sure you're okay, Mom?" Catherine asked as we neared the block to my apartment.

"I am," I said. "Sorry."

"Was that Adele on the phone back at the restaurant?"

"It was," I said with a sigh. "She told me Jean-Marc is getting married."

"Seriously?" She looked appropriately shocked. "That's terrible."

"Well, I suppose it's good for him," I said ruefully.

"I'm sorry, Mom."

"No, it's fine. I've barely heard from him in a year. I should have expected something like this."

"You really liked him."

I sighed again and focused on the front of my apartment building now blurred with the mist of tears in my eyes.

"I really did," I said.

It was midafternoon by the time we got back to the apartment. I felt as if we'd been gone all day. Haley put Robbie down for his nap and I put away the groceries while Cameron watched French cartoons. Todd and Catherine retired to the bedroom. I was relieved not to hear angry voices from behind their door.

After I'd showered and made myself a cup of tea, I felt better about Adele's shocking news. I really should've expected it and scolded myself because I was obviously holding out for a miracle with Jean-Marc and now that possibility had been firmly squashed, to say the least.

Now that he was getting married, I could wholeheartedly and completely let him go and begin to move on.

Haley joined Cameron in the living room watching television. Catherine emerged from the bedroom and followed me into the kitchen.

"About dinner tonight," she said.

I turned to her. "Would you and Todd like an evening to yourselves?"

"Would you mind?"

"Not at all. I think it's a great idea."

She lowered her voice.

"I guess you've figured out that Todd and I are trying to work some things out."

"Do you want a recommendation for some places nearby?"

"We were thinking maybe a dinner cruise," she said. "What do you think?"

"I think that would be lovely. You'll need reservations."

"Todd's already made them."

I could tell she felt better. There was more color in her cheeks and her smile didn't seem as forced to me. I reasoned that jetlag and staying with the in-laws would be stress enough to get the most loving couples sniping at each other.

I really tried to believe that too.

10

With its reputation as the most romantic river in the world, the Seine always felt like a surprise to Catherine with its fetid odor and murky olive-green color. She remembered reading that the river flowed into the sea, but as stagnant and listless as it always looked to her, she found it hard to believe that it had enough force.

She let Todd lead the way to the table since she knew things like that were important to him. He'd spoken very little on the cab ride over. She would've preferred to walk—the weather was hot but it felt good on her skin. Unfortunately, her mother had mentioned it was a nice walk and that was all Todd needed to hear to insist on calling for a taxi.

She hated how he behaved when he was around her mother. She hated her mother seeing him like that. Although truth be told, he'd been acting that way more and more regardless of who was around.

They sat at their table which was positioned close to the front of the boat and quickly gave their menu selections to the waiter.

Catherine watched the famous Paris landmarks slide by—

the Orsay museum, the Louvre, Notre-Dame.

She looked around to smile at a few of the other passengers in the first floor dining room with them. From the conversations she could hear, they all spoke English and mostly American English.

She looked back at Todd who was once more focused on his phone.

"Is something happening back at the office?" she asked.

"Huh?" He looked at her and frowned.

They'd had five full minutes of noncombative conversation in her mother's guest room which had led Catherine to believe that the night, if not the entire visit, might be salvaged. But aside from those few minutes, Todd had been markedly distant with her.

"This was *your* idea to take this cruise," she pointed out to him.

"Are you not enjoying yourself?"

"I'd enjoy it more if you'd put down your phone."

He sighed heavily and made a drama of laying his phone—face down—on the table. Before she knew she was going to do it Catherine playfully reached for his phone and looked at the screen.

A text message was there.

<miss u desprately>

Todd snatched the phone back before she could look to see who the message was from.

"How dare you?" he said, his eyes protruding, his voice now raised and sputtering.

But Catherine didn't see the picture of rage that everyone else in the dining room must be seeing. What she saw was guilt and shame flooding his features.

"Are you...are you having an affair?" she asked, dumbfounded.

"Don't be ridiculous," he said, quickly jabbing at his phone either to close out of his text messages or delete the message stream.

In spite of the heat on the boat, Catherine felt a sudden coldness that seemed to start in her stomach and expand outwards. For a moment she couldn't think of what to say. Virtually hours before they climbed onboard the airplane to fly to Paris she'd caught him reading her phone and when she challenged him on it he accused her of having a boyfriend. She'd been so hurt and offended by the accusation, it never occurred to her that he might have made it to assuage the guilt he felt about his own adulterous behavior.

"I can't believe you," she said. "I put up with your homicidal jealousy and baseless accusations for years and now *you're* cheating on *me*?"

"I'm not cheating on you. You're paranoid. That's what twenty-four hours with your mother does to you. It's not healthy. Not for you or Cameron."

Catherine stared at him in disbelief. For the last several months she had told herself that she could put up with anything for Cameron's sake. It had been a long and painful year.

"I want a divorce," she blurted out, surprising even herself.

He folded his arms across his chest. "You're crazy."

Catherine felt breathless, empowered, terrified. She also felt as if everything was moving too fast, as if the boat had ramped up its speed and any moment the breadbasket and vase full of summer daisies would go flying off the table. She felt an irrational urge to grip the table and hold on with both hands.

"This is your mother's doing," Todd said, his face twisted into a contortion of disgust.

Catherine stared at him and saw for the first time how much he loathed her mother. She was astounded she hadn't seen it before.

The waiter appeared and set down two plates of *foie gras*

with toast spears and raspberry sauce and poured two glass of champagne. For a minute Catherine felt like laughing at the absurdity of it.

"I'll accept your apology when you're ready," Todd said, flapping out his napkin on his lap. "Meanwhile, I've rebooked our flights back to Florida. We leave first thing in the morning."

"No," she said, staring at him in incredulity.

"You can stay if you want," he said matter of factly. "But Cameron's coming with me."

"Why are you doing this?" she asked.

"I'm taking care of my family," he said, jabbing the table with his index finger with every word. "When the lockdown comes I'm not going to be trapped here."

"That's not what I'm talking about, Todd. What happened to you? To us?"

He looked at her, his face devoid of emotion, his eyes so cold they took her breath away.

"You can ask that after all the men you've been with during our marriage?"

Catherine felt lightheaded, her mouth dry at the accusation.

"There's been no one!" she said, leaning toward him earnestly as if that might make him believe her.

He patted his phone.

"Well, it doesn't matter now, does it?" he said smugly.

Catherine snatched up her champagne glass and tossed it into his face. He jumped out of his seat.

"You crazy bitch!" he shouted.

He angrily attempted to brush away the liquid from his t-shirt, then flung down his napkin and turned and stalked away.

"You'll be sorry!" she shouted at his retreating back.

Catherine watched him go until he disappeared around the corner and she was alone at their table—quivering with rage and a horrified realization at what had just happened.

11

The beauty of July in Paris—once you balanced out the ungodly heat in the middle of the day—was that it doesn't get dark until quite late. Nowhere else in the world does that matter more than in Paris where there is so much architectural and natural beauty on display.

I thought of Todd and Catherine on their boat cruise. I've taken that cruise or another just like it at least three times and it never fails to amaze. Plus, in the summer, the eerily beautiful sights of Paris's treasures and historic monuments are fully visible.

I checked the kitchen clock and saw it was after nine.

"Time to head home, Haley," I called to her from the kitchen. She and Cameron were playing a board game at the dining room table.

Dinner with Haley and the boys had been delightful and I'd again had to face the fact that that was because Todd wasn't there. I loved seeing how Cam and Haley and Robbie all interacted together. They behaved with each other as if they'd always been together and were already a family.

On the one hand I loved seeing that. But on the other hand it made my heart hurt a little too. First for Robbie who would miss Cam when he left, but also for Cam who had no siblings to buffer the agony of what his parents were putting him through.

But I was also sad in a way for Haley who had no siblings either and who often appeared to spend her time with Robbie less as his caretaker and more as a big sister. She'd miss Cam when he left and I'd miss that contented scene at dinner of the three of them laughing together.

"You don't need to come downstairs to wait with me, Missus B," Haley said as she slipped her backpack on.

I snapped the leash on Izzy.

"Izzy and Cam and I will all come to wait with you. Robbie's asleep and he'll be fine for a few minutes on his own."

After watching Haley climb into her Uber and after reminding her to text me when she got home, Cameron and I let Izzy water the pavers of my building's courtyard.

I dropped my hand to his shoulder.

"I am so glad to have you finally with me in Paris," I said. "I've imagined this moment for so long."

"Me, too, Grammy. I had it circled in purple on my calendar for months."

"So did I," I said, giving him a squeeze. "Were your friends jealous?"

"They were!" he said with a grin. "Can we get some souvenirs tomorrow? I said I'd bring some back."

"I know just the place," I said. "And if your mom and dad want to go off to lunch tomorrow, I'll take you to Parc Monceau."

"I wish we could've gone today."

"I know, but we'll go tomorrow."

"I really like Haley. She's awesome."

"She really likes you too, darling. I can tell."

He took Izzy's leash from me and the two of us reentered the apartment building. I was struck with the bittersweet feeling that my dearest, most beloved grandson had just had a single evening's respite from not having to act like a grownup with way too much on his shoulders.

12

Catherine sat at the table and chewed her nails. Todd had been gone for at least fifteen minutes and she could see the boat was heading back to the dock.

Should she go after him and tell him she didn't mean it? Should she suggest they try counseling again?

She knew he'd always been irrationally jealous and in the early years they'd even talked about it. But it had gotten worse as the years went by. Recently she would walk into a room at their house and catch him hurriedly putting her phone down. It was discouraging to see but a part of her always thought *Well, at least he's embarrassed about being caught.*

That time, it seemed, was past.

She looked around, her vision blurring with tears at all the famous monuments and structures she'd always dreamed of seeing one day and couldn't believe she was finally here looking at the Eiffel Tower—only miserable and heartsick. Todd had spoiled everything.

No, that's not fair. It's how we are when we're together that spoils everything.

She felt like letting her head fall into her hands at the table but she'd already caught a few people looking her way. They'd made a spectacle, that was for sure. Even though Catherine wasn't meeting their gazes, she knew the people in the dining room were pitying or condescending. Suddenly, she couldn't take it another minute. She got up abruptly, leaving her untouched plate of duck *confit* and *foie gras* and all the prying eyes behind her.

As soon as she stepped outside on the upper deck the river air seemed to slap her in the face; it was pungent with the scent of fish and diesel oil. She walked quickly to the railing and scanned the western side of the river.

The Eiffel Tower loomed over her in a ghostly dark shadow transforming before her eyes from one of the city's most magical landmarks to something threatening and eerie. She glanced down the railing but didn't see anyone who looked like Todd.

The boat was maneuvering close to the cement rampart in order to dock where it had launched from. Catherine took in a big breath of the foul river air as if to somehow fortify her for the confrontation she knew was coming.

She imagined he would be waiting for her outside the sight-seeing office. It irked her that he was making such a big dramatic performance of this.

Why not just wait for me on the boat? The public fight was embarrassing enough.

She was tempted to walk to the other side of the boat to find Todd, but a stubborn splinter of annoyance jabbed her.

Why should I track him down? Why are we still playing these stupid games?

Instantly an image came to her of her mother opening the apartment door, all smiles, asking her how their night went.

Catherine let an involuntary groan escape.

Her mother would take no joy in how things had devolved

tonight. Catherine knew that. But she wouldn't be surprised either.

Catherine stared into the oily murky green of the Seine, watching the foamy wake of the boat.

Is this really how it ends? On a beautiful summer evening with the setting sun sparkling on the water on a boat in Paris, surrounded by lovers and elderly tourists?

She sensed him before she saw him. And she knew before turning and before he said a word that it wasn't Todd behind her. She felt a light tap on the shoulder.

"Madame?" His voice was velvety soft, nearly a whisper.

Catherine only moved her head to glance at him. He was slim with molten brown eyes and a full sensuous mouth. There was a tiny spatter of what looks like blood drops across his t-shirt. She put a hand up to shield her face against the dropping sun rays as they bore down on her.

In spite of the warm air swirling gently around her a wave of cold rippled across her skin.

I looked in on Robbie in his crib in my bedroom and then on Cameron, sleeping soundly in the guest room before returning to the living room and the book I'd been trying to read for the last ninety minutes.

I'd already assumed that Todd and Catherine's evening had been a roaring success. I even assumed that the dinner cruise had segued into a late night martini bar visit and possibly even an impetuous check in at a charming pensione or hotel with a vacancy.

That was all well and good I thought as I sat back down on the sofa and picked up my book as Izzy rearranged herself next to me.

But it didn't explain why Catherine hadn't texted or called

to tell me not to worry. And it didn't explain why Catherine hadn't responded to any of my texts to her.

Something is wrong.

It was nearly one in the morning and there was no explanation for why my daughter hadn't come home or explained to me what was going on.

I stood up again and double checked the locks and the burners in the kitchen but I knew everything was turned off. I looked at my phone again and put in another call to Catherine. It went straight to voicemail.

Is it possible—remotely possible—that they're having so much fun caught up in the moment that they've forgotten all about letting me know?

No. It wasn't possible.

Should I start calling hospitals?

Just the thought sent a shiver of fear straight through me. I checked the time again and then turned on the television to see if there had been some sort of local disaster I was unaware of.

Turned out, there was.

"It's a mystery," one of the bubbly newscasters was saying.

Suddenly I saw a B-roll of video of one of the *bateaux-mouche* sightseeing boats while the news anchor continued to talk. I felt my skin go suddenly clammy.

I found myself standing up, the remote control clutched in my hands as the video switched to what look like live footage of a tourist boat parked along the rampart of the Seine. Police lights had been erected and police caravans were parked alongside the office.

My heart pounded in my chest until I thought I couldn't breathe.

"It was suggested that the death happened as the boat was returning to the launch site," the bubbly news anchor said. "They are still looking to notify next of kin."

I put a hand to my mouth, my fingers trembling, at the same time I heard a firm rapping on my front door.

13

Two uniformed policemen stood on my doorstep along with one man in plainclothes. I started to shake my head as soon as I saw them.

No. This isn't happening. This can't be happening.

Robotically, I moved to make sure both bedroom doors were closed before turning back to the police who had now entered my apartment.

"You are Claire Baskerville?" the detective asked me. He was an older man with a pot belly. I was relatively sure I'd never seen him before and I thought I'd met all the Paris detectives.

"Is it my daughter?" I asked breathlessly. "My daughter Catherine Stone?"

"Sit down, Madame Baskerville," the detective said. "It is not your daughter."

I nearly whimpered in relief as my legs gave out beneath me and I sat down hard on the couch.

"Then what...?" I watched as the two policemen opened the bedroom doors and peered inside before checking both bathrooms.

"What has happened?" I asked, as nausea began to spread through me.

"When was the last time you saw your daughter, Madame Baskerville?"

"I...I saw her at five, I mean seventeen hundred hours today with my son-in-law. Please tell me what has happened. Where is my daughter?"

"Is your daughter here, Madame?"

"Here? No. I just told you. She and my son-in-law went on a sunset cruise on the river. I saw on the news that there was an accident of some kind?"

I didn't think I could handle one more moment of their questions without knowing the truth.

Where is Catherine?

I picked up my phone and called her number again and again it went to voice mail.

"What has happened?" I said, my voice rising shrilly.

"There has been an accident," the detective said. "A man has fallen off one of the river tourist boats."

"A man? Is it Todd? Is that what you think?"

I can't believe I didn't have Todd's phone number or that I was only now thinking of calling him.

"We will need you to identify the body, Madame," the detective said not unkindly.

I put a hand to my mouth, the full horror of what he was suggesting washing over me.

"Oh, my God," I whispered.

"There was identification in his wallet but we need corroboration."

Tears pricked my eyes.

"Is it Todd Stone?" I asked hoarsely.

"We will need you to confirm that," he said. "But yes, that it what we believe."

14

The next morning, I rolled out of bed having not slept a wink. I sat on the edge of the bed my head still humming with disbelief and shock. The morning only put a painful glare on the shocking news of last night. Because I needed to arrange childcare the police had allowed me to wait until later this morning to come to the morgue to identify Todd's body.

I still couldn't believe it.

Todd had died in a boating accident on the Seine.

And Catherine was missing.

The police were dragging the Seine.

For Catherine's body.

I'd literally run from the room to retch into the kitchen sink when they told me.

How can this be happening?

I dressed quickly and texted Haley to ask if she could come this morning. She wasn't scheduled to come until this afternoon—I think she even had school today. If she couldn't come, I'd ask Geneviève. But Haley responded that she would be at my apartment within the hour.

I went to the kitchen to make coffee, but a noise made me look up. I saw Robbie walking out of my bedroom. I groaned. This was the first time he'd gotten out of the crib on his own.

"Grammy?" Cameron said as he came out of the guest room. His hair was sticking up around his head and he was still in his pajamas.

"Good morning, sweetheart," I said, going first to Robbie to remove his diaper. He was toilet trained by day but was still in pull-ups at night.

"Where are Mom and Dad?" Cameron said. "They didn't come home last night?"

"I think they got a hotel room," I said. "They were out late and didn't want to bother us."

I was nowhere near ready to have this conversation with him.

"Really?" He frowned. "That's weird."

"Sweetie, can you help Robbie find something to wear today? I'm putting waffles in the toaster. And Haley will be here soon."

Cameron turned to Robbie.

"Come on, Robbie," he said. Robbie ran bare-bottomed toward the bedroom.

My heart fell at the sight of the two of them. How was I going to tell Cam about his father? What in the world was I going to say? His world would collapse.

And his mother? Where was she?

What am I going to tell him about Catherine?

I picked up my phone and called the police. They said they'd contact me with any information but I knew they only called when they wanted something. If I didn't call, I'd never find out anything.

I found myself praying they hadn't found anything last night. I didn't think I could bear hearing on the phone that they'd found Catherine's body in the water. I nearly hung up when I was put through to a recording and told to leave a message. I left my number and the reason for calling.

When Robbie and Cameron came back to the living room, Robbie was dressed in a matching set of cotton shorts and a t-shirt, and Cameron was pulling on a t-shirt over his jeans shorts. I quickly found a channel for them to watch. I thought about telling Cam not to change the channel in case he turned on the news but thought that would just make him suspicious.

Where could she have gone? Why didn't she come home?

I called Adele but only got her voicemail. It was possible that meant she was working the accident scene. Adele's company often took up the slack for the Paris police department when they got too overloaded, which they nearly always were.

I finished making my coffee and the boys' waffles as I fought the racing panic and dread that threatened to overpower me.

I watched Cam as he laughed at the TV and my heart clenched. Today I would confirm the tragedy that would change his life forever.

15

The Paris police station is situated on one of the most expensive pieces of land on the planet. It is set right in the heart of Paris—in the center of the Seine—a block from Notre Dame Cathedral. The actual building blends into its surroundings by appearing on the outside as if it had always been there. The interior where I was sitting was much less romantic or attractive.

One of the first things I did last night when I found out that Todd might have been involved in a deadly accident was contact the US Embassy. I'd been assured by the night consular officer that a representative would be present with me this morning but so far no one had shown up.

It was possible that a tourist boat accident didn't qualify as one of the things that got the state department interested. In all honesty, I'd worked with them before on various expat cases and hadn't found them inordinately helpful. But in those instances a death wasn't normally involved.

I'd been ushered into an empty anteroom off a long bleak hallway to wait for the detective in charge of the case. I don't know whom I was dealing with last night—probably the night team—but today a totally different detective stepped out of the hallway to shake my hand and thank me for my assistance.

The new detective was blond, cleanshaven and young, no more than thirty-five. He wore a button-down shirt open at the neck with slim cut jeans and leather braided loafers. His eyes were clear blue and sharp as if they would miss very little. The badge swinging from a lanyard around his neck identified him as Capitaine Roger Bonnet.

This was the first time I'd been to the police station since the last detective in Bonnet's position had been reassigned to Normandy. I still had no doubt as to why Victor Muller had been reassigned. It was my personal belief that my father made it happen in his continuing quest to rid the world of people who annoy me.

Muller and I had had a very public argument about whether or not he should get to sleep with me. It was exactly the sort of thing that tended to seriously set off Daddy Dearest.

Bonnet led me to his office.

"How were your daughter and her husband getting along?" he asked after we'd seated ourselves, him behind his desk.

I stared at him, dumbfounded.

"What are you suggesting?" I said. "You think *Catherine* pushed Todd overboard?"

"We are considering every possibility."

"Well, you can *unconsider* that possibility! It's absurd! Does that mean you haven't found her?"

My eyes smarted with tears. I'd been living with the terror that any moment now they would find my daughter's body in the Seine.

"No, Madame, she is not in the river."

I gulped painfully in relief. I closed my eyes and for a moment I thought I might faint.

"May I get you a water, Madame Baskerville?"

"No," I wheezed. "What you can do is find my daughter."

"We are doing everything we can in the regard," he said. "And we expect to locate her soon. Now, back to your son-in-law."

"I don't understand how this could happen," I said. "Todd was an excellent swimmer and those tour boats are not that tall. How in the world could he have died from the fall?"

"He died because he was already in the process of dying before he went into the water."

"What does *that* mean?" I asked, frowning in confusion. "Are you saying he had a heart attack or stroke of some sort?"

"No, Madame."

The detective steepled his fingers over his desk as if analyzing me.

"The medical examiner believes the cause of death was the six-inch stab wound to his heart."

16

I f there are worse things than a visit to a police morgue, I can't think of what they might be.

Every time I'm forced to go to one of these places for one reason or another, I find myself ruminating over the fact that the smells and sounds of a morgue are almost always worse than the things you see there.

Or maybe it's neck and neck. Because it's all pretty horrible.

As I stood at the viewing window staring into the main theatre of the police morgue, I felt a ringing in my ears and an unnatural calmness settle in my bones.

Through it all my head continued to re-run the detective's statement that the boating accident victim had not died accidentally.

Stabbed and pitched over the rail into the water?

Who would stab Todd?

Last night the police had said that Todd's wallet was found on the body. So it wasn't robbery. Who would stab someone for no reason?

After my interview with Bonnet I made another call to the

Embassy, this time a much more insistent one, since it looked like we were now not only dealing with a possible homicide—and I swallowed hard at the thought—but also a missing persons case.

In all my dealings with the embassy here in Paris—especially having to do with missing persons cases which are the majority of what I do for the expat community—I have found the foreign office personnel to be generally polite if specifically useless. There were too many forms to fill out, too many hoops to jump through, and too many similar cases in the most popular and one of the most populous cities in the world for them to do more than go through the motions on one more lost tourist.

I put a hand to my mouth and fought the impulse to double over as if in physical pain.

Where is she? Why hasn't she come home?

If Todd truly had been stabbed in a senseless attack, did Catherine witness it? Was she wandering the streets of Paris dazed and shell-shocked?

Standing beside me at the viewing window of the police morgue, Detective Bonnet cleared his throat. The noise brought me back to the reality of the moment.

Maybe that's the reason why I was still on my feet and going through the motions of somewhat normal behavior. My brain had literally shut down on registering what was happening around me.

But that was about to end with a bang.

The sterile room before me was completely furnished in metal—handles, tables, sinks, gurneys. The autopsy table had pride of place and sat with its raised edges designed to catch the inevitable escape of bodily fluids. Technicians wearing green gowns, booties, masks and hairnets moved around the room turning on and off sink taps or carrying mysterious vials and bags from one cabinet to another.

Lining the room was a wall of silver handles that hid the dozen or so coolers where individual bodies were stored.

My stomach roiled ominously and I gripped the windowsill in front of me that overlooked the room where the boating accident victim's body lay on the gurney.

It was shrouded in a sheet and had been positioned close to the viewing window.

"Are you ready, Madame?" Bonnet asked.

Not trusting my voice, I simply nodded.

Let's just get this over, I thought. *I need to put this in my rearview mirror. Then get me out of this place of horror.*

Of course I knew it had to be Todd. He hadn't come home last night. This body was found with Todd's driver's license and credit cards on it.

And yet when the dour-faced technician pulled back the sheet and revealed Todd's face, I felt as if I'd had the air knocked out of me.

My eyes filled with tears and an uncontrollable shudder swept through my body at the thought of telling Cameron.

"Well, Madame Baskerville?" Bonnet prodded almost gently.

I swallowed past the lump in my throat.

"It's him," I said in hoarse whisper. "That's my son-in-law Todd Stone."

17

The outdoor café where I went after my visit to the police morgue was a modest bistro, slapped together with whitewashed walls and rickety tables whose paint was peeling in various stages. I thought of it because it was on the Île de la Cité near where the police *Préfecture* was located.

I sat down at the table and felt the heat from the July day crush me. I held my phone in my hands as if it were a lifeline, as if any minute my daughter would call me to tell me she was fine. I was sitting to give myself time and to steady my nerves before going back to the apartment to talk to Cameron and tell him that his daddy was never coming home.

And that I didn't know where his mother was.

I ordered a large Americano with a shot of whiskey and put in a call to Adele.

"Oh, Claire," she said when she picked up. "I am so sorry this is happening to you!"

"Have you heard anything?" I asked in an emotion-choked voice.

My mind was whirling in confusion and pain. *How can I tell Cameron his daddy is dead? What happened on that boat last night? Where is Catherine? Why is her phone turned off?*

I rubbed my arms in spite of the heat.

"I will tell you what I know, *chérie*," Adele said gently, "which isn't much."

"It's more than I know."

"You know that no other bodies were found in the water?"

"Yes, the police told me."

"There is no forensic indication that there was another attack like Todd's."

I grabbed at her words like they were a lifeline.

She's saying there's no sign that there was another violent attack.

"So where is she?" I asked plaintively.

"The police believe she left the boat."

"Without Todd? That makes no sense!"

"Eyewitnesses said Catherine and Todd had a screaming match at their table," Adele said. "They report seeing him walk away from her."

I sat there at the café table, the sun beating down on me, stunned as I envisioned it in my head. Todd and Catherine had not been getting along. I knew that. So last night they fought, and Todd stormed off.

I felt suddenly so sad for both of them and so desperate for answers as to what had happened.

"So Catherine might not have known what happened to Todd," I said.

"Maybe not."

My eyes filled with tears. "But then, where is she?"

"I think, more importantly," Adele said, "the question is, if she didn't know that Todd had been killed, why did she run?"

~

All the way home from the café, Adele's words rang in my head: *If Catherine didn't know that Todd had been killed, why did she run?*

But Adele wasn't a mother and she couldn't intrinsically understand the mindset that Catherine would have been operating under. I don't care if my daughter took a battle axe to Todd in full view of the whole boat.

There is just no way she would run off and leave Cameron behind.

It was inconceivable.

By the time I got back to the apartment with Indian takeout, I was already so exhausted I could barely stand. Cameron had called me twice and after confirming with Haley that everyone was safe, I gave vague assurances to him on the first phone call and let the second one go to voicemail.

Haley met me at the door, Robbie on her hip and Izzy jumping at her feet.

"What's going on, Missus B? You were outta here this morning like you had a fire cracker up your...tail."

"Very colorful, Haley," I said, setting the takeout down on the counter. "Can you organize lunch? I think today's a good time to introduce Robbie to Indian food."

"Oh, wow," Haley said peering into the bags of heavenly scented lamb biryani and chicken tikka. "Guess we'd better double-wrap his butt before he goes to bed tonight."

"Where's Cameron? You haven't had the TV on, have you?"

"Chill, Missus B. I've monitored it every minute. Only bizarre French cartoons about cockroaches. He's in the bathroom."

As she spoke, Cameron came flying out of the bathroom, his trousers still unzipped.

"Grammy!" he said. "Where's Mom and Dad? I've sent about a million text messages and nobody's answering!"

"Come here, sweetie," I said, opening my arms to him. "I want to tell you something."

He froze at my words and I could tell he was jumping ahead. I held my breath for a moment and tried to push the fear away. I led Cameron into my bedroom, afraid that the guest room with his parents' clothing and personal affects would be too evocative after I told him what I must.

"Where are they, Grammy?" he said, his voice quavering.

I led him to the bed and put my arms around him and held my face close to his.

"Darling, I'm afraid there's been an accident."

I waited until Cameron had cried himself to sleep—well, honestly, we both did—before I slipped out of the bedroom at a little after eight o'clock in the evening. Robbie was asleep in the guest room. Haley was in the living room watching television. I told her what had happened.

"Oh, man," she said. "Poor Cam. I can't believe it."

"I know," I said. "Is there any way you can stay the night? And maybe tomorrow?"

"Sure. Wow. I can't imagine how bad he must feel."

I watched her face and realized she was actually imagining how *she* might feel if she'd gotten such terrible news. Haley had a somewhat estranged relationship with her parents. However, they were all trying and I got the sense that, after this, Haley might even try a little harder with them.

"Did you get enough to eat?" I asked, reaching for Izzy's leash.

"Yeah," she said. "I can take her, Missus B."

"Thank you sweetie. But I need to make a call. Can you keep an ear out for Cameron in case he wakes?"

"Yeah. Where's his mom?"

"Nobody knows," I said, trying to get out the door before I broke down in front of her.

I hurried down the stairs to the foyer and then to the courtyard outside where I let Izzy wander while I called Bonnet. He didn't pick up so I left him a message and tried to think what else I could do.

Adele had not worked the crime scene—I still couldn't quite comprehend the fact that Todd had been knifed last night —but she had plenty of contacts who could tell her what was going on.

I depended on that.

On the way back upstairs I saw that Geneviève's door was open. She was waiting for me.

"I can't stop," I said. "I'm worried that Cameron will wake up."

"*Chérie*, I cannot imagine what you are going through right now."

She stepped forward and lightly touched my arm.

"How did you hear?" I said, feeling the tension I was holding in my body ease just a bit.

"The police canvassed the building this morning," she said. "They seemed to think that Catherine was hiding here somewhere."

"They think it's suspicious that she's gone missing after a big fight with Todd," I said wearily. "And he ends up dead."

"What can I do to help?"

I heard a low rumble of voices coming from inside her apartment. Noel and Bill were of course still with her.

"I'll let you know if there's anything," I said turning wearily to go back upstairs.

"*Chérie*, have you heard the other news?" Geneviève called after me.

I stopped and turned to look at her.

"Other news?" I asked, bracing myself.

"Never mind, *chérie*. It is not important."

"Just tell me, Geneviève. Has something happened?"

"I think we slept through the official notification last night. Paris is officially in lockdown. Nobody in or out."

18

Day One of the Lockdown

The next morning I sat next to Cameron on the couch watching television while Haley dressed Robbie.

It seemed that the boating accident and Todd's death had moved off the news circuit, thank God, and the only thing anybody wanted to talk about now was the lockdown.

All of the news anchors urged calm and patience, saying the lockdown could be anywhere from three days to a month. Unlike the previous lockdowns that the government had imposed, people were allowed to come and go freely within Paris but no one was allowed to enter or leave the city. The lockdown would have to be long enough to stanch the projected flow of infections coming from the cities into the rest of the country.

One news channel talked about the people already pouring into hospitals with symptoms of the new virus. Another told the story of how the lockdown, which had been hinted at for the last day and a half, had gone into effect without warning at twenty-two hundred hours the night before.

One newscaster reported that the government regretted not being able to give more formal notice of the impending lockdown. All roads, tracks or airways in or out of Paris, Lyon, Marseille, Nice and Nantes were frozen.

I switched the channel to find some kind of cartoon or children's entertainment for Cam. I found the cartoon about the goofy cockroaches that Robbie liked, and hoped that the sheer lunacy of the premise would at least distract Cameron.

I don't know why I bothered. He wasn't interested and nothing was going to sidetrack him from the terrible blow he'd been dealt.

"Where's Dad?" he asked in a small voice where he sat beside me. He was mindlessly massaging Izzy's back. "Can I see him?"

I caught my breath, not sure how to respond. "He's with the police for now," I said.

"Why?"

"They have their procedures."

"But I'll be able to see him?"

I caught my breath at the thought. Could an eight-year-old really handle seeing his dead father? I know children do at funerals, but even then I always thought the practice was macabre.

"We'll see," I said.

My phone rang and I snatched it up. The urgency of my movement startled Cameron and alerted him to what I must be thinking.

"Is it Mom?" he said with a waver in his voice.

"No," I said, getting up from the couch. "It's overseas."

He nodded and went back to staring at the cartoon and petting Izzy.

I took the phone out into the hallway.

"Hello?" I said.

"Is this Claire Baskerville?" a woman's voice said on the other line.

"Who's asking?" I asked.

"My name is Tonya Stone. I am Todd's older sister."

My stomach dropped. I should have called Todd's family. I don't know what I was thinking. They must have been informed by the Paris police. I could only imagine how terrible that was for them. Before I had a chance to apologize Tonya cut me off.

"I'm not saying any of us are surprised that this has happened," she said bitterly. "I told Mama he should never have married that woman."

At first I didn't process what she was saying. But she went on so that there could be no doubt.

"The police said Catherine killed him and then ran off," Tonya said.

Regardless of what the police might be thinking I was sure they said no such thing to this woman.

"What do you want?" I said coldly, all hope of family unity and mutual grief gone.

"We want his body returned so we can have the funeral. You speak French so you can make it happen."

"I'm sorry," I said. "The Paris police will let us know when they can release the body which they can't right now."

Since it's an active murder investigation.

"I'm just saying my family will never forgive her when they find her," Tonya said. "And she'll deserve everything she's got coming to her."

I hung up and stood in the hallway, my skin vibrating with revulsion but also fear. These were Cameron's relatives. His aunts and uncles on Todd's side. These were people he had a loving relationship with. At least up to now.

I came back to the living room and saw that Haley had taken my place on the couch. Robbie sat next to her and

Cameron was huddled up by her side. She looked up at me and smiled and I was never more grateful for her in my life.

I went to the dining room where I pulled out my laptop. The police weren't keeping me informed but if Tonya's phone call was any indication we would all soon be actively working to find Catherine—but for very different reasons.

First, I emailed Adele and told her about the call I'd received from Todd's family. If she had any fresh news, I figured she'd be able to tell me in greater detail in an email. Meanwhile, I went to the online new story of the boat accident and found the name of the tour boat company.

As a private investigator, I have many tools at my disposal that the average person does not. Frankly, some of those tools are not absolutely legal or, should I say, there's a gray area I'm sometimes forced to work within.

I wasn't sure how long it would take me but I knew the manifest of that night's boat outing was somewhere accessible on the Internet. I didn't know what it would tell me, but I knew it was a start: find the people who were on the boat with Todd and Catherine that night.

At the very least somebody must have seen something.

My email dinged. It was a new message from Adele.

Hey, Claire, How are you? I know that is a stupid question but I do not know what else to say. Do not worry about Todd's family. I hear they are calling Bonnet a lot too and he's dodging them. I also heard that the family wants to actively help the police in putting together a case against Catherine.

I stopped reading for a moment and felt my heart fluttering in my chest. I wasn't surprised. This was essentially what Tonya had told me on the phone. But it still took my breath away to see it in writing.

Between you and me it's of course idiotic for them to look at Catherine for this but you know the Paris police. In the absence of real leads, they typically default to idiocy.

My eyes blurred with tears as I read on.

I know how upset you must be, Claire. But try to keep the faith. A lot more facts are bound to shake out. This is early days.

Not for Catherine it isn't, I couldn't help thinking.

I closed out of my email with Adele's words burning in my brain that the police intended to do everything possible to find my daughter.

Everything possible, so they could charge her with murder.

19

L ater that afternoon Cameron and Haley and I took Robbie in his stroller to Parc Monceau. It was only a few blocks from my apartment and yet once there I always felt a world away from anywhere. Complete with pyramid, arching stone bridges and even a carousel, it had become my go-to for any and all moments in my Paris life: happy ones, confused ones, sad ones.

And whatever today was.

Even among all the flowers and greenery of the park it was still quite hot. I sat down at a wooden table with a hastily packed picnic spread out before me.

I was heartened by the fact that Cameron had actually eaten most of his lunch. Aside from the fact that he spoke very little, I thought I could see signs of that resilience people always talk about when they reference kids weathering horrific events.

I wasn't sure what my plan was just yet. I just knew that I needed to hurry up and think of something.

In any missing person's investigation, the first twenty-four hours are critical. In fact, many law enforcement believe that if you don't uncover a lead during that time, the chances are almost nil that you'll recover the person at all.

We were eight hours away from Catherine being missing twenty-four hours.

Cameron walked to the edge of the duck pond to watch the ducks and I turned to Haley.

"Do you think you can handle watching both boys on your own for a bit?"

Haley shrugged. "Sure."

I looked over again at Cameron as he gazed into the distance and reminded myself that the best way to help him was to find his mother. The best way to help both of us.

"I'll meet you back at the apartment in a couple of hours," I said. "You've got your phone on you? And charged up?"

"Of course."

I looked back at Cameron and saw tears coursing down his cheeks. He wiped them away quickly. I wanted to run to him and press him into my arms. But if he was trying to be brave and hold it together, he wouldn't thank me for making it harder.

"Are you sure?" I said to Haley. "I'm not sure what he needs right now."

"He'll be fine, Missus B," Haley said, finally looking me in the eye. "Robbie and I got this."

From my apartment, the Paris police station was somewhat on the way to where the sightseeing boat was moored. I didn't hold out much hope that Bonnet would see me—let alone help me —but on the wild chance that he might, I needed to try.

I waited for twenty minutes for him to see me from where I waited in the lobby, but he never came out. I imagine if I'd been willing to sit there for an hour or more he might speak to me, but I keenly felt the hours and minutes ticking by.

I didn't have time to waste.

Discouraged but trying not to let it weaken me, I walked letting the force of my feet hitting the pavement give me courage and strength for the full twelve blocks to the office for the tourist boat company on Port de la Conference at Pont de l'Alma. It would have saved time to take a taxi or even the Metro, but I needed to walk.

The business office for the *Companie de Bateaux-Mouches* looked like it had been a Roman washhouse in another life. Ancient stone formed an irregularly shaped square building with a new metal door in the middle of one wall.

My understanding was that one purchased the boat tickets and then came into this building to register before walking through the building as a conduit to the boat embarkation point.

I shouldn't have been surprised to see that the office was closed today. After all, a man had just died on their boat. *Of course* it was closed.

I pulled out my phone and called the number painted on the office door, but only got a recorded message explaining the steps for booking a reservation. When there was a beep which indicated I should give my details, I hung up and called Adele.

She answered immediately.

"Do you have news?" I asked breathlessly, feeling as if every door I'd tried to open today had been slammed in my face.

"I am glad you called, *chérie*," Adele said. "Yes, I have news. Good and bad."

"For the love of God, give me the good news first," I said as I leaned against a nearby wall for support.

"CCTV camera footage shows Catherine leaving the boat."

Even though I always felt in my bones that Catherine was alive, the news that she'd been seen alive that night nearly prompted another breakdown in me. The relief was so massive I had to sit down for a moment on a nearby bench.

Catherine is alive! Hold onto that. You can live with anything else.

"Oh, my God, that's amazing news, Adele. Thank you. What's the bad news?" I asked the question not believing for a moment that there really could be any bad news now that I knew she was alive.

I was wrong.

"She wasn't alone."

At first I didn't think I understood what she was saying. Fear jabbed into my heart.

"Someone took her!" I gasped.

Of course! That made the most sense!

But whatever positivity I was managing to eke out from that theory was quickly extinguished by Adele's next words.

"Except," she said, "you can see on the video that she's not being dragged away."

"What...what do you mean?" I asked, blinking rapidly in confusion.

"Claire, she's definitely leaving with this guy of her own volition."

20

Catherine's head was pounding as she shifted on the filthy mattress and looked toward the window where a hazy filter of light was seeping in from the outside. She blinked in bleary confusion into the light.

Suddenly it all came back to her.

The terrible night, the shocking news that Cameron had been hurt, the man who was helping her...until she realized he wasn't helping her at all.

She felt gripped by an intense claustrophobia. Pain seemed to radiate from her chest and throat and she fought down the terror that threatened to engulf her. Taking a long breath she looked around at her surroundings.

She was in a small unfurnished room. A single window above her was grimy and unreachable. The floors were peeling linoleum and the walls were stained and dank. Across from where she lay on the mattress was the kitchen which amounted to no more than a sink and a small stove. She heard the sound of a dripping faucet either in the kitchen or from the other side of the only other interior door, which she assumed must be the bathroom.

"I'm thirsty," Catherine called, more to find out if she was alone than to actually get water

From across the room, she heard the bathroom door eased open. As it began to slowly move, she sat up and looked frantically around for anything she could use as a weapon.

"Do not be afraid," he said.

She realized with shock that he was handsome. He had a thick head of black hair and probing, almost kind eyes. Middle Eastern or maybe Indian. She recognized him as the man from last night.

He held a bottle of water in one hand and approached her as if she were a wild animal. He seemed more fearful of her than she was of him.

She took the water from him and saw his hands were shaking. She took a drink. Her head still hurt and for a moment she tried to remember if he'd drugged her. She remembered when she left the boat with him, her heart bursting out of her chest in the urgency and fear at what he'd told her.

He said Cameron had been in a car accident and that he would take her to the hospital where he was. She should have realized it wasn't likely that Cameron would be riding in a car. Her mother didn't even own a car! But her mind hadn't been working. All she heard was that Cameron was hurt.

It wasn't until they reached his car and it wouldn't start that Catherine pushed through the veil of panic and began to doubt him. Her doubts had taken longer than they should have. She'd been so protective of Cameron for so long that when this stranger told her he was hurt, she'd reacted without thinking. All she knew was that she had to get to her boy.

It wasn't until they got on the bus that she realized everything felt all wrong.

But by then it was too late.

Because by then the man had switched from "I will take you to your son" to "Come with me or I will kill him."

She remembered sitting on the bus and reaching for her phone. He snatched it from her and tossed it out the window of the bus.

That's when she felt the sting. Something sharp in her arm. He must have had the hypodermic ready because after that she remembered nothing more. She only registered hazy sights and sounds after that. And feeling so tired she could barely walk.

"What do you want with me?" she asked.

He shook his head helplessly.

"I know you speak English. You spoke it last night."

"No talk," he said and wiped his hands on his pants in agitation.

She felt her breaths catch in her chest.

Was this human trafficking? Was he going to try to sell her?

He looks nearly as terrified as I feel.

She licked her lips.

Which makes him even more dangerous.

"I have to use the bathroom," she said, standing up and instantly putting a hand on the mattress as she felt woozy.

"Okay," he said, stepping away from her to clear a path to the bathroom.

She took two steps when she heard a noise in the hallway. Women's voices. She caught his eye and knew he'd heard them too.

To reach the bathroom, she had to walk past the front door. As she did, she could hear the sounds of women laughing on the other side.

Suddenly, she lurched for the front door and wrenched the doorknob.

"Help!" she screamed. "I'm American! Help!"

She felt his hands hard on her shoulders as he grabbed her and spun her around. She clawed his face and neck with her nails, still screaming.

He brought her down violently onto the mattress and slapped a huge hand across her mouth. She writhed and fought until her muffled cries turned to defeated whimpering sobs.

21

That night Haley stayed for dinner but it was a sad, glum event.

I'd spent most of my day mentally falling down a very scary rabbit hole of what-ifs and if-so's, the result of which was that I was now an anxious, nearly-hysterical wreck.

I had no idea where my daughter was and I could not imagine how she could have just left the boat and not contacted me.

Regardless of what the video showed Catherine doing, there was no doubt—*as in none*—in my mind that she had not gone willingly. I don't know how to work that out. I just know it like I know I'm her mother. I know she would not have left without letting me and Cameron know.

She had to have been taken against her will.

And when I went down *that* particularly nasty rabbit hole, I always came up with the same answer.

Philippe Moreau.

I don't know why he would take Catherine but I can't imagine any other way this scenario makes sense.

I would give anything—years off my life, a leg or an arm

even—just to be able to call him up and plead with him. But I have no way of contacting him.

After Haley got both boys to bed—and they both fell asleep quickly—I did the dishes to try to lose myself in the chore. Then, giving up, I opened up a bottle of *Côtes du Rhône* and took it and a glass to the dining room table where I opened up my laptop.

Because of what I do for a living—basically find people who don't want to be found—I had no trouble tracking down the sightseeing boat's manifest for that night—complete with addresses for all the passengers.

I looked at the list of names I'd found.

There were seven couples. No singles.

All were obviously tourists except for the possible exception of one couple. All were registered either with a VRBO or Airbnb rental or at a hotel.

All except for the one couple where an address was not given.

I looked at the names and could only guess at the nationalities but I would soon know that too. Seven couples, fourteen people in all.

This had to mean that the man who left the boat with Catherine had come on board with someone else. It was imperative I talk to the woman he came on board with.

Seven couples, minus Todd, Catherine, and the mystery man, also meant six sets of two eyewitnesses, minus one. Eleven people to talk to—not counting the serving staff. In my experience, waiters and waitresses see an awful lot more than people think.

I wrote down the addresses as I found them on the Internet and then pulled out a paper map of Paris and marked on it where they were all staying.

Since they were tourists, most were staying on the right

bank—the second and eighth arrondissements—except for one couple who was staying in a rental in the Latin Quarter.

I looked up the hotel and saw it was in a nice neighborhood near where the sightseeing boat was moored. I reviewed what I found.

Two couples were staying at Airbnbs, one couple was staying at a VRBO apartment, and two sets of two couples were registered at an area hotel.

And then there was the couple whose address line had been left blank.

I drilled down on that line and found the reason for the ambiguity was that the guest's handwriting was not legible at the time of registration and the person who registered him didn't bother asking for clarification.

I felt my skin tingle as I studied the two names who registered without giving an address.

Ali and Ariel Qasim.

My pulse raced.

Those were Arabic-sounding names. And my father lives in Dubai.

I took in a shaky breath and refilled my wine glass. Tomorrow I'd visit every one of these people on my list and check them off one by one. But I was now fairly sure that Ali Qasim was the man who came onto the boat with a false name and left with Catherine in tow.

I looked again at the other names.

John and Sugar Brennon—probably American—were staying in a rental apartment; Mark and Mindy Sanderson— also probably American, were also staying in a rental; Matthew and Julie Marksdown—possibly Brits, also a rental; Susan Scibetta and Barbara Simpson—either American or British, were staying at the Seine Hotel; Margie and Denise Leverson, obviously related somehow, were also staying at the Seine Hotel, so possibly they were traveling with Susan and Barbara.

That made things easier.

And then there was Ali and Ariel Qasim.

I looked up the name Qasim on the Internet but there were thousands living in Dubai alone. I found no evidence of the two names linked—Ali and Ariel—no marriage licenses, in fact no trace at all of an Ariel Qasim.

My standard rule of thumb is if I don't get a whisper of a hit on a name I'm looking for, then it's probably a fake name. That wouldn't really be a big surprise if Ali and Ariel Qasim was the kidnapping duo. But something bothered me about that.

I kept looking at their names and then it came to me—what kind of a Middle Eastern name was *Ariel*? If you were going to give a false identity so as not to arouse suspicion or curiosity, wouldn't you have chosen something more clearly Arabic? Like Farah or Aisha or Aaliyah?

Where the hell did *Ariel* come from?

Unless it was her real name.

Without seeing the CCTV video I didn't know if the man on the video looked Middle Eastern. I didn't know if any of the couples I would meet and question tomorrow looked at all like the man in the video. For that matter I didn't know if any and all of the men on the boat were accounted for.

I found myself looking back at the list of names and wondering if the police were questioning them. Surely they would be. But even if they were, I still needed to talk to the passengers myself since the cops wouldn't be interested in sharing with me what they found out.

And the questions they'll ask will be very different from mine.

Because our goals are very different.

I had a huge job ahead of me tomorrow. I had to locate and question all of these people and hope that one of them saw something that might help me find Catherine—and I needed to do it with the clock steadily ticking down.

On top of all that, the radio said the lockdown would

include a curfew. Everyone needed to be off the street after eight o'clock in the evening. I needed every minute I could use, but if I was caught out after hours I would be lucky if I were only fined.

There would be no way I'd ever find my dear girl if I were locked up.

My arms and legs began to tingle with fatigue as I put my head in my hands and let the agony of what I feared most ripple through me.

A week from today and this will all be over.

If I get her back, it will just be a horrible memory as we work to put her and Cameron's life back together.

But if she's not back...

My shoulders bent inward and I felt bowed by the weight of my despair as tears coursed down my face.

Suddenly Izzy stood up and went to the door. This was not the way she normally goes to the door to tell me it's time to take her out. The hairs on her back were up and she was staring at the door intently.

Just as I realized that someone was at my door, I heard the soft rap on the other side of it.

I stood up slowly, knowing it was too late for it be Geneviève. Without knowing the security code downstairs nobody else would be able get into the building.

Izzy wasn't barking or even growling. But neither was she budging from her guard post.

I approached the door cautiously and raised up on tiptoe to peer through my peep hole before ripping off the security chain and flinging open the door with more strength and speed than I could have imagined I still had left in me.

There on my doorstep stood Jean-Marc.

22

I couldn't process that he was really here, in my living room, with a backpack over one shoulder, his dark brown eyes probing mine.

"How did you get here?" I asked, not really caring how.

"The lockdown, you mean?" He shrugged.

Tears pricked my eyes. I felt a warmth spread through my chest. I was so grateful to see him and it was all I could do not to throw myself into his arms. Perhaps he realized that because he reached out to take my hand and gave it a squeeze.

"I am sorry, Claire," he said.

I didn't ask him how he knew. Of course he knew. I searched his face to see if there was anything different about him since the last time I'd seen him, or since he'd decided to marry again. But there was nothing.

He held up a paper bag with a bottle in it and then turned to the kitchen.

"Who is here?" he asked as he poured two glasses of Philbert brandy to the rims.

"My grandson and Robbie and Robbie's babysitter."

He nodded and then led the way to the couch in the living

room. Izzy jumped on the couch and Jean-Marc ran his hand affectionately over her head. I sank onto the couch next to him.

"First tell me how you are," he said, pushing the glass of brandy toward me.

"Devastated," I said. "Terrified."

He nodded. "Drink. And tell me what you know."

I took a sip of the brandy. I'd already had too much wine but my head never felt clearer.

"Todd was stabbed two nights ago on a boat cruise on the Seine," I said, working to keep my voice stable. "He was pushed overboard and Catherine was seen leaving the boat with some man."

"Eyewitnesses saw this?"

"Not that I know of. It was captured on a CCTV video."

"Have you seen the video?"

I shook my head and felt a tremble of relief ripple through me. Everything was going to be better now. Jean-Marc was here and he was going to help me find my daughter.

Jean-Marc pulled out his phone and then turned to me.

"I didn't get a chance to grab dinner tonight," he said.

"I have Indian food."

He smiled at me and turned back to his phone while I got up to make him a plate. I could hear him talking in a low voice on his phone but his French was too fast for me to understand.

I returned to the room with a heaping portion of heated up panipuri and tikka masala and set it before him. He was just disconnecting the call.

I took another sip of my brandy, feeling it burn all the way down, and waited.

Somehow, ever since he'd come the minutes didn't feel like they were ticking by quite so quickly. I felt as if I was able to rest while someone else picked up the baton. I felt nearly six seconds of peace before he handed his phone to me.

"Press *Play*," he said and then leaned in next to me to watch the video with me.

Once the video started I heard street noise and birds in the audio. The disembarking point was a ramp half submerged in the water and a set of steep stone stairs leading up to the embankment.

I saw a couple appear in the frame from the boat and hurry down the ramp toward the stone stairs. I recognized Catherine immediately. There was no doubt it was her and I felt my heart catch in my throat to see her. In fact, I must have made a noise because I felt Jean-Marc's arm go around my shoulders.

Catherine was wearing the same linen slacks and blouse she had worn when she left the apartment that evening.

I played the video over again, watching my daughter hurry down the gangplank, her companion on the far side of the camera, his face obscured. Both moved quickly and deliberately.

Catherine was clearly *not* with him against her will. Half the time she was a step ahead of him.

"The cops think he's her lover," Jean-Marc said as the video ended with the two disappearing up the stairs and into the street. "They believe he killed Todd and then he and Catherine escaped together."

I replayed the video again.

"The guy's Middle Eastern," I said.

"It's hard to tell from the video."

"He's Middle Eastern. My father sent him."

Jean-Marc took his phone back and put it on the coffee table before reaching for a piece of naan.

"Why would he do that?" he asked.

"Who knows why he does what he does?" I said, fighting to keep my voice low so as to not wake the children.

But why else would Catherine leave with a stranger in the middle of a date with her husband?

After Jean-Marc had eaten, I collected the dishes and put them in the sink. I hated for him to leave now that he was here, but he said he was staying nearby. It was then that I found myself wondering if his fiancée was with him, perhaps waiting back at the hotel for him to return?

"You have informed the US Embassy?" he asked.

"I did. They told me to let the Paris police handle it and they would help with shipping Todd's body back to the US once it was released."

They'd called me earlier today and I'd felt so disheartened by their response that I'd actually forgotten about it until now.

"I just keep asking myself, why would she go with him?" I murmured.

"That is also the question the police will need answered," Jean-Marc said. "Or they will jump to their own answers."

"One possibility comes to mind," I said. "And that would be any number of a thousand different tricks that involved Cameron."

He nodded. "A desperate mother does not stop to ask questions."

"Exactly. She just runs to her child."

He patted his pockets as if he was forgetting something and then stood up.

"I will back in the morning. And we will think of a plan."

I walked him to the door.

"I've got the manifest of all the people who were on the boat that night," I said, although of course now that Jean-Marc was here, my night's work was unnecessary. He would be able to get all the names and addresses straight from the Paris police.

"You were planning on talking to them?" he asked as he stood at the door, preparing to take his leave.

"I was. All except for one, a Middle Eastern couple with no confirmable address."

He nodded.

"I'll go with you," he said.

I felt a warmth rush to my face at his words. It was all I could do not to kiss him.

"Thank you, Jean-Marc. I won't forget this."

"Try to get some sleep, Claire. You will need to be sharp in the coming days. If for no other reason, then for your grandson's sake."

He didn't say *we'll get her back*. He knows he can't promise that.

How I wish he would.

"I will," I said, already resisting letting him go. "Thank you again. You don't know how much your coming means to me."

He bent over to give Izzy's ears one more tousle and then turned to me.

"There is one bright side," he said.

"Please, tell me," I said, feeling a lump form in my throat.

"The lockdown has bought us time. Until it lifts she will still be in Paris."

I hadn't thought of that and it gave me a glimmer of hope.

"How long will the lockdown last?" I asked.

"No telling. Possibly a week. Maybe less."

I nodded. We only had until they lifted the lockdown to find her.

After that she would disappear into the mists of the Middle East.

Lost to us forever.

23

Catherine watched the man move around the kitchen. She noted that he was careful not to look at her.

After he'd wrestled her to the floor, he'd lain on top of her, his hand over her mouth until the women in the hall had gone and Catherine had spent herself with her tears. Then he carried her back to the mattress where she lay unresisting as he bound her hands with zip ties and put duct tape over her mouth.

She lay there on the mattress for what must have been hours, helpless and spent. Through her despair and burgeoning fear, she heard him vomiting in the bathroom. But she took no hope or pleasure from that. The man was desperate. His desperation seeped out of his pores, his eyes, and in his every gesture.

He was going to do something terrible to her. And regardless of how conflicted he seemed to be, it wouldn't stop him.

He stayed in the bathroom for an hour or more. Eventually, the stress and the exhaustion of her ordeal overwhelmed her and she slept.

When she woke he was in the kitchen, moving quietly as if

trying not to wake her. Catherine dragged herself to a sitting position and glared at him over the tape. She knew he wouldn't look at her and see the full strength of her fury and loathing.

Finally, he stood with his back to her and leaned against the kitchen counter, his head down as if praying or trying to gather the strength to do whatever he needed to do next.

Catherine inched to the far edge of the mattress and drew her knees up into her chest. She had no defense against him except to kick him when he came for her.

He turned and looked at her and rubbed his hands down his pants. Jeans. Lees. Not the sort of jeans anyone in the US wore any more. She wondered idly if he bought them in a *souk* or village market in some far-off third-world country.

"I will remove the tape from your mouth," he said. "If you promise not to scream."

She stared at him for a moment and then nodded. It was then that she smelled the unmistakable scent of garlic and onions. He'd been preparing a meal.

He came over to her, again careful not to meet her eyes, and gently tugged the tape off her mouth.

"You said my child was hurt," she said, her voice breaking to reference Cameron.

"I am sorry," he said, taking a step back but finally looking at her face. "How would you have come with me otherwise?"

"How did you know I had a child?"

"I was told."

"Who told you?"

"I cannot say."

Catherine looked away and fought for strength, for fortitude, for hope. She *would* escape. Of that she had no doubt. She would find a way because she had to.

"I still need to go to the bathroom," she said.

He backed away as if to clear a path to the bathroom. She scooted to the edge of the mattress and stood up and felt instantly woozy. She closed her eyes for a moment until her head cleared.

"My hands?" she said, holding her bound hands up.

"I'm sorry," he said. "And the bathroom door does not lock. I'm sorry."

"You're sorry about a lot," she said as she moved unsteadily to the bathroom.

As she passed him she looked at the skillet of hot grease and vegetables on the stove. She gauged her chances of snatching it up and throwing it at him but the steps to the stove and then to him and then to the door didn't add up.

Not with her as unsteady as she was. He saw her look at the skillet and went to stand in front of the stove. She turned toward the bathroom.

There would be another time.

There had to be.

24

Day Two of the Lockdown

I had hoped that Jean-Marc would come to the apartment so that he could see Robbie—although I imagine Robbie wouldn't remember him—but he suggested we meet at the address of the first boat passenger we intended to interview.

Telephoning typically saves time but leads aren't followed up on the phone. An old mentor of mine back in Atlanta—an ex-cop who'd turned to private investigation work—used to tell me that DNA and fingerprints didn't solve cases. They only supported the findings you uncovered from walking the streets and knocking on doors. Shoe leather, he use to say, was always the foundation of the successful detective.

Normally I'd have chosen to go first to the address furthest away and work my way back. But Jean-Marc suggested we start with the address closest to my apartment. I made a printout of the map of where all the boat passengers were staying—except for the Arabic couple.

John and Sugar Brennon were renting an apartment in the ninth arrondissement, so that's where we elected to meet.

The problem with Airbnb—or any short term rental company as far as the Paris city authorities see it—is that people who rent out their flats for brief stays reduce the housing available for people who need economical lodging for long term stays. I think the hotels in the city might have weighed in on the problem too, but the upshot of it all meant that all tourist rentals were now carefully monitored by the city government.

The sun was still high in the sky, but here on this pleasant residential street lined with classic Haussmann apartments its golden light filtered through a leafy canopy of sycamore trees and cast dappled shadows all around.

Paris is always beautiful, I thought miserably. Even when you were having the worst day of your life.

Jean-Marc was waiting for me at the corner of rue de Londre, not far from my apartment in the eighth. I hadn't asked him last night if he was taking a leave of absence to help me. I'd made up my mind not to question him too much. He was here and he was helping. None of the rest of it mattered.

He greeted me with a nod—not the typical double kisses I'd once been used to from him a thousand years ago—and we made our way to the apartment of the concierge on the ground floor.

In the old days, every Paris apartment building had a concierge who lived in the building and served as a sort of doorman. A concierge would accept packages and convey messages. If a building had a concierge, there was little need for an electronic security system. For me to have gained entry without Jean-Marc, I would have had to sneak past the concierge.

And trust me, that is no easy feat. These people take their jobs seriously.

Jean-Marc showed her his police credentials and asked for the apartment number for Mr. and Mrs. Brennon. Within moments we were having the door opened for us onto a small but natty two-bedroom apartment.

JB Brennon was a rugged, stout man with a ruddy complexion and prominent cheekbones. His wife seemed the mirror opposite of him with a diminutive heart-shaped and very pale face.

"It was all so terrible!" Sugar Brennon said, her southern accent laced thick with an overly sweet drawl. "We couldn't believe it when we heard about it."

Jean-Marc and I were sitting in their comfortable, color-coordinated living room with two cups of hot coffee before us.

"So you didn't see anything?" I asked.

"Well, no," she said, glancing at her husband as if for confirmation. "But I had a headache and was ready to come home. Nobody said anything about...you know...a man falling overboard."

I told myself not to be disappointed. They were our first interview after all.

"Did you notice *anything* unusual on the trip?" Jean-Marc asked.

"Not really," John Brennon said jovially. "It was all pretty much what I expected."

"Well, except for the fight," Sugar said, again looking at her husband.

"Oh, yeah," he said. "Yeah, that was intense."

I stiffened in surprise at her words. "What fight?" I asked.

"This young couple—American by their accents—were fighting," Sugar said.

"Screaming at each other," her husband said.

"And then he stormed off," she said.

"What did they look like?" Jean-Marc asked.

"She was a pretty little thing," John said. "Her husband was tallish. With glasses."

"No glasses," Sugar said. "I don't think. Anyway, sorry we

can't be more help. Was the couple related to the man who fell overboard?" Then she gasped. "Oh, don't tell me! Was *he* the one who died?"

"Unfortunately yes," Jean-Marc said as we stood up. "Thank you for your help. Is the lockdown preventing you from going home?"

"No, we planned on staying two weeks anyway," Sugar said with a smile. "It won't interrupt my shopping one bit!"

The next interview wasn't much more helpful. Staying in a studio rental in the Latin Quarter, Mark and Mindy Sanderson, also American, had also seen the fight and heard shouting at the launch site when the tour was over.

"I'd lost my sunglasses," said Mindy Sanderson, a chubby blonde in a bright pink set of matching shorts and floating top. "So we were some of the last ones off the boat."

"This guy was shouting," said Mark, a balding but affable man in his early forties. "Screaming that someone had fallen in."

"Do you know who was shouting?" Jean-Marc asked.

"The pilot, maybe?" Mark said, glancing at his wife, who shrugged.

I hadn't forgotten the boat pilot. In fact, if he was the first one to see Todd's body in the water, he would be a key person to interview.

Aside from possibly embellishing the fight just a bit—or possibly presenting it more accurately—there was nothing more to be learned from the Sandersons.

It was late morning by this time and Jean-Marc and I decided to stop for an early lunch. It seemed that both of us had failed to eat breakfast—I was so nervous and overwrought it was an agony even to think of food.

Our next interview was back across the Seine, so we stopped at a little place a few streets off the Champs-Élysées to eat.

I ordered an omelet with fries and a Coke. Jean-Marc ordered fish with a glass of wine. I couldn't help but think sadly of the café where I'd eaten with Todd and Catherine just three days ago.

"So far nobody saw Todd fall," I said. "But they all heard the fight."

"Was there a doubt that they fought?" Jean-Marc asked.

I shook my head. "No, they were having problems. That definitely scans."

"What were the problems about?"

"I don't know. She didn't share that with me."

He held my gaze for a moment too long and I leaned across the table to him.

"Yes, their marriage was going through a rocky patch. But there was no way Catherine would stab him! And push him overboard? The father of her child? She went back to the States last summer specifically to try to make it work with him!"

The waiter returned with our food but I was no longer hungry. I was pretty sure I was not going to be able to find my appetite ever again.

"Calm down, Claire," Jean-Marc said taking a sip of his wine after the waiter left. "No one is accusing Catherine of killing Todd."

"The cops are saying her *lover* did the killing which is nearly as bad and you know it!"

Jean-Marc made a face that I'd seen him make many times before. It sometimes meant *you're right,* but it could also mean *no way is that true.* I suppose other French people have the answer key to knowing how to interpret this look but I still don't know and I'm sure no matter how long I live here, I never will.

"You should eat," he said.

I forced myself to eat a forkful of the omelet and then picked up my phone to text Haley. I sent a text to Cameron too. I hated leaving him alone now of all times. Every time I reached out to him to encourage him, it helped buck me up too. I couldn't think of what I would do, what either of us would do, if we couldn't find Catherine. I couldn't go there.

Not until I had to.

An hour later Jean-Marc and I were knocking on the door of Matthew and Julie Butterworth, who were renting a one-bedroom in the eighth arrondissement not far from the Champs-Élysées.

When Matthew Butterworth opened the door, he smiled broadly.

"Come in, come in!" he said in an Australian accent. "Jules will be right out."

He ushered us into the living room.

"The police have already talked to us," he said. "I'm afraid we weren't able to help very much."

Julie Butterworth entered the room with a tray of teacups and a teapot. She was blonde with a carefully made-up face and wearing a linen sundress. Jean-Marc stood up until she set the tray down and seated herself.

"I am Capitaine Jean-Marc LaRue," he said formally to them both. "And this is Claire Baskerville. It was her son-in-law who died on the boat you were both on."

"Bloody hell," Matthew said. "That's rough."

"I'm so sorry for your loss," Julie said as she poured our tea.

"We are asking everyone who was on the boat," Jean-Marc said, "if they saw anything—anything at all—out of the ordinary."

The couple looked at each other and both shrugged at the same time.

"Not really," Julie said. "It was a fun tour. Up until then, of course."

"Did you hear the moment when they discovered someone had gone in the water?" I asked.

"Not really," Julie said, a response I found a little frustrating. *Well, you either did or you didn't*, I wanted to say.

"When did you find out that one of your group had gone over the side?" Jean-Marc asked.

"I guess when we were at the dock," Matthew said. "We were still finishing our desserts, so we weren't the first ones off."

"And that's because you took so many ciggie breaks," Julie said pointedly.

Matthew didn't answer but I could see he wasn't happy with her comment. But Jean-Marc saw something more.

"I hate to ask, Mrs. Butterworth," Jean-Marc said. "But do you have any more milk? This seems to have gone off."

Julie jumped up, horrified, and grabbed the creamer issuing apologies as she hurried to the kitchen. Unlike the other apartments we'd visited today, the kitchen was around the corner and out of earshot of the living room. Jean-Marc turned to Matthew.

"Did you see something on your cigarette break?" he asked.

Matthew's face looked resigned and ashamed all at the same time.

"Not really," he said in a voice that seemed to say otherwise.

Jean-Marc glanced toward the kitchen and by doing so wordlessly reminded the Australian that these questions could just as easily be happening after his wife returned.

"Okay," Matthew said, dropping his voice. "I saw the bloke who'd been fighting with his wife, okay? He was at the railing."

"Was he alone?" I asked.

"No, he was talking to some Arab dude."

I felt my heart speed up and a warmth flushed through my body at the revelation.

Todd had been talking to Ali Qasim!

"I didn't hear what they were saying, you know?" Matthew said. "But you know how you can tell with body language? The American was super pissed off."

"Pissed off in general?" Jean-Marc asked. "Or pissed off at the man who was with him?"

"Definitely with the Arab guy."

He was talking about Todd's murderer. I felt myself suddenly awash in emotion hearing it—even though I'd already imagined the killer had to be the mysterious Ali Qasim.

"Did you see the Arab man attack the American?" Jean-Marc asked him.

"No! Nothing like that," Matthew said in a hoarse whisper, glancing over his shoulder in the direction of the kitchen.

"Give me a break! I would've told the police if I had. I only noticed the two of them for a second before I knew I had to get back to my wife. She hates me smoking."

That explained why Jean-Marc had contrived to get rid of Julie for a few minutes—so that her husband could be a bit more honest with us. I don't know how Jean-Marc saw that. Maybe it's a guy thing, but in any case I was grateful he'd picked up on it. I don't think I would have.

Afterwards, we stood for a moment on the street in front of the Australian couple's apartment building. I felt like I was vibrating with expectation. We were piecing it together. It was taking forever, yes. But we were getting there.

"It was Ali Qasim," I said firmly to Jean-Marc. "It has to be. Todd went to the railing after his fight with Catherine. He was attacked there by Qasim who then went looking for Catherine."

I wracked my brain trying to imagine what the man—a total stranger!—could have said to get her to accompany him and leave Todd behind on the boat.

"Didn't you pretty much know that anyway?" Jean-Marc said.

I looked at him and wondered why he was attempting to tamp down my optimism.

"Yes, of course. But now we have a witness."

"But not to the killing. The Australian only saw them arguing. That makes his observation circumstantial."

"Okay," I said with frustration, "it's true nobody saw Qasim *stab* Todd. But if we can track down people who remember seeing Catherine during the crucial time, she'll at least be in the clear for Todd's murder."

"Claire, no." Jean-Marc said as he threw up his hands in frustration. "As far as her innocence is concerned, Catherine's whereabouts is irrelevant! She left the boat with the presumed murderer. At worst she's an accomplice. At the very least..."

"Okay, fine," I said briskly, trying to shake off the crowding emotion that was beginning to brim up inside me. "What's our next move? Do we track down the pilot?"

"The police will have already spoken with him."

"They've already spoken to all the boat passengers too," I pointed out. "But that isn't stopping us from talking to them again."

He shrugged as if to say that of course I was right. What he didn't say—because he didn't need to—was that we'd found out nothing helpful despite our efforts.

"I need to make a call," he said. He turned away with his phone and walked a few yards away to make his call. As I watched him, I realized he was right. There was no way to look at this that wasn't devastating. Not for Catherine, at least, and that was all that mattered.

But as I looked at the earnestness in Jean-Marc's face as he spoke on the phone, I realized that at least half of what I was trying to do right now—put together the pieces to try to construct a scenario of what had happened—was to keep myself from imagining what it was my daughter might be enduring right now.

25

Catherine stared at the light creeping in from the lone window over her mattress and tried to guess the time before turning to confirm it on the digital clock on the stove in the kitchen. The light looked milky and hazy. It was hard to tell if it was morning or late afternoon because the pane was so dirty.

She lowered her head to rest on her arms in front of her.

Todd and Mom must be going out of their minds!

She couldn't even bring herself to think of Cam. Every time she did she felt weaker, more enervated.

A noise from behind her made her turn to see her captor as he entered the kitchen from the bathroom where he typically stayed. She saw a cardboard box on the counter where she watched him extract a small bag of rice and a rotisserie chicken. She didn't remember seeing a refrigerator in the kitchen.

He'd gone out at least twice but she'd been asleep when he left each time.

As he turned on the gas flame on the stove and set a skillet on it, she studied his face.

She worked to commit his features to memory, believing that the time would surely come when she'd be able to tell the police what he looked like. He had no tattoos that she could see, but he kept his arms covered, even in all this heat.

He was clearly Middle Eastern, so perhaps that was a cultural thing. He wore nonbrand sneakers and his hair and beard were neatly clipped. He wasn't homely. In fact she found herself shocked to realize he was actually nice looking. She felt a pulse of anger as the realization came to her. She didn't want to think anything nice about this monster.

Just thinking the word *monster* gave her a stab of anxiety.

What does he want with me? Why are we here?

It was true that he hadn't touched her except to help her to the bathroom or physically subdue her that first day. He'd repositioned her bonds so that her hands were in front, but the duct tape was still securely in place.

He was taking no chances that she would scream.

She waited until he turned to look at her, which he did with chilling regularity, and lifted her hands to get his attention. He walked over to her, a pained look on his face, and eased the tape off her mouth.

"My husband will be going out of his mind," she said. "And my son! Please! He'll be so afraid that I didn't come home! How can you be so heartless? Do you not have children of your own?"

He looked startled at her speech as if surprised that she would appeal to him personally. His hand hesitated by her face as if not sure whether to tape her mouth shut again or let her say more.

Catherine heard her last words echo around in the small, dank apartment.

Do you not have children of your own?

"Why are you doing this?" she whispered, feeling a tear streak down one cheek.

"Please no talk," he said, glancing at the tear before gently reaffixing the tape to her mouth.

He went back to the kitchen and Catherine felt the disappointment like a gut blow. She looked at the single window over her mattress—the only one in the apartment and too high up to easily reach. She reminded herself of the walk into the apartment—even though she'd been groggy and barely cognizant—and tried to remember the walk through the outside lobby, foyer, courtyard and street. She realized after a moment of trying to remember that she was only remembering the features of her mother's apartment.

She'd counted the steps from her mattress to the door and had calculated the seconds it would require to unlock it...but he was always just a step or two away from her. There was no way she could escape with him here. And he always waited until she slept before he left the apartment.

She watched him pull the skillet off the heat and divide the food between two plates.

I need to not panic or give up. Find out his mission and why he's doing this.

It occurred to her that screaming out "I'm an American" to the building residents might have the opposite desired effect. She honestly didn't know what the average French person thought of Americans. In her own experience, it was hardly fondly.

As she watched him pull spoons and condiments from a drawer, she thought of how furious Todd must have been when he discovered she'd left the boat without him. How long before he realized she was in trouble?

Or would that be Mom suggesting that my disappearance couldn't possibly be normal?

Regardless of who did it, surely they would have gone to the police by now! It had been nearly twenty-four hours.

Surely somebody saw me leaving with him! There are CCTV cameras everywhere over here!

She stared at the door to the apartment and felt a flutter in her belly as she embraced the thought.

Surely the police will come bursting through that door any minute!

Surely to God they will.

26

I t was the smell of mildew more than anything that struck me when Jean-Marc and I stepped into the office of the Companie de Bateaux-Mouches near Pont de l'Alma. Otherwise the place was very plush and elegant. Even so I half expected to feel my shoes squish when I stepped on the carpet in the company manager's office beside the quay where the sight-seeing vessels were moored.

Jean-Marc and I decided that he would do the talking in this interview. It was one thing for me to take the lead when we were talking with tourists—most of whom were American— but the pilot of the tourist boat would likely have zero patience for anyone remotely resembling a tourist. And we needed him to take our questions seriously.

The manager of the Companie de Bateaux-Mouches was waiting for us in his office with another man, by the looks of him the boat's pilot. He was thirty or so with thick curly hair, stubble on his chin and a smile on his sunburned face. He struck me as someone who'd found what he liked to do and was doing it.

Jean-Marc showed his police credentials and we all shook hands.

"Our lawyers have advised us to stick to a prepared statement," the manager said. "I have sent it to your office."

"We are not here to blame anyone," Jean-Marc said. "We just need a clearer picture of what Monsieur Bocuse saw that day."

"I saw a body bobbing in the water," the pilot said.

"Henri!" the manager admonished. "You are to say nothing!"

Henri shrugged. "I saw what I saw. I didn't put him there."

"What is the route you take on these tours?" Jean-Marc asked Henri who looked at his boss before answering.

The manager frowned but decided the lawyer's statement wasn't necessary to cover such a benign question.

"We start at Pont de l'Alma," Henri said. "We go south and then turn back at Notre-Dame."

"And there was nothing unusual on this leg of the tour?"

"From my end? Nothing at all."

I knew the police had thoroughly questioned the waiters on the boat, which in many ways seemed more useful than talking to the pilot. All he'd seen was the body. They might have actually witnessed the attack.

"And then?" Jean-Marc prompted.

"And then we swung back and headed upriver past the d'Orsay and the Eiffel Tower before heading to the debarkation point."

"How long did the whole tour take?" Jean-Marc asked.

"Ninety minutes."

"And when did you notice the body?"

The manager shifted in his seat but didn't object.

"Just as I was bringing it in to the ramp."

"By the position of where you saw the body, would you guess that it had gone in relatively recently?"

"Yes. Within a minute perhaps of my seeing it. Otherwise, with the current, he would've been headed for the bulkhead down by Pont de Bir-Hakeim."

He grinned as if he'd made a joke but my stomach churned at the image he created.

This was Todd he was talking about.

I felt a bubble of perspiration form on my forehead, but Jean-Marc was already standing to signal the end of the interview.

"Thank you, Monsieur Bocuse," he said, nodding to Henri before turning to the manager. "I will need to talk with the table servers as well."

"Absolutely not," the manager said, rubbing his forehead in agitation. "The police have already taken their statements and the company lawyer has made it very clear that we need to do no more."

∾

"I can get copies of the statements from the boat's table servers," Jean-Marc said from across the café table where we'd gone after the interview with the boat pilot. It was long past lunchtime, but Jean-Marc convinced me that a snack and a rest would do more for us than rushing on to the next set of interviews hungry and weary.

I had to agree. The results of our interviews alone were enough to deplete us.

"That's good," I said. "Although I'm sure they're all going to focus on the screaming fight between Todd and Catherine."

"Yes, but there may be something else of note."

When our meals arrived, Jean-Marc directed his attention to his plate with the single-minded focus with which I've found most French people address their food. I took a moment to call Haley to see how Cam was doing.

"He's fine," she said. "We're watching TV and Madame Rousseau is making us *poulet de Provence*.

"Okay, good," I said. "Please let Cam know he can call me any time he wants."

"He knows."

After that, I concentrated on getting food into me so I didn't pass out during the rest of our afternoon's interviews. Unlike most detectives, the information I was hearing wasn't just factual to me or the bricks I needed to build a case. Every time I heard some stranger describing a scene that involved Todd and Catherine, I felt like weeping.

I felt desperate when they talked about Catherine, because these strangers had seen my darling girl since I had and that was painful. And when I heard them talk about Todd, I felt swamped with guilt for how much I'd disliked him and how a part of me has actually thought of how much easier life will be now for Catherine and Cameron.

I truly hate myself for thinking that. But it underscores how today's work was so much more emotional for me than any investigator doing the necessary groundwork of a case.

"Are you okay?" Jean-Marc asked, frowning at me over his steamed mussels.

"It's just hard," I said, hearing the quaver in my voice.

"Of course," he said, still watching me.

I took myself in hand then. This was a job that needed to be done and if I let my emotions take the lead, it wouldn't get done properly. And if there was ever a case where I needed to be at my best, this was it.

I forced myself to push away the image of Todd bobbing along in the wake of the romantic boat cruise.

"I wanted to congratulate you on your engagement." I said in a rush. I hadn't realized I was going to say it until it came out of my mouth.

Jean-Marc made an odd guttural sound and stayed focused on his plate.

"Adorlee has helped me a lot these last months," he said.

"How did you meet her?"

He glanced up at me.

"She works in the department. She is assistant to the medical examiner."

He turned back to his plate as if to stress that he'd said all that he intended to say on the subject. I felt a heaviness settle into my chest.

"Well, I'm glad you have someone to help you," I said, turning my attention to my artichoke risotto, my stomach suddenly feeling unnaturally queasy.

I'm glad you have someone to help you get over the pain I caused you.

27

I looked down the street of immaculate upper-class apartments, each carefully crafted to represent the epitome of Parisienne style and design. The windows and balconies of the apartments looked down onto the little gardens which were full of geraniums and climbing roses. The wealthy of the Left Bank lived here.

I glanced at Jean-Marc as we walked down the street toward the hotel.

"Do you miss it?" I asked. "Paris?"

He looked at me in surprise and then looked around the street and shrugged.

"I do not think about it."

That sounded like a lie to me. The question was why did he bother telling it?

The Seine Hotel clearly strove to fit into the setting of its elegant neighbors. As I crossed the street, I saw the builder's plaque on the corner which read 1865. The front door, flanked by two massive marble pillars, was walnut with elegant brass fittings.

The only people left to interview that day—besides the mysterious Qasim and his companion—were the four women who were staying in the hotel.

It was late afternoon, which led me to hope we'd find the women in. If they were like most tourists my age, the big push to see museums and to shop and eat lunch would happen early in the day. If they did rouse themselves for an evening activity —like say, a boat tour—chances are they would be napping or resting in the afternoon.

We stepped into the lobby with its gleaming marble tile with decorative inserts and plush couches and chairs and went immediately to the sweeping front desk which was manned by a grim-faced hotel clerk.

Jean-Marc flashed his badge, which only increased the grimness in the man, but he quickly called up to the hotel guests we needed to see.

We were in luck. Not only were all four women in, but I'd been right about them knowing each other.

We took the very modern elevator—one that could fit more than two people in it—to the second floor, and walked down the thick carpeting to the room door belonging to Susan Scibetta and Barbara Simpson—widows and childhood friends.

They opened the door and welcomed us in. Behind them we could see that they'd opened the door between their room and the next so that the other eyewitnesses on the boat—sisters Margie and Denise Leverson—could join us.

The exhaustion I should have felt from my already very long day was not registering with me yet as I sat at a desk chair in Susan and Barbara's room facing all four women who sat on the two queen size beds. Jean-Marc stood beside me.

They introduced themselves and told how they knew each other—through a knitting club in Indianapolis.

"We're sorry to interrupt your trip," I said. "But we're trying to talk to everyone who was on the boat that night."

"You're not interrupting our trip," Susan said with a shrug. "It's the most excitement we've had since we got here."

I turned to the group.

"We understand a young couple had an argument in the dining room," I said. "Did you see it?"

All the women nodded.

"We didn't want to stare, you know?" Denise said. She was a heavyset woman and wore a bright floral day dress. "But they were shouting."

The other three women nodded again in agreement.

"She threw a drink in his face," Susan said.

"That was so shocking, wasn't it?" Margie said. A pinched-faced woman with pulled-back and overly dyed hair, she looked around at her friends who again all nodded.

"We tried not to look, didn't we?" Barbara said. "It was such an unpleasant scene to witness."

"He stormed off, I guess to cool off," Margie said.

"And the girl just sat there for the longest time," Susan said. "She finally left, I guess to go look for her husband."

"I hope she wasn't thinking of apologizing," Denise said. "It sounded as if she had every right to throw that champagne at him."

"Well, marriage is long," Barbara said. "They might *both* have apologized."

"You act like you're the only one with a long marriage," Margie said.

"Longer than yours anyway," Barbara said with a sniff.

"Girls, girls!" Susan said. "It doesn't matter who's been married how long."

"Said the ninety-day wonder!" Denise snickered.

Barbara clapped her hands.

"Enough!" she said, making it clear who was the leader of the group.

She turned to me and Jean-Marc. "We heard all the commotion when we got off the boat about a body being in the water but we didn't see anything ourselves."

"Did you leave straight away?" I asked.

Barbara seemed a little embarrassed by the question.

"Well, the night was still young and we were curious," she admitted.

"And then the police showed up and it's a good thing we did hang around," Susan said. "Because they wanted to talk to all of us."

"That's when we heard that the body was one of the passengers," Margie said with a shiver.

After that there was some discussion about whose idea it had been to hang around which seemed about to devolve into an argument among the four.

I stood up.

"Thank all of you," I said. "You have been very helpful." Although truthfully I wasn't really sure how helpful the discussion had been. They basically only confirmed that Todd and Catherine had fought on the cruise.

Which of course we already knew.

Barbara got up to let us out.

"Thank you for telling your story a second time," Jean-Marc said. "We appreciate it."

"I think Margie felt a little guilty, you know?" Barbara confided as she stepped out in the hall with us.

"Guilty?" I said. "Why?"

"Well, when the cops came to talk to us that was before we knew they were looking at the young wife as the murderer."

I'm sure the blood drained from my face at her words.

"Where did you...where did you hear that?" I said in a breaking voice, my chest suddenly squeezing me with dread.

"Oh, I don't think it's official, honey!" she said, hurriedly. "It was one of the policemen who told us. Denise saw him standing out front of our hotel yesterday and the two of them got to talking. Her French isn't bad—she majored in it in college as she never fails to remind us. Anyway, the cop said the young woman we'd all seen screaming at her husband was being held for his murder."

"That...that's not true," was all I managed to sputter out.

"Well, Denise might have gotten that wrong. Her French isn't *that* good and she's been having memory issues lately. But she definitely got the idea the police thought the young woman killed her husband. Although how she pushed him over the railing I have no idea!"

"You said Margie felt guilty about something," Jean-Marc said, trying to steer her back to the original point.

"Oh, yes, she did," Barbara said. "Because I'm sure she never would've said what she did if she'd known the police thought the girl killed him."

I literally thought I might scream in frustration and Jean-Marc must have sensed that because he put a hand on my arm as if to calm me or restrain me, I'm not sure which.

"What did Margie say?" he asked her as calmly as I never could have managed.

"She told the police what we all heard but I guess had forgotten until just that moment."

"And that was?" Jean-Marc asked.

She looked over her shoulder in the direction of her friends inside.

"She told them what the young woman yelled at her husband."

"Which was?"

Barbara looked truly grieved to have to tell us. She shook her head sadly.

"She said she'd make him sorry."

28

W alking away from the hotel, I felt a warm breeze blowing in off the river, bringing with it the smell of fish and refuse. It was late afternoon but still hot and I could feel my linen blouse sticking to my back.

After our full day of interviewing witnesses I have to say I can't remember feeling as disconsolate and exhausted as I did on the walk back to my apartment.

I appreciated that Jean-Marc didn't comment on the threat that Catherine was overheard making to Todd. The fact was, that was the kind of thing people said in a fight.

But when one of them ends up dead, those words can come back to haunt you.

If not indict you.

When we reached the corner of my street, rue de Laborde, I dug in my purse for my front door keys.

"You're welcome to stay for dinner," I said.

He hesitated but shook his head.

"You need to rest," he said.

I didn't think it was necessary to point out that *resting* was hardly likely, but I wasn't going to push him if he preferred not to come up.

"I just wanted to say again, Jean-Marc," I said, choosing my words carefully—tears were my default response to everything these days, especially heartfelt expressions of gratitude, "how much I appreciate what you're doing for me."

"Claire, *non*," he said. "Of course I would come. And you mustn't give up."

The word *yet* hung in the air between us.

"I'm not," I said.

Suddenly he held up his finger and began patting his pockets to indicate he was getting a call. I watched him pull his phone out and speak into it in a low voice. Finally he hung up.

"That was Bonnet," he said. "They believe they have found his car."

I felt a fluttering sensation go through me at his words. This was the first real break we'd gotten yet.

"There was no registration or identification in it," Jean-Marc said. "And the battery was dead which would account for its still being parked there."

"Where did they find it?"

"On rue Goethe, not too far from the *Bateaux Mouches*. Nobody else on the street owns it and a few of the vendors say they'd never seen it before. It wasn't stolen so we should be able to get an identification on it."

"So what's the takeaway?" I asked impatiently. "Does it mean he and Catherine fled on foot?"

"It looks like it."

Was that good or bad? Did that make our job easier or harder?

One thing was for sure, as leads go, it was at least more than we had a few seconds ago.

But it was still a very tiny needle in an absolutely colossal haystack.

29

That night I made macaroni and cheese for the children and a green salad. Haley had essentially moved in with us for the past few days and I don't know how I would've managed without her. Geneviève had come up to make them lunch today. I invited her, Noel and Bill to come up for a bite to eat, but she declined. I know she was thinking she doesn't want to add to my stress at the moment.

Once the kids had eaten and were settled yet again in front of the TV, I was about to take Izzy downstairs to wet the pavers when a bloodcurdling scream projected out over the television cartoon laugh-track.

I hurried into the living room to see Robbie on Haley's lap and Cameron standing on the couch shrieking at the television set. Robbie began to cry and Izzy began to bark. I went to him and took his hand.

It was like he was in some kind of trance, the way he was staring at the television. His face was mottled with red blotches and he seemed to be gulping for air.

"Cam, sweetie," I said, running my hand up the back of his

neck. When he was a baby, this motion used to calm him instantly on those rare occasions he became fretful or unhappy.

He looked at me as if in a panic.

"Grammy," he said, gasping, his eyes on mine in desperation.

"I know, my darling," I said, feeling tears gather in my eyes. "I know it hurts."

"I want Mommy. I need her."

"I know, angel. We'll get her back. I promise you."

"You...you promise?"

Would he ever forgive me for this lie if I couldn't keep it? Will I even care if it means a world without Catherine?

"I do, sweetie. I promise."

He turned to me and held out his arms and I gathered him into mine and held him tight. His body was rigid until he broke down in long agonized sobs.

"Just a little bit longer," I whispered to him.

I caught Haley's startled look and tried to smile to comfort her. Robbie had stopped crying but he was looking at Cameron as if he was someone he didn't know. He burrowed deeper into Haley's arms.

Somehow Haley understood what to do next. She gathered Robbie up and took him into my bedroom and closed the door. I pulled Cam onto my lap on the couch and rocked him. Words weren't necessary. I'd said everything I could say, lies or not. He had to get through this interim the same as the rest of us. Any way he could.

No, make that the same as me. Nobody else would be as devastated as Cam and I would be if we never saw Catherine again. Nobody else's world would be as impacted as ours. I held him tightly and when he finally stopped crying, I realized that holding him helped me too. I held him like that while Izzy, her leash still attached to her collar, snuggled beside my hip.

Spending time with Cam made me feel weaker. When I was

around him, I saw only too clearly the agony that awaited both of us if I were to fail. When I was out of the house, talking to people, following whatever meager clues I had, I had what Cam didn't—the feeling that I was moving forward, getting closer.

I hated that I couldn't be here for him when he was hurting the most. But I only had a few hours to find her. It killed me to choose those hours—useless and futile though they may well prove to be—over Cam. Especially in his hour of deepest need. I prayed that my abandoning him now when he was so fragile wouldn't damage him forever.

But mostly I just prayed that we find his mother.

For both our sakes.

Cam's meltdown had done him in emotionally and physically and he fell asleep in my arms. It occurred to me while I was holding him that if Catherine's kidnapper had lost the use of his car, he might not just walk to wherever he needed to go. He might, instead flag down a taxi.

After a while I disengaged and covered Cam with a blanket on the couch. Haley had bathed and put Robbie to bed. She was in the guest room now reading a book.

As soon as I ran Izzy downstairs and back up, I got out my laptop and went to find the list of taxi cabs companies that served the area of Paris nearest the sightseeing boats' debarkation points.

There were only three major companies which didn't seem too daunting. But what about Ubers? Would the police have a list of all the registered Uber drivers in the city?

I looked at a map I had printed out and drew a tight arc around the spot where Catherine and her kidnapper had entered the street from the boat ramp as well as the spot where his car was found. There wasn't a taxi stand nearby, so if they hailed a cab this circle I'd outlined was the most logical place for them to have found one.

As I was poised to call the first cab company I realized that there was no way they were going to give me the information I needed. No dispatcher would give out that information without an official request from the police.

Just as I was about to pick up the phone to call Jean-Marc to see if he could manage that from his police contacts in Paris, I saw he was calling me.

I answered the phone with a hushed voice although I could hear by Cameron's snores that he was sleeping deeply.

"Hey," I said. "I was just going to call you. I need you to get me a green light to talk to the cab companies in the area so I can find out if any of them picked up a fare that might have been Catherine and Qasim."

"Okay," he said.

There was something about the way he answered—and the fact that he'd called me first—that made me realize he must have news.

"What's happened?" I asked.

"I've got the CCTV footage of everyone getting on the boat," he said. "I'll bring it over tomorrow."

"Have you seen it?"

"*Oui.* Like the manifest, it shows everyone we've already met coming on board in twos."

"Even Qasim? Are you able to see his face?"

"No, he kept his face averted. But the boat's ticket taker remembered his companion calling him *Omar.*"

I clasped my hands together and was nodding my head before he finished speaking.

"So he gave the sightseeing boat purser a fake name!" I said.

"A different one, anyway."

"What do we know about her?" I asked.

"The police are working on finding her. No luck so far."

"*How* are they working? Using facial recognition software?"

"Claire, no. The video is too blurred."

"Can Detective Bonnet get me a photo of her from the footage?"

"How do you hope to find her if the police cannot?"

"It's not that the police can't do it, they won't bother! They've got Catherine and this Omar guy in their crosshairs! I'll take this woman, Ariel's photo and walk up and down every street in a ten-block radius to the boat ramp until I find someone who remembers seeing her."

I didn't need him to tell me how futile and time-consuming that sounded—and how little time we had. I appreciated he didn't say it because it wouldn't have changed anything.

"What else do you know about Omar? Does he live in Paris?"

"First we do not know that that is really his name. And it is only a first name. There is no record of any *Omar* on any flight manifests coming into Orly or Charles DeGaulle. Or he could've come in through Nice or Marseille or even the Chunnel."

"But if he used a fake name on the boat tour, why would he use his real one to fly?"

"Because he'd need a passport to fly. It's a lot easier to give a fake name to a tourist boat that doesn't demand any kind of formal identification. In any case, it's more likely he drove into France since we know he had a car."

I wanted to throw my hands up and scream.

Two steps back, a half step forward. Arghh!

"Do you think *Omar* is his real name?" I asked.

"We have no way of knowing."

"But if his companion called him that—"

"We are just guessing," Jean-Marc said impatiently. "He could just as easily have given *her* a fake name too."

"But then why give a *different* fake name to the boat purser?"

"All good questions, Claire."

My jaw began to ache from how hard I was clenching it.

"There has to be something more on him. This guy didn't just spring from nowhere," I said, feeling my muscles tighten as if in readiness for something. "He exists. He has a trail."

And no matter what it took I was determined that I was going to find it.

30

C atherine felt as if she were wilting in the heat. With no air conditioning and the only window in the apartment closed, there was only a small oscillating fan on the dining table to provide relief. Directed at her as she ate, it only pushed her hair around her face in waves of stale, warm air.

He'd left the tape off the last time she ate and that at least helped.

She knew he was watching her from the kitchen as she ate the chicken and rice meal he'd prepared. She pushed her plate away, determined to eat only enough to keep her strength up. She stood up and walked to the bathroom, knowing he was watching her every move, knowing he wouldn't stop her.

She closed the bathroom door firmly behind her. She'd already examined everything possible in the room. There was only a sink and a toilet. The mirror over the sink was solidly affixed and she could see no way to get any piece of it into her hands.

After she emerged from the bathroom she went to the mattress, refusing to look at him. She collapsed on the mattress, feeling the heat and the futility pound into her like competing pistons.

"I'm dying from the heat," she moaned. "I need air."

"I have water," he said, turning and retrieving a water bottle from one of the cabinets.

"I can't endure this heat. I'll have a seizure," Catherine said as she reached for the water bottle. A line of sweat dribbled down her brow. She drank but her mouth still felt dry, her heartbeat was racing.

Am I having a heart attack?

He stepped on the mattress and, reaching up to the window overhead, opened it. Instantly Catherine felt a gentle wave of cooler air flow down to her.

"Thank you," she said, then drank thirstily from the bottle of water.

He stepped away and sat at the table with his phone. He appeared to be texting someone. Every so often he glanced at her. His looks were the thing that made her think he could be persuaded. He was careful to make sure she was as comfortable as he could make her under the circumstances.

There's a human being beneath that nervous and determined façade.

"At least tell me your name," she said.

He looked up from his phone and cocked his head as if in surprise or confusion.

"If you truly are going to hand deliver me to whomever you're working for, it won't matter if I know your name."

"My name is Rashid."

"Is the man who hired you Arabian too?"

"Enough questions."

"Rashid, I have a little boy who needs me. A precious little boy who needs his mother."

"Please, stop."

"I know you're not a monster. Maybe you have a child too. If you need money, if it's about money—"

"It's not money!"

She bit her lip and felt her mind start to race.

How was she going to reach him if money didn't matter?

"Then why are you doing this? Is someone making you do this?"

"No one is making me do this."

He was pacing now and rubbing his face, glancing at her and at the door as if expecting someone. She noticed a light sheen of sweat on his face that she hadn't seen before. He was agitated. Something in her told her to push him. Something told her she had to disrupt what was happening somehow.

"If you are going to sell me to people who are going to turn me into a sex slave—"

"Stop! That's not what will happen!"

"Says the liar and the kidnapper! Don't tell me it's not about money! You're going to sell me to sex traffickers! Why else would you do something so despicable!?"

"I am following orders!"

She stared at him and she could see the shame in his face as he realized what he'd said. He was only following orders. But something motivated him to follow the orders. Something motivated him to treat her like this, to wrench her away from her son. Something or someone powerful.

"Whose orders?"

"I can't tell you that."

"Why? I'm a captive. How could it possibly hurt for me to know? Who am I going to tell?"

He just shook his head and turned away from her.

Somehow she needed to convince him not to follow the orders. She needed to make him see that disobeying his orders was a higher calling.

She needed to make him care about her.

"My boy is eight years old," she said. "He likes science and reading. He likes playing catch with his daddy. Do they play catch where you come from, Rashid?"

He looked at her, his face stark with indecision, his eyes blinking as if trying to decipher her words.

"Rashid? I asked you if children play catch with their daddies where you come from?"

"Don't...don't say things like that."

"My little boy is named Cameron. He is a sensitive, kind boy. He believes in God. Do you believe in God, Rashid?"

"Yes, of course, I do. You don't know how this is..."

"How this is hurting you? Torturing you? I see it, Rashid! I see how you don't want to take me away from my little boy! I see that you are a good person!"

"No more talking!"

He continued pacing, his eyes on the door even more as if tempted to run out of it.

"What are we waiting for? Is someone coming?" she asked. Her voice sounded panicked even to her own ears. "Where are you taking me?"

"No one is coming. No more questions!"

He swiveled on his foot and jerked open the apartment door and bolted through it as if on fire. The sound of the door slamming rang in her ears as she waited for the echo of his footsteps outside to recede and then disappear.

He never left her alone in the apartment while she was awake. It was at that moment that she realized that in his hurry to get away from her questions he'd forgotten something.

Her heart began to pound as she turned to confirm what she was sure she would see.

He'd forgotten to close the bedroom window.

31

Day Three of the Lockdown

The moment Jean-Marc entered the *Préfectorate* on the Île de la Cité he was greeted by old friends, people he'd worked with for nearly thirty years. He'd kept in touch with a few of them after he moved away—unfortunately most reminded him too much of the Chloe years—but now it seemed as if they were all greeting him as a returning comrade. The sort of homage one reserves for a visit of a long-retired veteran.

He'd just agreed to have lunch at some undetermined time in the future with a man who'd served as his temporary partner at some point in the past decade when the department secretary approached him where he sat in the hallway to tell him that Capitaine Bonnet was available to see him now.

She led him down the hall and Jean-Marc found himself oddly relieved when they passed his old office. It pleased him to see that Bonnet might have taken his position but not his space.

He'd heard about Bonnet's immediate predecessor, a Victor

Muller, who'd been in the job less than six months before requesting a transfer to Normandy. Not everyone could handle the intensity of the case load of Paris Homicide, as Jean-Marc well knew. His own workload in Nice was much less demanding than he was used to. For some people that was ideal. Jean-Marc found it less so.

The secretary opened one of the doors along the hallway and stepped back to allow Jean-Marc to enter the office. The man seated at the desk facing the door stood up immediately but did not step around the desk to greet him.

"Capitaine LaRue," Bonnet said, stretching his arm out across his desk to shake hands.

Jean-Marc shook hands as the secretary turned and left them, closing the door behind her.

"Please sit," Bonnet said. "I am delighted to finally meet you, Capitaine LaRue. Your name is spoken of often in the ranks."

The man's condescending body posture along with the smirk that Jean-Marc wasn't surprised to see told him that his reputation had definitely preceded him.

Exposed two years ago for taking bribes, he'd have lost his job then and there if it hadn't been for the success and resulting publicity that came from uncovering a police mole, a human trafficking ring and the closing of two high-profile murder cases, one of them involving an American tourist—Claire Baskerville's husband.

The mole had been Jean-Marc's partner, the human trafficking ring had operated as a result of Jean-Marc's own willingness to turn a blind eye to what was happening, and the murders had both been solved by the relentless determination of Claire Baskerville.

In the end it had been his connection with Claire that had saved his career if not his reputation—although the bullet he'd taken when it all came together hadn't hurt. The longstanding

pity he'd garnered for his crippled wife had also helped to mitigate the consequences of his crimes.

In any case, Jean-Marc was under no illusion that the Paris
homicide department as a whole had spoken well of him.

"I am grateful for your time," Jean-Marc said. "I know how
busy you must be with the murder on the tourist boat."

"Yes, although we are confident of our suspect," Bonnet
said.

"In custody?" Jean-Marc asked innocently knowing
perfectly well she wasn't.

"Not yet. But soon enough."

"Any leads?"

Bonnet smiled, a facial grimace that showed only teeth and
no emotion. Jean-Marc knew his relationship with Claire—the
mother of Bonnet's prime suspect—was well known—
certainly to Bonnet. He would have to play this next part
delicately.

"A few, yes," Bonnet said. "But I am sure you have more
than your share of unusual cases on your own field."

This was Bonnet not-so-gently reminding Jean-Marc that
he was no longer a detective in Paris.

"Yes, of course," Jean-Marc said. "Although at the moment I
am on leave."

"That was a surprise to your commandant, I understand?"

So he's checked up on me.

"So how can I help you, Capitaine?" Bonnet asked, clearly
tired of playing around and ready to find out what it was Jean-
Marc wanted.

"I need an assist from the Paris police," Jean-Marc said
easily.

"With regard to what?"

"As I'm sure you know, I am friends with the mother-in-law
of the victim in your tourist boat case."

"I am aware."

"She has asked for my assistance in speaking with the cab companies who were in the area the night of the accident."

"You mean the night of the murder," Bonnet said.

"Yes, of course."

"She is perfectly free to contact any public cab company she feels inclined to," Bonnet said.

"She believes, as do I, that the cab companies would be more forthcoming with their answers with the weight and influence of the Paris Police behind her."

Bonnet stared at him.

"Have you contacted these cab companies yet?" Jean-Marc asked.

"We have not."

"Do you have a problem with *my* contacting them?"

"You mean as a private citizen?"

"No, Capitaine. As I said, I require the blessing of the Paris police department in order to encourage the cab companies to answer my questions."

"What kinds of questions would you be asking?"

"Specifically, did any of their drivers pick up a woman fitting the description of Catherine Baskerville Stone and a Middle Eastern man?"

Bonnet's eyebrows shot up and he smiled.

"Perhaps it sounds more like the sort of thing your department should handle?" Jean-Marc said.

There were at least three cab companies operating in Paris with around two hundred cars each. Not to mention Uber drivers. It would take him hours to contact them all.

"Unfortunately," Bonnet said, almost sadly, "I do not have the manpower to assign to such a task."

"But you don't mind if I do it," Jean-Marc said.

"Not at all. Of course you will share anything you discover pertinent to the case."

"Of course."

"I'll have my assistant send you the list of taxi companies and registered Uber drivers in the city," he said with a smile. "There are quite a few of them."

Knowing when he was being dismissed, Jean-Marc stood up.

"Thank you, Capitaine," he said.

"Of course," Bonnet said, standing up to shake hands again. "I am honored to have the chance to work with the famed Jean-Marc LaRue."

If Jean-Marc weren't so focused on getting started calling the companies, he might have taken just a few seconds to punch this grinning orangutan in the nose.

But he didn't have the time. As it was, there was no way he could meet up with Claire today.

32

Cameron seemed better this morning after his good cry last night. I'm not saying I think he was going to be okay. He can't be okay. He had lost both his parents in one night. Unless we found Catherine soon, I don't think he's ever going to be okay again.

Geneviève came upstairs with Noel and Bill this morning after breakfast. They were planning on taking Haley and the boys to the park and then lunch. I was so grateful to them. Between Geneviève and Haley, I thought Cam would manage okay today, and the outing would help take his mind off things for a little bit. An exhausting day and an early night sounded like exactly what was in order.

As eager as I was to see the CCTV video that Jean-Marc had found, I was impatient to start showing Catherine's and Ariel's photos around. It was the most time-consuming—i.e. hopeless —part of the investigation, but nobody else was going to do it if I didn't.

Before I left the apartment, I hugged Cam and tried to will strength and hope into him for his day. He smiled at me and it broke my heart to think he was trying to appear strong for *me*.

The morning was blessedly overcast as I made my way to the neighborhood where Qasim's car was found. As I approached, I could see the grey stone bulwark that heralded the Seine straight ahead of me.

The first block nearest to where the *bateaux-mouches* were based was full of cafés, souvenir shops and restaurants. There was a steady stream of people here—office workers, shoppers, and tourists.

A few hundred yards ahead, the street narrowed and the shops disappeared to reveal only apartment buildings on both sides of the road.

I pulled out my phone and typed in the exact address Jean-Marc had given me for the location of the car, then waited for the data to download. Finally, my GPS pinpointed the street which wasn't far away. Following the screen directions, I turned a corner and was startled to see an enormous church in front of me. The sign on the church read *American Cathedral in Paris*.

Honestly I am continually surprised that there are so many gorgeous churches in this city. It seems as if they pop up on every street.

I hurried down the block, my eye on my phone screen as my GPS led me past two more side streets. Finally I came to a street where the lane ended in a small square which was hemmed in by several cafés and shops. There was an enormous plane tree in the center of the square and a small dry fountain anchored off the northern side. Curious, I approached and found a large granite plaque attached to the fountain which read in French:

On this spot the Gestapo gunned down five young people who spoke for France. August 21, 1944.

I rubbed the goose bumps off my arms. These people had died mere hours before the city was liberated. I stared at the plaque for a long minute before moving away. The square felt sad to me and reminded me that this city had held its share of heartbreak and tragedy.

I'll be damned if it was going to take any more of my loved ones.

I hurried past the square and quickly found the spot on the next street over where Qasim's car had been found.

I stood by the fender of the car that was now in the spot and looked down the residential street to the cross street a block away, rue de Freycinet.

This is where Catherine and her abductor left from.

I brought up the photo that Jean-Marc had sent me of Ariel. It was pretty fuzzy, but I was hoping that her uncommon name would also help people remember her. I was convinced it must be her real name because no operative worth her salt would attempt to pose as a Middle Eastern couple and give a name like *Ariel.*

My working assumption was that Qasim had walked from this spot and gone to the *bateaux-mouches* so I would walk toward the river from here. Along the way I stopped at every store and café on the block. I didn't just talk to one waiter, I talked to every single person, including bus boys, working at each café, showing them both Catherine's and Ariel's photos and asking if either woman looked familiar to them.

Most of them assumed my questions had to do with the death on the sightseeing boat. While I typically find most Paris waiters about as helpful as Vladimir Putin with hemorrhoids, almost every one of them seemed as if they were at least telling the truth.

I stopped mid-morning for a cup of coffee and to get off my feet. I spent the break scrutinizing the photo of Ariel, specifically her clothes. Even though the photo was indistinct, I could tell her clothing wasn't very nice. Her shoes looked more like shower shoes than proper footwear. Was this a clue?

When the waitress came to my table to see if I wanted anything else I showed her Ariel's photo.

"Have you ever seen her?" I asked.

"Why do you want to know?" she asked, her eyes narrowing.

"I think she might be in trouble," I lied.

She frowned at me and I could tell she didn't know whether to believe me or not. The thing about not speaking a foreign language like a native is that it is much harder for the native speakers to tell if you're lying. Comes in very handy in my line of work.

"She looks familiar," she said finally and then picked up my espresso cup and walked away.

I am always so impressed with people who can remember faces. I do not have that ability. I suffer from a brain anomaly called prosopagnosia that makes it impossible for me to remember anyone's face. Which was *not* a plus in my line of work.

Still, if the waitress thought she recognized Ariel, even if she wasn't sure, that might mean that Ariel frequented this area or even lived around here. That was my hope anyway.

I received a text from Jean-Marc saying that Bonnet had green-lighted our talking to the cab companies in the area and telling them we were working with the police in an active murder investigation.

I'd have preferred it if *Bonnet's* people could have talked to the cab companies since it was still going to be much easier for these cab companies to blow me off than it would be if a police officer was asking. I'd hoped that Jean-Marc could meet up with me but his text put an end to that hope. He was tied up for the rest of the day.

I checked my watch and saw it was already edging toward lunch time. I didn't have time for a sit-down meal. I'd have to stop at a kiosk and grab a crepe or slice of pizza. I had heard no update as to when the lockdown would lift. Every evening the news reported that the government was extending it another twenty-four hours and every day I sweated out the minutes like they were my last—*or Catherine's.*

I felt like I'm being killed by inches although of course every time they extended the lockdown I was grateful and relieved for the extra time.

I tried calling a couple of the cab companies from the café. Not surprisingly, they were not interested in talking to me, no matter how much I stressed that I was working with the police. *I* wasn't the police and they knew it. Most of them hung up on me and I stopped trying after four attempts.

Feeling a sense of heaviness in both legs and a general feeling of discouragement, I paid for my coffee and headed out again down the street. I'd already done three streets on this block which didn't feel like very much except I'd had to talk to every single person I'd run across—even sometimes just random people waiting to cross the street. Turns out French people appreciate being accosted even less than Americans.

I went to the sandwich shop next door and ordered a *jambon sandwich.* I showed the waitress Ariel's photo and got the usual head shake. I found a bench a block away and quickly wolfed down my lunch. I couldn't imagine what a sight I must have made.

The French feel very strongly about not eating on the run. To see an older woman sitting on a bench pushing a ham sandwich into her mouth like it was some kind of contest to see how fast she could eat it must have made them wonder why I didn't just wear a sign saying *I'm American.*

Any other time I might have given a royal crap what they thought. Right now I just needed the calories to get through the afternoon.

The rest of the day was a mind-numbing panoply of pavement and cobblestone pounding, head shakes, hair salons, *tabacs* laundromats, green grocers, souvenir shops, stationery stores, wine boutiques and clothing stores.

As before, most people were vaguely helpful, if not exactly friendly, but nobody had seen her. By the time I sat down on another bench around five in the afternoon, my back aching, my feet throbbing and my heart doing all it could to stay steadfast, I knew I was done, at least physically.

If President Macron didn't extend the lockdown, I would just have to live with it but today I could do no more.

I dragged myself on legs of cement to the Pont d'Alma Metro and as I pulled out my Metro pass to go through the ticket stile, I decided I needed one more rejection to be the cherry on my cake. I went to the encaged ticket seller and showed her Ariel's picture. She shook her head and waved me away so that the person behind me could buy his ticket.

I turned back to the ticket stile, passing a security guard along the way who was watching me somewhat suspiciously. More to prove to him that I wasn't some reprobate, I approached him, showed him the photo and asked him if he'd seen her.

I was so sure that his answer was no that I was actually turning away when he answered me.

"*Oui,*" he said.

I turned back to him, not sure I'd heard correctly.

"*Quoi?* You have seen her?" I asked, pushing the photo back at him.

He jerked his head in the direction of an elderly woman on her knees on a blanket, a hat in front of her.

"Sometimes she begs here," he said. "Mostly I chase her off."

"*This* woman," I said, pointing at the picture and not truly believing that I'd finally gotten a hit. "You've seen this woman?"

"*Oui,* Madame. That woman. Ariel."

33

C atherine hit the ground hard, her breath exploding out of her on landing.

There was broken glass and debris under her knees and hands where she'd fallen but it was her right ankle that commanded her full attention. White-hot agony seared up her ankle to her brain.

She hadn't meant to scream when she hit the ground and now she heard the echo of that scream ringing in her ears. She clawed her way to her feet using the broken brick of the building to haul herself up.

And then she remembered.

Her scream wasn't the only thing she'd heard. Seconds before she'd slipped through the window she'd heard a noise behind her.

Had he come back?

She looked down the alley. It was open at both ends. But which way to go?

She felt gripped by panic and indecision combined with the desperate urge to *hurry*. She took a tentative step forward and felt the pain shoot up her hip, dulling her brain in its intensity.

Hurry! Just go!

She hobbled a few more agonizing steps, pushing into the pain. It couldn't be broken or she wouldn't be able to do even this much!

A flash of color at the end of the alley made her jerk her head up. *People were walking by!*

A sound behind her made her stumble involuntarily forward in desperation and anguish.

"Help me! Help me!" she shrieked.

A woman at the end of the alley forty yards away stopped and stared and then hurried away.

"No!" Catherine screamed, the pain from her ankle all-encompassing now. She had to stop. She couldn't walk on it. But she had to.

One more agonizing step and she heard him behind her. Her panic exploded in her chest and she moaned out loud as she felt his hands on her shoulders.

"No!" she whimpered again, her stomach lurching in nausea and despair as he pulled her almost gently to the ground among the broken glass and the weeds.

34

That night Geneviève made *boeuf bourguignon*. She and Noel and Bill and the children sat around the table and I couldn't help but feel the bizarrely festive feel to the meal in spite of the circumstances. Everyone was reaching out to distract Cameron—especially Noel. I felt my heart go out to the man and his efforts for a grief-stricken boy he'd never known before this week. I was keenly aware of how I'd been ready not to like Noel because he hadn't contacted Geneviève for so long.

People truly are so much more complicated than the sum of their parts, I thought as I watched Noel make a coin disappear for the children. Because I like him, I could see that maybe there were extenuating circumstances for his estrangement with Geneviève.

I got a sharp stab of guilt then, remembering how I'd never liked Todd. I am pretty sure I hadn't been fair with him.

Robbie burst out laughing at the coin trick which in turn made everyone else laugh too. I was struck by all the love and warmth so palpable around the table.

As for Geneviève, I saw that she seemed genuinely happy to

be sitting next to her son again. While lately conversation had been naturally stilted because of the tragedy we were all dealing with, she'd dropped a few nuggets of information about Noel and Bill's plans to move to Paris. I knew that if it had been normal times, she would have told me everything in detail.

I prayed that time would come for all of us.

After everyone left and the children were in bed, I went to my own bedroom to look at the CCTV video that Jean-Marc had sent to my laptop.

I studied for the hundredth time the face of Ariel as she stepped on board the boat with Omar. The security guard at the Metro station had suggested I visit the homeless shelter on rue du Chemin-Vert in Le Marais. If I hadn't been bone tired and afraid of being caught out after the curfew, I would have gone right then. In fact I nearly called Jean-Marc to see if he could meet me at the train station.

But I needed a break. My legs ached and I kept having sporadic dizzy spells that I could only attribute to my stress and maybe lack of quality calories. I'd be good for nothing if I wore myself to a frazzle.

And I needed to see Cam. I'd stayed in touch with both Haley and Geneviève all day and gotten frequent reports on him. But I needed to see with my own eyes how he was doing. I needed to hold him in my arms.

I felt much better after getting off my feet for a few hours and enjoying a good dinner. Plus I'd seen Cameron smile a time or two tonight and that did more for my spirits than anything could. I'm not saying he was going to come out of this unscathed—that was impossible—but I was betting everything I had on the whole children-are-so-resilient adage. I prayed with all my heart that it was true.

As for me, I wasn't going to get off so easy.

I'd had a glass of wine at dinner and worried mildly that it might put me to sleep, I was so tired, but the stress quickly overpowered any possible drowsy tendencies it might have had.

I glanced at the clock and saw it was ten o'clock. Jean-Marc had called earlier in the evening and I'd put him off. I'd needed to be with Cam—really *be* with him. And now I needed to get back to work.

I pulled on my running shoes and changed into a loose pair of jeans. I didn't want to look like I'd just stepped out of one of the designer departments of *Galleries Lafayette*. I didn't want anything about me to be the reason why Ariel wouldn't talk to me.

I checked on Haley and the boys in the guest room. Robbie and Cameron slept together in the guest bed. Haley was sitting in an armchair by the window with a book.

"Everything okay?" I whispered.

"Sure."

"I'm going out for a bit."

"What about the curfew?"

"I'm going with Jean-Marc."

"Oh, okay."

"You'll be fine?"

"Of course."

She really did look at me like she couldn't imagine why I was making such a big fuss out of leaving. Maybe she was right. The longer Catherine was missing, the more I started to second-guess my own instincts.

"I won't be long," I said and then tiptoed out of the room. I went to the kitchen and made myself a cup of coffee in my French press. While I waited for it to steep, I called Jean-Marc back.

"So what happened today?" he asked.

"I found Ariel," I said, barely able to conceal my excitement. "She's a homeless person who solicits."

"Did you get her full name?"

"The guy I talked to didn't know her full name, but he matched her picture to her name."

I poured my coffee in a mug. "If she's a prostitute," I said, "wouldn't that mean she's got a record?"

"Yes, if she's been arrested. The cops aren't always so particular on solicitation."

"Even in the tourist district?"

"We'll find out when we talk with her."

"Can you meet me there?" I asked, knowing he would say yes, knowing I would go without him if he didn't.

He probably knew that too because he didn't bother reminding me of the curfew.

"I'll meet you at your place in fifteen minutes," he said.

35

L *e Cité des Anges* was like any homeless shelter you might see anywhere in the States. The entrance way opened up to a communal space filled with competing television sets, vending machines, coffee machines and walls lined with bulletin boards and computer kiosks for Internet access.

A check-in counter in the center of the room gave me the feeling of walking into a very shabby hotel. Several people, mostly women with small children, sat on the worn couches and chairs clustered around the TV sets in the common room.

Every eye tore away from their screens to stare at me and Jean-Marc as we made our way to the counter where a waspish older woman with bone-white hair watched us approach.

"Bonsoir Madame," I said to her, presenting the photograph I had of Ariel. "We are looking for this woman. Is she here?"

The woman glanced at Jean-Marc as if accurately assessing that he was a policeman.

"There's a curfew," she said acerbically. "Where else would she be?"

"She's not in trouble," Jean-Marc said. "We just have a few questions."

The woman grunted and turned to point to a woman sitting alone with a book on her lap in the far corner of the common room.

"Ariel Dominion?" I said, approaching her with my hand outstretched. There are few French who can resist a handshake. It was hardwired into their DNA.

Ariel looked just like her picture. She had brown hair worn to her shoulders and a wide generous smile. Her eyes looked sad to me though. Right now they looked hunted.

She shook my hand but looked at Jean-Marc. Just like the woman at the check-in counter, she knew he was police right away.

"I don't know anything about anything," she said, her jaw set.

"You're not in trouble," I said. "Tell her, Jean-Marc."

"You are not in trouble," Jean-Marc said.

I sat on her cot. I'd already asked Jean-Marc not to speak unless he felt he absolutely had to. I could tell my instincts had been right about that.

"My son-in-law was the person who died on the boat tour that you were on," I said, watching her face ignite into fear and suspicion. "We know you had nothing to do with that," I stressed.

Of course we didn't know that at all, but her clamming up before we could find out wouldn't help anyone.

"I'm going around asking everyone who was on the boat what they saw in hopes that someone might have seen something that can help the police with their investigation."

She seemed to soften just a bit.

"I didn't even know it happened," she said. "Not until later that night when I saw all the police crawling over there."

"My daughter was with her husband that night," I said. "They fought loudly in front of everyone."

Her eyes widened.

"That was your daughter?" She glanced at Jean-Marc again and I was a hair away from asking him to wait outside. Just his presence seemed to be disturbing her.

"I know they fought," I said. "Did you hear it?"

"Heard it and saw it. She threw a glass of champagne in his face."

My vision blurred for just a moment before I forced myself to stick out my chin and resist the nearly constant impulse to weep. I hated hearing how upset Catherine must have been. I hated knowing that Todd had a glass of champagne flung in his face moments before he was stabbed to death. I hated everything about everything I was hearing.

"We've talked to everyone on the boat," I said. "Now that we've talked to you—and you've confirmed what everyone else said—we have only one more person to talk to and we can't find him."

She gave a shrug as if to say *what is that to me?*

"He was the man you came on board with," I said as gently and as non-threateningly as I could.

She stared at me for a moment and then closed her eyes as if the real reason for our visit had just been revealed to her

"You are looking for Omar," she said.

I felt a tingle of hope. At least she wasn't going to try to lie about it. I least I didn't have to pull out the CCTV video that showed them together.

"Do you know where we can find him?" Jean-Marc asked.

"Sorry, no."

That was it. That was all.

Like hell it was.

"How is it you know Omar?" I asked.

"I don't know him."

I didn't have time to count to ten but I took a beat.

"Then how is it you were on a date with him on the boat that night?"

She snorted.

"He approached me on rue Freycinet and asked me if I wanted to make a hundred euros and get a free meal. I said yes."

My heart beat faster when she said the name of the street. That was the street that abutted rue Goethe where his car had been found.

"And you didn't know him before that?" Jean-Marc asked.

"I just said that, didn't I?" she said, curling her lip at him.

"So the two of you had dinner—" I began but she interrupted me.

"Wrong. I went to our table without him."

"He didn't eat with you?"

"No. Which was fine with me. I ate his *foie gras* too."

"What time was that?" Jean-Marc asked.

She made a face at him but I waved away his question. I could easily find out through the boat service what time the first course was served.

I pulled out my phone with a screen grab of Omar leaving the boat with Catherine.

"Is this the same man you got on the boat with?" I asked.

She squinted at the screen.

"*Oui.*"

"Do you remember seeing the woman he was with?"

"She was the one fighting with her husband."

"Do you know where they went?"

She gave me a puzzled look. "How would I know?"

"Because you came with him," Jean-Marc said. "Were you

not surprised to see he'd left without you? Did you know he intended to leave with this woman?"

"I told you," Ariel said. "I didn't know him and after we got on board we split up."

"And you never saw him again?" I asked.

"*C'est ça.*" *That's right.*

I don't know what I was expecting. I felt like holding my head in my hands but forced myself to go on.

"Can I see the hundred euros he gave you?" I asked.

"I spent it."

"All of it?"

Ariel glowered at me and Jean-Marc jumped in.

"Is there anything you can tell us about the guy?" he asked. "Anything at all? Was he anxious? Was he looking around? Did you get the idea he was by himself?"

"He spoke with some kind of an accent," she said with a shrug. "Now that you mention it, he acted nervous."

"One last question," I said. "You were overheard calling him *Omar.*"

"Because that's what he told me his name was."

"But he registered himself as Ali at the *bateaux-mouche* office," I said.

"Yeah, I noticed that."

"Didn't you wonder about it?"

"No. I only wondered how I got so lucky to get a free meal and a hundred euros."

I felt a sharp pinch of discouragement at hearing that. If Ariel was *not* working with Omar, and it very much appeared that she wasn't, then he would not have given her his real name. So Omar, like Ali, must be an alias.

I swallowed hard at the realization. Two names that meant nothing, that led us nowhere.

"So you don't know if Omar was his real name," Jean-Marc said as if clarifying my own thoughts.

"*Au contraire.* I know for sure it wasn't his real name."

I had been looking for my business card in my bag when she spoke and I stopped at her words. I felt my skin tingle.

"How do you know that?" Jean-Marc asked.

"I pay attention to certain things, Monsieur," she said, smoothing the stains on her polyester pants as if attempting to preserve some dignity even in the homeless shelter where she was sitting. "In my life, it is necessary. I pay attention to a man's eyes who says he wants to be with me—in case what he really wants is to rob me or maybe cut my throat. I pay attention to where the police in my neighborhood eat—so that I can make sure I stay away from there. And I pay attention when anyone, male or female, opens their wallet for whatever reason."

A light flickered on in my mind.

"You saw his identification," I said already groping in my purse for my billfold. I pulled it out and found a twenty-euro bill inside. I held it out to her but Ariel just looked at it and frowned.

"Now that I think about it," she said, looking into my eyes, "I'm not sure I got that good a look at it."

I took out four more bills and dropped them on her lap with the first bill.

"Rashid Abadi," she said, picking up the bills and folding them. "Are we finished? There's usually a line at the showers."

Without waiting to hear our response, she stood and walked out of the room.

As I stood up, Jean-Marc was already on his phone calling his people at the *Préfecture.* I watched Ariel walk away, her shoulders back, her chin held high.

My heart was pounding. Inch by inch we were covering ground. Getting closer. But were we going fast enough?

Jean-Marc disconnected and I turned to him but he wasn't smiling.

"So?" I said. "Who is he?"

"There is no *Rashid Abadi* registered on the ICD," he said.

The ICD stood for International Crime Database. It was the equivalent of the NCIC in the US. Essentially it was a list of all missing persons, violent offenders, terrorists, foreign fugitives and firearm dealers in the world. Basically, any bad guy there is outside of the US and Canada.

"Damn it!" I said feeling like I wanted to slam a door or scream or both.

"It's not all bad, Claire," he said.

"How is it not all bad?" I said, whirling on him. "We have a name but can't use it to find the guy!"

"Not finding his name on the ICD means he doesn't have a criminal record," he said, nodding as if his words at least conveyed hope.

But I wasn't in the mood to be mollified.

"Neither did Ted Bundy," I said bitterly. "It didn't mean he wasn't going to be a problem."

———

36

Somewhere in the building Catherine could hear a television program with a laugh track. It was late, she knew that much, but she didn't have the energy to lift her head from the mattress to find the stove light.

What did it matter what time it was?

The muted laugh track erupted again at some place in the building and Catherine tried to imagine normal people living their normal lives while she lay on a stained mattress, her hands tied, waiting for whatever horror was in store for her.

Ice packs were strapped to her injured ankle and two blankets, still with their price tags on, covered her to fight the chill the packs caused. Catherine shivered in spite of the blankets and shifted uncomfortably on the mattress closing her eyes against the memory of the moment when he recaptured her.

The memory of that sickening feeling of thinking she was about to break free and then the horror of feeling his hands on her as he pulled her back from freedom was almost too much to bear.

Tears stung her eyes at the memory.

I was so close.

He'd picked her up in his arms murmuring ridiculous apologies the whole way and trying not to hurry in order not to call more attention to them both.

Catherine had arched her back as she fought him, nearly falling out of his grip when he'd pushed her against the alley wall and brought his face close to hers.

"Do not fight me," he'd said, nearly imploring her.

She was not going back inside! She raked his face with her nails and tried to head butt him when he turned her around, her face to the wall. Her ankle screamed at the maneuver and she paused long enough to catch her breath, to steady herself against the pain in her foot when she felt him pull at the elastic at the waist of her pants.

For one harrowing moment she thought he was going to rape her there in the alley but then she felt the shocking prick of the needle as it went into her hip.

She screamed in frustration and desperation and he snaked another arm around her throat and clapped a hand to her mouth.

All the while he kept saying over and over again *I am sorry I am sorry I am sorry.*

Now as she lay on the mattress with no idea of what time it was but knowing it was night, her head spun in the aftermath of whatever drug he'd given her.

She didn't know where he was. He usually slept in the bathroom, getting up every hour or so to check on her.

The sadness that enveloped her felt complete. The world actually felt as if it had stopped spinning. Everything was in slow motion. Her chin trembled as she fought another bout of weeping. It didn't help. It didn't make her feel better.

She licked her lips and suddenly realized that her gag was off. He must have assumed she'd sleep for longer. But even with the gag off, how did that help? The people in this building didn't hear her when she screamed in broad day light. They would ignore a nighttime scream just as easily.

In spite of her trying to resist them, tears coursed down her cheeks. Her ankle throbbed and she felt her face sting where he'd held her against the wall before he injected her.

She breathed in and out trying to quell her sobs, not wanting to wake him, not wanting to alert him to the fact that he needed to gag her again. When he didn't come, she took in a long breath and forced her mind to think of what she'd learned from her failure to escape.

She pushed past the lump in her throat and the pain in her jaw, trying not to weep, and forced herself to review what had happened. He must have come back to the apartment and seen her jump. There was no other explanation how he could have been right behind her. And then he easily caught her and...

She felt a tingle of excitement as she realized what the difference had been.

He'd caught her but he'd done it gently. *He hadn't tackled her* which surely would have been the easiest and fastest way to stop her? Instead, he'd stopped her and pulled her down to the ground. Was that because he could tell she was hurt?

Her mind raced as she tried to fill in the rest of what had happened pre-drug.

She remembered his profuse apologies and how he'd tried to carry her before giving up and turning her to the wall to inject her.

He was trying not to hurt me.

That explained why he hadn't assaulted her yet in four days. And why he apologized before he fed her, led her to the bathroom, untied her, gagged her.

He's been told not to hurt me.

Catherine lay on the mattress and tried to think what this new insight meant and how she could possibly use it.

That's his weakness. He doesn't want to hurt me.

Right now her brain hurt too much and was too fogged from the drug to see how she could use this insight. But later, when she was stronger, when she wasn't so thirsty, when her ankle wasn't hurting so much, later, she would use it against him.

She heard a creak coming from the bathroom. He would be in soon to check on her. She closed her eyes to feign sleep. He wouldn't put the gag on her while he thought she was asleep for fearing of waking her.

She heard his footsteps as he walked carefully to the mattress and then stopped. He paused for a moment and gingerly repositioned the blankets around her and checked the ice pack on her ankle.

Then he stood for a moment and after a while she heard him turn and leave the room.

She kept her eyes closed and let the sadness sift through her body as if it were penetrating every organ, every muscle, coating them in heartache and hopelessness.

Squeezing her eyes shut even tighter Catherine prayed desperately that this agonizing night would soon be over.

And that it might, by living through it, please God, bring her one day closer to seeing her boy again.

37

J ean-Marc walked me back to my apartment. We weren't challenged along the way about the curfew and we saw plenty of police, in tandem and also solo. There must be something about the police that they're able to see their own kind even in the dark, even from a hundred yards away. Or maybe the police we passed had better things to do than stop every couple they saw walking by at one in the morning.

Both Jean-Marc and I kept to our own thoughts as we walked. Although we'd identified the man with Catherine, those thoughts were not positive ones.

When we stopped on the street in front of my building, I turned to him.

"What did Bonnet tell you?" I asked.

"Nothing helpful."

I studied him for a moment.

"He told you he wants Catherine for Todd's murder," I said.

"Essentially."

I looked away and felt the weight of the day's failure press in on me.

"None of the cab companies will talk to me," I said.

"But they are talking to me," he said.

I turned to him with hope etched across my face. "Really?"

I could tell he was sorry to get my hopes up.

"They need to reach out to their drivers," he said. "It's going to take time."

I wanted to scream because of course time was the one thing we didn't have.

"I can't believe this Rashid guy is not on any crime register anywhere," I said. "Did your people check everywhere?"

He sighed and threw up his hands in a gesture of frustration.

"The name is a common one," he said. "You will have trouble yourself tracking it down."

He knew me well. He knew I would go straight to my laptop tonight and try to find a Rashid Abadi somewhere in the world. Jean-Marc was telling me I was going to find thousands.

"So now what?" I asked.

"Now you rest."

"You know what I mean, Jean-Marc," I said with a touch of censure in my voice.

I can rest when I'm dead.

Or when Catherine is.

"What's the next step?" I asked.

He ran a frustrated hand through his hair. It was a gesture I'd seen him do many times before. It was one of disappointment and helpless irritation. I'd rather stab a fork in my eye than see it tonight and know what it meant now of all times.

"Give me the night to sleep on it," he said. "We'll come up with a plan tomorrow."

I nodded miserably. We were running out of time. We didn't have time to *sleep on it*. We needed to wake up tomorrow and hit the ground running.

"Sure, okay," I said.

I turned away before he could say or do anything that was going to break my heart, like reach out to give me a hug or even touch my arm or give me a sad reassuring smile. I couldn't handle that.

I pushed the code on the security panel through the wrought iron gate. When it buzzed, I slipped inside. I still didn't turn around, but Jean-Marc didn't walk away until I was halfway across the courtyard to the front door of the building.

Upstairs in my apartment, I checked on all the children and then took Izzy downstairs one last time before peeling off my clothes and falling exhausted into my bed.

It had been an interminably long day. And mostly a frustrating one. I'd intended to look up *Rashid Abadi* on my international people-finder site, but decided to set my alarm for five in the morning—less than three hours from now—and do it then.

On impulse I got out of bed and walked to the window of my bedroom. I looked up into the night sky. The moon was visible there, a half-moon that was glowing brightly. I wondered if Catherine was seeing the same moon wherever she was.

I prayed for her to have comfort and faith. I prayed for her not to give up.

I prayed the same for me.

I took comfort in the knowledge that I'd gained today that Catherine was likely still alive, but I lost that thin wisp of solace as soon as that thought spring-boarded me inevitably into my next thought—which was that my father had to be involved somehow.

I didn't know what I could do about that or if I should take comfort in the fact that he was less likely to abuse and murder her than if she'd been taken by sex traffickers.

My dreams that night were not peaceful.

Jean-Marc went back to his hotel and climbed the steps to the registration desk. He asked for his key from the night clerk and was handed two messages from Adorlee. That surprised him since he'd spoken to her earlier in the day.

It was late and he was tired. In fact, nothing felt clear in his mind.

The day hadn't been a total loss but it had yielded little in the way of a promising lead. None of the cab companies he'd called had the information he wanted immediately at hand. But they agreed with Jean-Marc that if a young American blonde woman and a Middle Eastern man had taken a taxi, the driver would likely remember them.

That supposed of course that they'd taken a taxi. If they hadn't, then he and Claire were back to the beginning.

Unfortunately the *clock* wasn't going back to the beginning.

He trudged upstairs to his room and tossed his wallet and keys on the dresser before sinking onto the bed. He looked at the messages from Adorlee. It was too late to call her back. He realized he was glad of that. He didn't want to call her back.

Was that because of Claire?

Of course he'd missed Claire this year. Of course he'd blamed himself for every time thoughts of Chloe and his duty to properly mourn her had instead turned to thoughts of missing Claire. When he heard about Claire's daughter's disappearance, there was no question he had to come.

He ran a hand through his hair and felt a wave of confusion. He'd had every expectation that he'd feel conflicted when he saw her again.

The problem was he hadn't felt conflicted at all.

He laid the messages on the bed and immediately saw there was one he'd missed. Frowning, he picked it up to try to decipher the desk clerk's handwriting.

If you want to find her, meet me at the Alcyon bicycle factory at three o'clock

Jean-Marc felt his adrenaline spike as he picked up the room phone and called the front desk.

"I have a message here," he said, squinting at the message. He read the message to the man. "How did this message come to you?"

"A phone call, Monsieur," the desk clerk said. "Delivered an hour ago."

"They gave no other information?"

"Only what was on the message, Monsieur."

Jean-Marc hung up and looked at the note and then glanced at his watch. It was one-forty-five.

An hour later Jean-Marc stood in the back lot of the old Alcyon bicycle factory in Nanterre on the outskirts of Paris. He'd looked it up on his phone as he rode here and found they'd stopped making bicycles in 1928. From the looks of the building, it had not been used for anything else since. The roof was caved in and the walls were covered in graffiti.

A single streetlamp illuminated a small patch of broken tarmac in front of the factory. The rest of the streetlights were smashed and broken glass was littered beneath them.

Even as a cop, even armed, this was the sort of place that sent all his senses into hyperdrive.

His gun was in his shoulder harness and he had a Taser on his belt. It had taken him longer to arrive than he'd expected. The buses weren't running at this hour and even with his police credentials it had been difficult to find a cab. As it was, because of the desolate location, the cab he'd hired refused to take him all the way. He'd had to jog the last three blocks on foot.

He wasn't late so he could only assume the author of the

note must be watching him to ensure he was alone. He hadn't been warned to come alone. He hadn't needed to be.

If he hadn't been so determined to ensure that Claire, who looked as if she was running on espresso and sheer willpower alone, got some sleep tonight he would have apprised her of the message.

He thought for a moment about calling Bonnet but the detective's veiled warning yesterday morning was still ringing in his ears. Bonnet wouldn't be pleased to be awakened or have any of his police resources used for a wild goose chase.

Besides, Jean-Marc was a professional. He could handle following up on an informant without needing to call for back up.

A sound off to his left made him turn. For an uncomfortable moment he was aware that he'd turned his back on his only unprotected flank. But instead of turning back around, he stood frozen and staring as he watched two darkened shadows walk toward him.

A heavy truncheon was visible in the hand of one of the men.

38

Day Four of the Lockdown

I ran the entire way from the street out front of the Hôtel-Dieu Hospital on the Île de la Cité to the fourth floor and down the long maze of brightly lighted hallways. I ran fueled by terror and disbelief and the memory of the cold-voiced hospital receptionist who'd called me this morning to tell me that Jean-Marc had been brought in late last night with significant injuries.

During the whole Uber drive, my mind was whirling with the sorts of nonsensical, useless things one thinks of during times like this—*I'd just seen him last night!*—as if nothing bad could possibly happen in the interim three hours—and *what was he doing out?*

If I'm honest, a part of me actually felt perversely betrayed by Jean-Marc since he'd insisted *I* take the night off, but he clearly hadn't planned to. I know that sounded sick since I was terrified of what I was going to see when I saw him. But a very big part of me was currently feeling all the terror that had been ramping up inside me for the last five days—which now seemed to have found an outlet.

The relentless hospital intercom announcements merged with the sounds of the continuous motorized whoosh sounds of doors opening and closing, phones ringing and the bleeps and pings of diagnostic equipment. Just the smell of the hallways—rife with the scent of cleaning supplies, alcohol, and hot food on the ubiquitous creaking meal carts—was enough to make me want to vomit.

I reached the nursing station, knowing full well that if they stopped me because I wasn't a family member—as they would in the US—I fully intended to barge my way past them anyway.

At least on that score I needn't have worried. When I told the stern looking nurse at the nursing station who I was looking for, she just indicated with her head which hall I should go down and said "*Chambre quatre cent.*"

I forced myself not to run, but I was still moving quickly when I reached his door. I nearly ran right into Detective Bonnet as he was coming out of the room.

He didn't look surprised to see me.

"He's lucky he still has his job after last night," he said when he saw me.

I hadn't known until this moment that whatever had happened to Jean-Marc last night had been because of Catherine's case. I'd feared it. I'd half-expected it. But now I knew for sure.

"He's doing your job," I said, trying to edge past him, my body tense with fury. "He's trying to find the truth."

"I know it is difficult for you to accept," Bonnet said, blocking my entrance to the room, "but we know the truth."

"You've indicted her without even hearing her side," I said between gritted teeth. "Are you even *trying* to find her?"

"Good day, Madame Baskerville."

He turned and left. If he had been here to take Jean-Marc's

statement, he must have committed it to memory because I didn't see any notebook in his hands.

When I entered Jean-Marc's room, I saw him in the hospital bed with his eyes closed. The metal siderails on the bed were raised and bags of fluid hung from an IV stand by the head of the bed. His head was bandaged and his leg was in a cast and raised in traction above the bed.

I looked at his face. A split lip, a black eye and at least two stitches over his other eye, his jaw darkly bruised. I had no idea what other injuries he'd sustained. Injuries invisible to the eye. I could see he had wires leading from under his sheet to the nearby monitor.

"It's not that bad," he whispered.

"Oh, Jean-Marc," I said, allowing my tears to fall.

"Stop it," he said, clearly trying not to move his mouth very much.

I pulled up a chair and sat down, slipping my hand under the sheet to gently take his hand. I hoped it wasn't hurt too.

"What happened?"

He licked his lips and I looked around the room for the cup and straw I knew I'd find. I positioned the straw to his lips and he drank.

"When I returned to my room last night, there was a message," he said and glanced at the chair in the room where I saw his clothes were. I went through the pockets until I found the note.

If you want to find her, meet me at the Alcyon bicycle factory at three o'clock

My heart hammered in my chest at the reference to Catherine.

"Did you show this to Bonnet?"

Jean-Marc grunted painfully. "For all the good it would do."

"He at least seems to believe that the assault is linked to Catherine's disappearance," I said.

"It doesn't matter," he said.

"Because he won't follow up."

"He doesn't see the point."

"You've been warned off the case, haven't you?"

"I'm on vacation. He can't warn me off."

I sat back down in the chair beside him and took his hand again.

"I can't believe this happened to you," I said, feeling an urge to hug him or stroke his hair and knowing that was the last thing I could do. "Tell me."

"They were not Middle Eastern," he said wearily. "Two were masked. I never even saw the third one."

I swallowed hard and tried to make sense of the fact that they were *not* Middle Eastern and finally decided that my father or whoever his agent was here in Paris had likely hired freelancers for the job.

Jean-Marc groaned and shifted uncomfortably. I knew I should let him get some rest. Or call the nurse for another hit of Demerol.

"How is Cameron?" Jean-Marc said as he closed his eyes.

"The same."

He needs his mother. I need his mother.

"What did they say to you?" I asked.

Jean-Marc opened one eye.

"How did you know?"

Of course they'd said something. It was a message. My father spoke in the language of sledgehammers. The beating wouldn't have felt like enough to him. He'd want to make sure I caught the subtext and the exclamation points too.

"What did they say?" I repeated.

"I didn't mention that part to Bonnet."

"Probably just as well."

I waited for a moment while he closed his eyes again. I

waited, not sure he hadn't fallen asleep when a few moments later he spoke again.

"You still here?" he murmured.

"I am. Take your time."

He sighed and then groaned at the expulsion of air.

"They said, *Stop what you're doing. Tell the American to stop too or she's next.*"

He licked his lips and kept his eyes closed as if the sentence had completely exhausted him.

In my mind there had never been any doubt that this was my father's handiwork. But he'd never threatened me before.

"It's a bluff," I said. "Or an improvisation. My father wouldn't hurt me."

Jean-Marc didn't answer. I wasn't sure if that meant he disagreed with me or if he'd drifted off again.

As I sat there and looked at his face—a face that is very dear to me regardless of the past year—I was reminded of what Geneviève said about family being whoever we say it is. It seemed to me that that was what Jean-Marc was telling me when he showed up on my doorstep in my hour of need. And now here he lay broken and suffering because of it.

"You know what I think?" I said softly, standing up and gently rearranging the sheets around him as I tried to break the spell of hopelessness that I felt begin to cascade over me. "I think these people are desperate because they know Catherine can still be found."

Jean-Marc didn't respond.

"I think we need to take what happened to you as a sign that we're on the right track."

He snorted and then moaned loudly as the resulting pain seized his chest.

"We have no leads," he rasped.

"They don't seem to know that. Maybe what happened to you means we're closer than we think."

Jean-Marc didn't answer. After a few moments I heard the slight burr of a snore coming from him and I was glad he was free from pain at least for a time.

I understand that Jean-Marc is trained to dealing in realities and practicalities. I get that he has to look at likelihoods and rational projections and go forward with actions based on them.

But I have a missing child. I can't afford to look at things too realistically.

Not without risking breaking down and becoming totally useless.

I turned and stepped outside his hospital room and took in a long fortifying breath. A couple of nurses stood across the hall talking and as I passed I heard snatches of their conversation.

"...promised it'll be lifted by nine tomorrow morning, thank God."

Her words hit me square in the chest. Nine tomorrow was less than twenty-four hours.

Less than twenty-four hours meant I had lost Catherine.

Because regardless of what I'd told Jean-Marc about what his assailants did or didn't know about our progress, the harsh, bitter fact was that we were no closer to knowing where she was.

39

The swelling had gone down on her ankle. But Catherine needed to make sure he didn't know it was better.

In the trips she made to the bathroom leaning heavily on his arm, she'd done her best to make him believe she could barely walk.

Once alone in the bathroom, she put her weight on it, leaning against the sink to test it. She could walk on it, painfully, but she *could* ambulate if she had to. Running however was out of the question.

Catherine stared at her image in the mirror. Her face was streaked with what was left of her eye makeup. Her eyes were red, her skin mottled. She saw what he must see. Someone terrified and weak. Her eyes flashed in defiance at her own self-assessment.

"You have a child who needs you," she said to her reflection and instantly felt a burst of strength surge into her.

"You are okay?" Rashid said on the other side of the door.

Catherine flinched at how close he was.

He must be standing there listening.

"I'm fine," she said, knowing if she didn't answer he would come in. "I'm not finished yet."

She quickly used the toilet with her hands still tied in front of her and washed them and used the threadbare but clean towel hanging on a rusty towel bar to dry them. She opened the door. He stood right outside it.

"Is everything all right?" he asked, glancing behind her into the bathroom interior.

She bit her tongue to stop herself from lashing out. She had to stop being so honest with him. She had to outfox him, not react to him. She had to lie. Be smarter.

"I'm fine," she said. "A little hungry."

His eyes lit up at that, which didn't surprise her. He'd spent half the morning making a stir-fry of some kind.

If she could make him think things were relatively normal with her, maybe he would lower his guard. Maybe he would tell her something that would make a difference.

He slipped an arm around her waist and she leaned heavily on him as he slowly escorted her to the dining chair by the kitchen. She hobbled and hopped and groaned as much as she dared but she could tell by the expression on his face that he believed her to be in physical distress.

At the table, she saw a box of Nurofen, the French brand of ibuprofen, and a glass of water. She instantly realized that he wanted her to see the box to know that the pills really were only ibuprofen.

As well he should, she thought trying to tamp down her fury at his giving her a sedative a second time in three days.

"Thank you," she said as she opened the packet and extricated two pills. He watched her as she took the pills with her water and then he removed the box.

Afraid I'll try to kill myself?

He went to the kitchen and brought back two plates of food and set one before her. It was yesterday's leftover chicken and rice. He handed her a spoon. She was hungry and so they ate in silence.

She knew if she looked up from her plate she would see him watching her. She needed him to believe she'd given up and had accepted her situation.

"Where did you learn to cook?" she asked.

He hesitated for just a moment.

"My mother."

"She must have been a good cook."

"She was."

"Is she still alive?"

"No."

"I'm sorry."

"She was an honorable woman," he said. "Everyone loved her."

"And your father? Did he love her?"

He looked at her in surprise which quickly changed to suspicion.

"My father was troubled," he said. "He was a brilliant man."

"Dead too?"

He focused on his food and didn't answer.

"What would your mother think of what you're doing?"

He took in a sharp breath as if slapped.

"If she could see you now," Catherine said, "would she be proud of her son?"

"Stop talking."

Rashid rubbed a hand across his face, flushed and tense, and pulled at the collar of his t-shirt. Catherine stared at him across the dining table until he finally tossed down his fork and pushed his plate away.

He doesn't want to be doing this. He feels guilty.

"How did she die?"

"Cancer."

"A son and his mother have a special bond," she said.

"Stop. Please."

"And yet you used this love—the love of a mother for her son—to trick me."

He looked at her and he was stricken.

"Don't apologize to me again," she said. "Don't embarrass us both. Don't humiliate your mother who is looking on you right this—"

"Stop it!" he shouted and jumped up.

"A boy needs his mother! My husband can't do it! My husband needs me!"

"Not anymore, he doesn't!"

The minute he spoke Catherine felt a ripple of ice-cold fear slice into her. Rashid looked at her from across the table with haunted eyes, his shoulders slumped as if trying to make himself smaller.

"What did you mean by that?" she asked.

He picked up his plate and retreated to the kitchen. Catherine stood up slowly at her place at the table.

"Answer me, Rashid!" she screamed. "What do you know? Where is my husband?"

When he didn't answer, Catherine picked up her plate and flung it toward the kitchen. He ran back to the table and stared at her, his hands going up as if in an attempt to calm her.

"Look, it was an accident," he said desperately.

Catherine felt for the back of her chair and fell into it, her legs turning to jelly.

"What do you mean?" she said in a whisper, her eyes drilling into him as if begging him to retract his words. "What...accident?"

"I'm sorry, Catherine," Rashid said, stepping over to her. "Your husband cannot help you."

Catherine forced her mouth to form the words. "Why not?" she whispered.

Rashid gripped himself in a hug as if needing to hold himself together.

"Because," he said, regarding her sadly. "I'm afraid your husband has died."

40

Geneviève was waiting for me in my apartment when I returned from the hospital.

"How is he, *chérie*?" she asked as I dropped my purse on the unfinished shelf table by the door. The twenty-four-seven cartoon marathon which had become the background music to this nightmare was playing on the television. Haley, Robbie and Cam were on the couch. Izzy was with them. She turned to wag her tail at me when she saw me.

"Broken ribs," I said. "And a broken leg."

Geneviève gasped. "Oh, *chérie*, no! What happened?"

We moved away from the living room into the kitchen. I felt suddenly exhausted as if fifty-pound weights had been attached to my arms and legs. I wasn't sure how I was going to get through the day, let alone the rest of the week, not to mention my life.

"He was lured out to some deserted area by an abandoned factory and beat up by three thugs. They told him to stop looking for Catherine."

I paraphrased the message that had been delivered. No sense in making it sound as bad as it really was.

"*Chérie*, these men knew where Catherine was?"

"I don't know. I think they were just sent to deliver the message."

"Do you..." Geneviève turned to glance in the living room where the children sat glued to the set. "Do you think they are safe?"

"I do," I said firmly. "My father wouldn't hurt children."

"And when it becomes clear you intend to ignore his message? What then?"

I felt tears threaten to overflow their banks. I'd worked so hard on the ride home from the hospital not to feel too hopeless, but I couldn't see how I could find Catherine in what amounted to eight hours until the next curfew.

I put my hands to my face and broke down. It was the combination of saying the terrible words out loud along with the sight of Geneviève's loving kind face that did me in. I sobbed silently into my hands while she wrapped her arms around me.

"*Chérie*," she whispered. "Have faith."

"I have none," I sobbed. "It's over. I can't find her."

"*Chérie*," she said firmly, giving my shoulders a light shake. "The lockdown has been extended another forty-eight hours."

At first I didn't register her words, but when she repeated them, they began to resound in my brain.

The nurses were wrong.

"Really?" I said, looking at her through my tears.

"Yes, *chérie*. Really."

There was still time.

I cried again, every bit as hard as before.

An hour later, after checking on the children and confirming that there was really nothing I could do to significantly change for the better how Cameron was feeling, I took my laptop into my bedroom and got on the Internet.

The first thing I did was look up Rashid Abadi's name on my people-finding sites and, as expected, found nothing. Or rather, found too many to be of any use. Closing out of the French finder site *Cherchez-Moi,* I focused instead on creating another map showing where the boat was, where it went, and where it launched from and returned.

I then noted the exact locations for the hotel and rental apartments for each of the boat's passengers that night, as well as Ariel's homeless shelter. I circled the spot where the car had been abandoned. Then I drew a line from where the car had been to the street rue Freycinet where Ariel had said Abadi picked her up.

I sat back and looked at what I had in front of me. The picture was an area of less than three blocks.

In my mind, *this* was the area I needed to canvas to find someone who'd seen Catherine and Rashid. There was no point in showing his photo. The only picture I had was too fuzzy.

I stared at my map which was very much like the one I'd created yesterday to find Ariel.

Someone has to have seen something.

I stood up and eased the kinks out of my back. It was bedtime for Robbie, but I'd heard Haley move about in the other room giving him his bath. I also heard Cameron's voice and so figured that he was staying close to her, which I was relieved about.

It was after eight o'clock and the curfew had already gone in effect. I hated to waste a minute of the reprieve we'd been given. But with Jean-Marc in the hospital, I couldn't expect not to be picked up if I tried to go out on my own.

A good night's sleep had some benefits too, I told myself. If I was able to sleep.

I went into the guest room where Haley and the two boys were settled on the bed with a book. Cameron looked up at me as he always did lately—with hope in his eyes—before turning away in disappointment.

"Mind if I join you?" I asked as Robbie held his arms out to me. I climbed into bed with all of them, Robbie on one side and Cam on the other, and I pulled little Izzy onto my lap. If it weren't for the curfew, I would have loved to have taken Cameron to the church around the corner.

Built in 1868, the Église Saint-Augustin was a beautiful building full of peace and soothing serenity. I'd gone there many a time to just sit and I always walked away feeling better and more grounded.

But even if there hadn't been a curfew, I knew I couldn't spare the time.

I needed to get back on the phone tonight calling more cab companies and then tomorrow I needed to go back to the neighborhood of the sightseeing boat office until I found someone who had seen Catherine and the man who took her.

There would be plenty of time later to sit in a church.

However it all turned out.

41

Catherine gripped the table with both hands and stared at Rashid. He stood in front of her, hugging himself, his head hanging.

"I don't believe you! He is not dead! You're just trying to make me give up hope!"

Rashid looked at her helplessly and lifted his hands in a gesture of futility.

"I feared he would not willingly have let you go otherwise," he said.

She stared at him, her eyes blinking rapidly as she tried to understand his words.

This wasn't happening. He was lying!

"I am begging your forgiveness," Rashid said. "I didn't mean for it to—"

"What? You *killed* him?" Catherine said. Her chest felt suddenly tight as if she was being constricted by a powerful force. "You killed Todd?!"

"Please do not scream," he said plaintively.

Suddenly she remembered the blood spatter on Rashid's t-shirt the night he led her off the boat. She'd been so intent on hurrying to Cameron that she hadn't thought about how Rashid had gotten blood on him. And then later he'd changed shirts and she'd forgotten what she'd seen.

Todd's blood. That was Todd's blood on his t-shirt.

The screamed welled up inside her chest and flew out of her in a powerful force. She grabbed her head and screamed louder.

Rashid ran to the kitchen and returned with the duct tape in his hand. He reached her, fighting past her hands, still bound, as she clawed at him. She drove her head hard up into his chin and he tasted blood and his vision clouded and the screams went on and on.

"You bastard! You murderer!" she howled as he finally wrestled her off the chair and onto the floor. She jerked her knee up hard between his legs but didn't reach him. Hating handling her like this, he pushed past her hands to position the tape over her mouth. It took him precious seconds to do it and as he did she carved ten jagged channels of bloody scratches down both his cheeks.

He grabbed her hands and held them as he watched her eyes, crazed, over the piece of tape that had finally silenced the awful screams.

"I'm sorry, *Habibti*," he said, holding her hands as she thrashed under him, trying to kick him, head butt him, reach him with her nails. His arms began to shake with the effort as her fury gave her a strength she hadn't had up to now.

She wrenched her hands away from him and turned away, her face to the floor and he heard her muffled sobs at least as chilling and haunting as her screams had been terrifying. He stood up and backed away from her, his hands briefly going to his face and coming back coated in his own blood.

"Forgive me, dearest one," he said as he staggered away from her, needing to get away from the heartbreaking sounds. He went to the door and turned to look at her. She never lifted her head, the weeping never abated. He eased out into the hallway and sank to a sitting position with his head against the door. He could still hear her crying and dropped his head in agony at the sound.

Catherine didn't care that he'd left. She didn't care what happened next. Todd was dead. Just the words reverberated around her brain and came crashing down upon her in a brutal barrage of guilt and shame and fear.

She thought of all the hopeful, agonizing hours when she told herself he was coming—*any time now!* She'd been so sure that he was working with the police to rescue her.

And none of that had ever been going to happen.

Todd had been dead by the time Catherine had gotten on the bus all those days ago.

And then a searing thought jolted her eyes open wide.

Cameron.

Cameron must know what happened to his father by now. Catherine forced aside the image of Cameron grieving for his father. She couldn't go there, couldn't see that. Not yet.

She wept again and with every shaking conclusive sob she told herself *Someone will pay for this. Someone will pay for these nights my boy has endured thinking he's lost both his parents.*

If it takes my life, I swear someone will pay.

42

Day Five of the Lockdown

Maybe because I knew this was very likely the last reprieve I would get on the lockdown, the day felt longer and hotter than just two days before when I had gone in search of Ariel. Every step felt like it was taking me further away from Catherine. I don't know why that was. A part of me thought there was something obvious I should be doing. But for the life of me I couldn't think what.

The plan today was for Geneviève and Noel to pick up Jean-Marc from the hospital and bring him to my apartment in the afternoon. Until then I wanted him to be able to sleep and heal so I refrained from calling him.

I never felt so alone walking the streets of Paris. I called Adele but the call went to voicemail and I assumed it meant she was working a crime scene and couldn't talk. I knew she'd call when she was able.

I tried not to talk to the same people I'd spoken with two days earlier. There was still plenty of neighborhood left to canvas that I hadn't covered. I went to every café and shop on every street in my mapped-out grid of streets in the area within a ten-block radius of the boat ramp. Whenever I stopped for a drink and to rest, I called the same cab companies I'd called yesterday. They were just as uninterested in talking to me today as they were yesterday.

What is it that Einstein said about doing the same thing over and over and expecting a different result?

When I found out that Jean-Marc had been working on this piece with the cab companies while I was knocking on doors, I felt better, but at the moment Jean-Marc was in a drug-fueled daze, his brain clouded with pain and pharmaceuticals. He couldn't call the cab companies and they wouldn't talk to me.

I resumed my walking, slower as the day dragged on, the sun beating relentlessly down on me as I walked from shop to shop.

As I walked away from a beauty salon—one where I'd shown Catherine's photo to every hairdresser, shampoo girl and client in the place—I received a text from Haley showing me a photo of Cam and Robbie sitting together looking at a book. Haley was so smart. Somehow she knew what it takes the rest of us a lifetime to learn.

If you want to ease someone's pain, let them help someone else.

The look on Cam's face was intense and focused on helping Robbie. I felt a rush of gratitude to Haley and a fragile hope that Cameron would have better days.

My phone rang and I saw it was Adele.

"Sorry I couldn't answer when you called before," she said by way of a greeting. "How are you?"

"I'm hoping you have some time for me," I said. "But no pressure if you don't. I don't want to get in the way of your work."

"I just finished a case. Until someone stabs somebody or shoots them, I'm all yours. *Mon Dieu*, Claire. I am so sorry. I didn't mean to say that."

"No worries, Adele. Please don't apologize. And I just need you for one night."

Because if I don't find Catherine by tomorrow night, I'll never need anyone for anything ever again.

I chased the dark thought from my mind and quickly caught Adele up to speed with what had happened to Jean-Marc, first to let her know why he couldn't come with me instead and also to let her know that there was risk involved.

I didn't *think* my father would hurt Adele but I honestly couldn't absolutely guarantee he wouldn't either.

Two hours later, the sun had dropped in the sky, but it was still light out and not yet curfew time. I sat on a bench and slipped my feet out of my sandals for a moment. My feet throbbed which surprised me since I walk all over Paris daily and have never felt effects like this.

I didn't have the mental energy to imagine what the difference could be. Perhaps I wasn't stopping and hydrating enough. Perhaps in my urgency and desperation I was hitting my footsteps harder than I normally do.

As I sat there, I pulled out a water bottle from my tote and finished off what was in there. The brief moment that my head was tilted to the sky I caught sight of a fluffy white cumulus cloud floating over the street.

My eyes stung as I watched the cloud and remembered a moment many years ago when Catherine had won top prize at her middle school science fair for her work on clouds. I remember thinking, as adoring parents do, that she was going to be a scientist when she grew up, that her fascination with clouds and weather in general would be the defining mark in my ebullient, precocious child.

Both Bob and I had sat in the auditorium that afternoon at

Henderson Middle School in Atlanta, so proud as we clutched each other's hands in pride and love at having created such an amazing creature.

She hadn't been expected to win. Two smart boys were favored and, while Catherine was well aware of that, she didn't let the fact derail her motivation as it might have others. She only knew that her project had fascinated her like nothing else had up to then. It was the passion and the creativity with which she'd presented her findings that won her the top prize.

My daughter is tenacious.

I prayed that stubborn trait was still there inside her somewhere. I prayed that the girl who'd stood on that stage all those years ago, that unlikely award in her hand and that determined expression on her face, was still alive and roaring somewhere in this city.

I got up from the bench and crossed the street. I'd already visited every shop and restaurant on that side. But as I crossed, I noticed that a flower seller had set up her retail stand on the side I had just left. I immediately turned around and walked back across the street. The flower seller was only one person, and hardly likely to make a difference. But if I didn't talk to her, I knew I'd drive myself crazy the rest of the night.

No stone unturned, I told myself. Not with only three hours left.

No stone.

I approached with pessimism and sheer exhaustion, reaching into my purse for my phone with the photo of Catherine and for my billfold. Unlike at the *cafés* and *tabacs*, I would pay the woman for a few posies for her time.

She wore her hair pinned up and while the effect should have been severe, it was actually elegant. Her face was weathered, but she'd taken the time to put on stud earrings, tiny violets in each ear. Her eyes were probing and quick.

There was something about her face that stopped me.

It was a mother's face.

I don't know why that thought struck me. But she was looking at me as if she were worried, as if she were curious about what I was doing. I couldn't help but think she was looking at me as if we had some kind of connection.

Maybe that was all created in my head after the fact. Maybe I've mythologized the whole encounter since the moment I crossed the street to talk to her.

Because when I showed her the picture of Catherine, she immediately started nodding her head.

"Yes," she said. "I saw her. With a man."

43

"Where? Do you remember where?"

It was suddenly hard to breathe and I had to restrain myself from grabbing her by the shoulders to make her talk faster. I glanced around the street. We were less than a block away from where Abadi's car had been found.

"They got on a bus," she said with no hesitancy. "The bus to Levallois-Perret."

I whipped out my map and pushed it in front of her.

"Where does the bus go?" I asked.

She squinted at my map and took a gnarled finger to draw a looping line far outside of the half-moon radius I'd drawn.

"Thank you," I said, tears in my eyes.

"*Bonne chance, Maman,*" she said as she handed me a single rose.

Good luck.

Within minutes of finding out that Catherine and Abadi had gotten on a bus when they left the sightseeing boat, I was on the phone to Geneviève and hurrying to the nearest Metro station. Geneviève and Noel had brought Jean-Marc to my apartment which was where they all were now.

When I'd originally suggested the idea to Jean-Marc that he stay with me, he said he'd go back to his hotel, which had made me wonder if his fiancée was staying with him there. But I didn't see her at the hospital, so that didn't make sense. In any case, I'd gotten a text message from Geneviève an hour earlier telling me that Jean-Marc had changed his mind about going back to the hotel.

"How does he look?" I asked her when I called her from my seat on the eastbound train heading home. It was July and would be many hours before dark. But the curfew was only minutes away and the train was empty.

"He has his pain medicine," Geneviève said, "And we've made him comfortable. Haley has moved the boys to your bedroom to give him the guestroom. She insists she can take the couch."

"Shall I pick up takeout?" I asked. "I'm on my way home now."

"No, Bill has picked up Chinese. You'd better hurry, *chérie*. The curfew."

"I know, I know. But Geneviève, I found someone who saw her! I found someone who saw Catherine that night!"

"*Vraiment, chérie?*"

"Yes. I'll tell you all about it when I get there. Is...is Jean-Marc up to talking to me?"

"I think he is asleep, *chérie*. Should I—?"

"No, let him sleep. I'll talk to him when I get there."

"That is good news, *chérie*," Geneviève said.

But even I could hear the hesitancy in her voice. A horrible thought wrapped around my entrails and gave them a slow, insidious tug.

Was I the only one who still thought we had a hope of finding her?

When I got home, my apartment was buzzing with activity. Noel and Bill had set the table and fed the children. Jean-Marc was awake, on the couch, his crutch leaning against the coffee table, an array of pill bottles on the side table.

I went first to Robbie and picked him up. Like Izzy, he and I have a routine which had been abandoned with all the horror of this week. The extra people and break from our routine had been enough to distract him up to now, but I knew children needed consistency.

Robbie wrapped his arms around my neck and lay his head on my shoulder. That told me he was tired, for which I was grateful, but I still felt a twinge of guilt that I'd had so little time for him since everything had happened. I sat down on the couch with him in my arms and Izzy instantly jumped on the couch and nosed her way under my arms for her own hug.

I smiled over Robbie's shoulder at Jean-Marc. I hoped he could tell by my face how glad I was to see him. He looked pale, his face stitched in barely disguised pain, but he smiled back at me.

"You have many people who have missed you," he said.

I gave Robbie a kiss and set him free, then searched the room for Cam but he was in the kitchen with Geneviève. I wouldn't worry about him for now.

"Geneviève said you found someone who saw them get on a bus," Jean-Marc said, shifting uncomfortably on the couch.

"You look miserable, Jean-Marc," I said. "Is there anything I can get you?"

"People are waiting on me hand and foot."

That was when I noticed the glass of wine by his hand.

"Should you mix pain pills with wine?"

He dismissed my question with an annoyed wave of his hand.

"So," he said. "This explains why we didn't get any hits on cabs in the area"

"It's good, right?"

He frowned. "Except we don't know where they got *off* the bus. And we don't know that they didn't switch buses. Or jump off and *then* grab a cab."

Hearing him say that deflated my earlier optimism. I knew he was right. My shoulders sagged at his words.

"But you have done good work, Claire. We are closing in, I think."

I knew BS when I heard it, but tonight I just didn't have the energy to pretend to be grateful for his effort.

44

F or the rest of the night, Haley kept the boys engaged
long enough for the adults to eat. I was indebted to
both Noel and Bill for pitching in. Bill was a big man
and helped Jean-Marc maneuver, while he was getting used to
handling his crutches.

After dinner, Geneviève insisted on doing the dishes with
Noel before leaving for the night. She'd given me a series of
hopeful looks all night long that I knew was her version of
supportive commiseration. But they only reminded me over
and over again that everyone was waiting for the other shoe to
drop and that it was most certainly going to bury me when
it did.

After she left, Jean-Marc hobbled into the guest room to
make a few phone calls and I asked Cam to come downstairs
with me while I walked Izzy.

The temperature had fallen a bit with the evening although
it was still warm. I let Izzy go to her favorite pavers over by a
large cement planter filled with geraniums. All of us in the
building were supposed to keep the courtyard garden tended

but only the Asian couple on the third floor really took care of it.

"How was your day today?" I asked Cam as I ran my hand through his hair.

"It was okay," he said, his eyes on Izzy.

We were both quiet for a few minutes. It occurred to me that Haley did such a good job of keeping Cameron engaged and distracted that perhaps he didn't get enough quiet time. Not that I want him to reflect too much. But children especially need a moment to catch their breath and decompress.

"I know they fought," he said in a small voice.

My gut wrenched at his words.

"Adults fight," I said. "Even ones who love each other."

"They loved each other," he said. "They did."

"I know, darling."

"I can't believe he's never coming home," he said, his voice quivering.

"I know, baby."

My body felt hot and cold at the same tight as I held him and felt his sorrow mix with my own. There is nothing worse than seeing someone you love in so much pain that you can do nothing to relieve.

He looked up at me, his eyes filled with tears.

"Am I going to live in Paris with you if you can't find Mom?"

"I'm going to find her, darling. I told you."

He seemed to study my face in the dark before turning away to watch Izzy.

Again, I know you shouldn't make promises. I've read all the books too.

The trouble is, I need to hear them as much as he does.

~

After the children were settled down for the night in the living room under blankets on the floor and the couch, I sat with Jean-Marc on the bed in the guest room. He'd already made it clear that he didn't feel my news about the bus was as earth-shattering as I did.

I tried to think that a part of that could be his natural pessimism after being so recently hurt. It must be hard to think of the next step in an impossible strategy when you were in the kind of pain I was sure he was in.

But I still needed a plan.

As I was helping Haley put Robbie down for the night, I'd caught a brief bit of the TV news about the lockdown. It seemed the government was determined to stick to its guns this time about reopening the country. Due to dramatic pushback from the citizenry in the cities who felt they were currently being held hostage, the government was promising to stick to its promise of lifting the lockdown in exactly twenty hours.

"Let's look at it from a different perspective," Jean-Marc said from where he lay on the guest bed, his leg propped up on a stack of pillows. "Let us put ourselves in this man's shoes."

"I'm listening."

"He paid a woman to get him on the boat so we know this was at least partially planned."

"You think he was following Catherine and when he saw she and Todd were in line to get on the boat he improvised? He went and found Ariel and got in line too?"

"Very likely. I think he was probably paid to kill Todd but possibly he merely feared Todd would interfere with his taking Catherine and so took his chance when he saw it."

I grimaced at the cold-blooded logic that could have sealed Todd's fate on what was supposed to have been a pleasant river cruise with his wife.

"He probably intended to take Catherine in his car," Jean-

Marc continued. "Either out of France or to a safe house, but two things derailed his plans."

"The lockdown happened," I said, trying to imagine how desperate Rashid must have felt when he got off the boat and realized he would not be able to get out of Paris that night.

"*Oui*, and his car battery was dead. Now what does he do?"

"He calls for orders from his employer and ends up jumping on a bus."

"Clearly a desperation move."

"Agreed. It definitely wasn't planned," I said, envisioning the likelihood of it happening this way. "He snags the first bus to come his way because he needed to get Catherine off the street and away from any CCTV cameras."

"Okay. So now he is on the bus, yes? I imagine at this point, whatever lie he told your daughter to get her to come with him has collapsed."

I felt a searing sting of fear at his words. Now would be the time when brute force or drugs would come into play to get Catherine where she needed to be.

I swallowed hard around the lump in my throat.

"The point, *chérie*," Jean-Marc said gently, "is that now he has no easy method of transportation *and* he cannot leave the city. He has a hostage who has probably become less compliant. He needs someplace to hide—to wait out the lockdown."

"The flower seller said Rashid was on his phone when she saw him," I said. "He was probably asking his handler where he should go. But how do we know where that is?"

I slumped into my chair feeling every muscle in my body go slack. As if it just didn't matter anymore. As if nothing did.

"We know the bus they got on," Jean-Marc said, tapping my knee to get my attention and distract me from my sinking thoughts. "And we know the route."

He hesitated and I looked up. When I did, I felt like I heard his unspoken warning reverberating my head: *Unless they got off before arriving in Levallois-Perret.*

I wiped away my tears of defeat and frustration.

"How far away is it?" I asked.

"Levallois-Perret? From where they were, probably around six kilometers."

That was bad. Six kilometers was a really long way to ride a bus with an unwilling, possibly hysterical hostage. Surely he would've gotten off before arriving at Levallois-Perret.

As if he could read my mind, Jean-Marc leaned over and squeezed my hand.

"I'll call the cab companies again," he said. "I'll ask for any driver who picked up a fare in this new area of the neighborhood during the same timeframe. If he did get off the bus, he'll have looked for a cab."

I let out a long sigh but found myself nodding, my heart trying not to listen to the words bombarding my head.

"Have faith, *Claire*. We are not yet beaten."

I looked at him—the very picture of *beaten* with his cast and crutch, his taped-up lip and black eye—and it was all I could do not to weep.

45

Day Six of the Lockdown

The next morning I spread out the map on the dining room table that showed the route of the bus. I realized that canvassing a ten-block radius was one thing, but there was no way I could cover anything but a small portion of the bus's roughly forty-block route.

Jean-Marc still wasn't up and because of his injuries, I didn't feel comfortable waking him.

Suddenly, as I stared at the map, I felt it hard to breathe. I'd been standing but now I sat down hard as if my legs wouldn't hold me another moment.

There was a tap on the door but I didn't bother standing and after a moment Geneviève came in with a bag of sugary *chouquettes*. Immediately Haley and the boys descended upon it and her. I watched numbly as the children greeted her and then took their pastries back to the living room where they were playing a game with the TV on.

Geneviève came to where I was sitting and pulled out a chair.

"What are your plans today, *chérie*?" she asked as she sat down beside me.

"I don't know," I said. "Honestly this job is too big for just me."

"Can Adele help?"

I took in a deep breath and felt a little better.

"I've got her on speed dial," I said. "But it's too big for the two of us. And before you offer, dearest Geneviève, it's too big for anything less than a squad of highly-trained detectives or maybe bloodhounds. In fact, it's impossible."

"Oh, *chérie*."

"Please don't tell me to have faith, Geneviève," I said, tears threatening as I looked at the map before me and digested exactly how impossible the task was. "The lockdown lifts in twelve hours and half of that is *after* the curfew. Jean-Marc can't come with me with his broken leg so I'm screwed."

"What will you do?"

"Oh, I'll still go out there and I'll stay until the cops arrest me for breaking curfew because there's nothing else I can do."

The sounds of the ever-indestructible Oggie and his felonious cockroaches came to us for a moment from the other room. The zany idiocy of the soundtrack made the harshness of my reality feel even worse. It was like a demon laughing while I was squirming on the rack.

Suddenly we heard a heavy crash that came from the guest room. I jumped up from the table, ran to the guest room door, and entered without knocking.

I'd expected to see the double-door solid walnut linen press armoire on its side on the floor. Instead I found Jean-Marc lying next to the bed, his crutches askew and his phone in his hand.

"I'm going to ask Bill or Noel to come help," I said.

"Wait, Claire," Jean-Marc said, grimacing in pain. He was wearing only boxer shorts and I suddenly realized I'd never seen his bare legs before.

It's possible he was realizing the same thing because he blushed and reached on the bed to pull his robe down.

"What happened?" I asked, feeling helpless. There was no way I was going to get him back on his feet on my own. Why wouldn't he left me ask Bill or Noel for help?

Within seconds the guest room door opened behind me and was filled with Haley with Robbie on her hip, Cameron, and Geneviève.

"Is everything all right?" Geneviève asked.

"Everything is absolutely wonderful," Jean-Marc said a little too loudly.

I'd never seen Jean-Marc sarcastic and, I have to say, pain or boxer shorts or not, I wasn't thrilled he was showing this side of him to the children. Then I saw he was actually smiling.

"What's going on?" I asked in bewilderment.

"I got a little excited," he said sheepishly. "And misjudged the distance from the bed to the dresser."

"Excited about what?" I asked.

He waved his phone at me.

"The cab company," he said. "I found them."

I was even more confused until I realized what he was saying.

"You called the cab companies?" I asked.

I'd had absolutely no expectation that he'd been in any state to do that. He must have done it last night while I was downstairs talking to Cameron.

"One of them called back with a hit."

Praying that I knew what he was about to say, I turned to Haley and shooed her and the boys out of the room.

"Let Detective LaRue get dressed," I said. "Geneviève? Can you see if one of your menfolk downstairs can come up and help Jean-Marc to his feet?"

Then I closed the door and it was just the two of us.

"Tell me," I said, trying not to get my hopes up.

"One of their drivers remembered them. A pretty American girl and a Middle Eastern man."

I clapped a hand to my mouth fighting down the burst of hope that had erupted inside me.

"We've got an address," he said.

46

Rashid felt the thickness in his throat as he fought the feeling of shame cascade over him.

He stood in the hallway of the apartment building where he'd spent the night curled up by the door listening to the sounds of her weeping because to do so was the punishment he deserved.

She'd finally stopped crying, but he couldn't take the chance that she was awake. He didn't want to upset her all over again.

If it wasn't for his sister, he would kill himself in front of Catherine. Happily, joyfully. He would take the knife and stab it straight into his throat to show her how much he cared, how his heart broke for her—not just for the loss of her beloved husband but also because she would never see her child again.

But he couldn't do that. Malek needed him.

Catherine's tears were the price of his sin and his baseness. Sweat popped out on his face as he thought of the moment he'd told her of her husband's death. Like a nascent life force he'd had no control over, the words had just erupted from his mouth.

He would never forget the look on her face. First, the look of sheer disbelief. And then the realization that what Rashid said was the truth.

He turned and laid his ear against the door and listened, but it was quiet inside. He groaned and stepped away from the door. He hated what he was doing. He would happily die to be able to let her go if only he could.

But there was sweet Malek.

He'd already botched this job in a hundred different ways, starting with telling the homeless woman a different name than the one he registered with the boat. It was just nerves but he couldn't afford nerves!

Malek can't afford it.

He glanced at his watch. It was a little after six in the morning. It was still quiet inside and he knew her well enough by now to know she slept late. A shiver of remorse reminded him that she might not today, since she'd cried herself to sleep earlier than usual.

He listened again at the door. He could hear no noise from inside and was relieved that he'd hammered shut the window. At least there was no way she could get out.

But he should hurry. Putting his ear against the door one last time to confirm that there was no noise inside, he turned and hurried down the hall and the long winding stairs to the front door.

He'd wanted to meet Khalil yesterday, but it had gotten late and he couldn't risk being out after curfew. That would be disaster for him—and for Catherine too, since she would starve to death in the apartment without him. He felt a small throb of pleasure thinking of how much she needed him, but guiltily extinguished the sensation as he stepped out onto the street.

He didn't deserve to feel good.

He pulled out his phone and called Khalil. His lip throbbed when it touched the phone and he winced. She had ripped up his cheek badly. He smiled at the thought. Even though the reason for it was sickening—and all his doing—it showed the spirit that Moreau prized in the girl. He was right about that. She was rare. One in a million.

"*Allo?*"

"*Ahlaan,*" Rashid said into the phone as he walked down the block. "Have you any news about what I should do about the car?"

He'd reported the dead battery two days ago and been chastised for allowing it to happen. But there had been no solution for the problem of how to get Catherine out of Paris once the lockdown lifted.

"I can get the battery replaced," Rashid said.

"No. The police already have the car."

Rashid's pulse raced and he heard the sudden sound of his own heartbeat thrashing in his ears at the thought of the police ripping the car apart, looking for clues, looking for him, for Catherine.

"You are to procure another car," Khalil said. "Park it two streets over from the safe house. Be ready to move as soon as the lockdown lifts."

"Where shall I get this car?"

"I don't know! Look on *Le Bon Coin*! Look at the sales ads! Do you have enough cash?"

"I think so."

Did he? Enough to buy a car? To last to the border?

"What about my route?" he asked, chewing his lip and feeling the pain shoot up into his head and making his eyes water.

He emerged from boulevard du Château onto an artery of cafés and shops starting to open for morning trade. He leaned against the wall, keeping his head down.

"It will be sent to your phone," Khalil said. "Basically you'll need to drug her again and put her in the trunk. Once you're in

Marseille, you'll hand her over to someone else. Instructions about that will be coming."

"Who? Who will be taking her?"

He couldn't help the sudden surge of protectiveness that shot through him.

"You don't need to know that. Just get her there."

Already Rashid's mind was spinning. They'd only given him enough for two doses of *Midazolam* and he'd already used both doses on her. He couldn't tell Khalil that she'd escaped a couple days ago—or that she'd injured herself in the process—that would be tantamount to signing his own death warrant. If he was lucky she wouldn't be limping by the time she got to Dubai.

But how was he to get her into the car undrugged? He scrubbed a hand down his face and felt his thundering heartbeat again, like a clawing animal trapped in a cage trying to free itself.

It took him longer than he'd expected to find the car. He'd sat in a café on the rue Baudin looking through the ads on his phone until he found one nearby for a price he could afford. It was listed for six hundred euros. It was a pile of junk but would probably get them to Marseille. It would mean he had no money for the trip itself but it would have to do.

He took a bus to the nineteenth arrondissement, found the car and paid for it in cash. He put petrol in it and bought water and some food and put them in the backseat. They might have to leave in a hurry, leaving their stores behind in the apartment.

The woman selling the car was as glad to hand over the car keys without much real examination on his part as he was to hand over the money. A grey 2009 4-door Renault, the car had sixty thousand kilometers on it, but Rashid didn't have time to find anything better. He'd already been gone too long from the apartment.

As Khalil had instructed Rashid parked the car two streets away from the apartment. Then he texted him that he'd gotten the car. Then he sat in it for a few minutes just to be alone with his thoughts and away from the misery and the guilt that awaited him inside the apartment.

His mind went back to Catherine's hopeless, heartbreaking tears last night and to her wails of grief. He reminded himself that *he* was the reason she was crying. He had hurt her beyond measure.

Could she ever forgive him? He shook that thought away. There was no reason that she should. After he delivered her to Marseille he would never see her again.

Finally, the heat beating down on him from the late afternoon sun, he got out of the car, locked it, checked that the street was as safe as he thought, and walked back to the main shopping district where he'd had coffee a few hours earlier.

Once there, he went to a local sundry and produce store and bought groceries, again keeping his chin down to obscure his face. He needn't have worried. The man at the register was uninterested in anything but his money.

Outside, he saw two members of the French armed forces saunter slowly by, their assault rifles at the ready.

His heart pounding, Rashid returned to the store to pretend to look at the shelves before stepping back out onto the sidewalk after the police had walked by.

That was close. He hadn't been paying attention. He couldn't allow himself to become distracted. Lives literally depended on it.

Minutes later, he walked down the street leading to the apartment building where Catherine waited for him, carefully confirming that nobody had followed him.

It was nearly sixteen hundred hours. He'd been gone for

several hours and was beginning to feel nervous about what he would find when he got back to the apartment. Just as he walked up to the front door and put the security code in, his phone rang.

It was Khalil.

"You have the car?" Khalil asked.

Rashid felt a flash of annoyance and worry. He'd already texted him that he had.

"I do," he said.

"Don't go out tonight. The lockdown is lifting soon. You will ruin everything if you are picked up for breaking curfew."

"You think I don't know that?" Rashid said, clenching his jaw. "I have never left the apartment after curfew."

"You are keeping her drugged?"

That caught Rashid off guard. Did Khalil think he had more *Midazolam* than he did? Was this a trick?

"There's no need," Rashid said. "She is cooperating."

"Really? I'll tell our employer. He'll be pleased. Make sure she stays cooperative."

How do I do that? Rashid thought desperately. *Right now she hates me.*

"Of course. No problem."

"He wants her unharmed. That's clear, yes?"

"Yes, of course," Rashid said. "And my sister?"

But Khalil had already hung up.

47

L evallois-Perret was not actually an arrondissement at all but a commune in the Hauts-de-Seine department of Île-de-France in north central Paris. It wasn't a great area as far as decent housing went, but it didn't really feel like a dangerous part of town. Or no more dangerous than any Paris neighborhood outside the tourist sections.

I'd argued with Jean-Marc half the morning about my going alone to the address he'd given me. He wanted to come too—of course—or for me to wait for Adele—unnecessary—or at least go with Noel or Bill—ridiculous. It all came down to the fact that Jean-Marc wanted desperately to go himself—which truly was impossible.

I seemed to have left all the activity of people and traffic behind. This street was typical of those in the Latin Quarter— claustrophobically narrow, with the apartment windows shuttered tight against light and noise. There were fewer cars and people.

I turned to look back the way I'd come. My heart was thudding in my throat now. Without really noticing it, the warm day had dissolved into an overcast one and the street was in creeping shadow. A sensation crawled across my skin like ants let loose over spoiled food. I rubbed my arms.

There was no doubt in my mind that the cab Jean-Marc had found had indeed picked up Catherine and her kidnapper. Jean-Marc had been able to talk to the driver and was told that the American girl was drunk off her feet and her Arabian boyfriend had had to practically carry her into the car. That dovetailed with the idea that Abadi had drugged Catherine to get her to come the rest of the way with him.

My job today was to confirm that they were at the address where the cab had dropped them. On the one hand, if I called the police and I was right, they would arrest Catherine. While that was vastly preferable to any other option short of a shootout, I was personally hoping for a different outcome.

In my mind—and I knew Jean-Marc feared this the most—I believed I would be able to reason with Catherine's kidnapper and extract my daughter without anyone coming to harm. I was absolutely confident that my father would not allow me to be hurt—or Catherine for that matter. I knew I could do this.

I would do this.

It had taken all the self-discipline I possessed to take the time to prepare for this confrontation. My phone was charged, my shoes were appropriate in case I had to run, and my clothes —in muted earth tones—were loose and chosen so as not to attract attention.

Even so, I feared every minute that I delayed that Abadi would move Catherine. I had no idea what his situation was, whether the place he was holding her—rue de Villiers—was his ultimate destination or just a temporary one.

Jean-Marc had done his best to try to keep my hopes deflated by saying there was every reason to believe Abadi wasn't so stupid as to give the actual address of his safe house to the cab driver.

I knew that. I was prepared for that.

But that still meant they were here somewhere. Catherine had been incapacitated so if the ultimate destination wasn't the address that Abadi had given the cab driver, it had to be close by. He wouldn't be wanting to carry her for blocks—that in itself would have garnered too much unwanted attention.

I glanced down the street. The address where the cab had dropped them off was a block away, but any of these apartments were possibilities. I tried not to believe that the address the cab driver had taken them to was the final destination. I tried to really listen to Jean-Marc when he advised me to accept that this nightmare wasn't over yet.

But I just needed so badly to believe I'd found her that deep down I couldn't really hear anything else.

I walked down the street, careful not to draw attention to myself, careful not to hurry. My phone vibrated in my pocket and I pulled it out to see I'd received a text from Jean-Marc.

<Macron extended lockdown to Wed morning>

Wednesday? That was easily another forty hours from now. I nearly laughed out loud.

I didn't need another forty hours. I didn't need another hour.

I walked with my head buzzing with images of Cameron crying tears of joy as he hugged his mother. I felt the indescribable feeling of my dearest child in my arms as I kissed her face over and over again.

We'd come so far, we'd endured so much, and now we were coming to the end.

I'd found her at last. And everything was finally going to be okay.

I stood in front of the address that the cab driver had given as the place where Catherine had been delivered. 650 rue de Villiers.

It wasn't exactly destitute but neither was it well maintained. Trash sat by the front door, which could be opened without a security panel of any kind. Inside was a dimly light foyer with more trash lining the floor.

I only had the street address, not the number for any individual apartment. But as I walked past the first ground floor apartment, I saw that the upper stairs had been blocked off by a permanent barrier preventing entry to the upper floors.

I felt a surge of excitement. This was the first piece of good luck I'd had. It meant I wouldn't have to go knocking on every door in the building to find Catherine—and alerting her captor that I was coming.

I turned back to the first apartment door I'd walked past and with joy and expectation mingling in my chest, I rapped loudly on it.

I knew Abadi might try to hide her. I knew he'd say he didn't know who I was talking about. I'd already cued up the video on my phone that showed him leaving with Catherine. I was ready for him. I had no doubt that when confronted with the evidence, he'd accept that it was over.

I waited and then knocked on the door again. I could hear something on the other side of the door. A furtive sound. A sound like someone was watching me from the peephole.

I felt my hands dampen and a fluttery feeling snaked its way into my stomach.

The door inched open and a young woman stood there.

I wasn't expecting someone besides Abadi. She didn't look Middle Eastern but she was clearly an accomplice. I pushed the door open and walked in, surprising the woman who stepped back and allowed me in.

"Who is it?" a man's voice called from an interior room.

I put my finger to my lips to the woman and she looked at me with fear and exhaustion. I walked further into the apartment, barely furnished, and heard the sound of a baby crying.

Even then, I refused to believe what my instincts were now telling me.

I walked down a short hallway until I found a young man, blonde, haggard and bleary-eyed, with a small baby in his arms. He turned to look at me with desperate expectation in his bloodshot eyes.

"Thank God," he said. "Did the lactation service send you?"

48

I stood with my back to the alley wall that faced the street. If I'd eaten anything for breakfast, I would've lost it as soon as I realized that the young couple with the baby inside the apartment had absolutely nothing to do with my daughter.

I called Jean-Marc, hoping he had something new to tell me. Hoping he wasn't waiting for *me* to tell *him* that it was the wrong apartment. Hoping maybe he'd even gotten the address wrong.

"I told you not to get your hopes up," he said. "It was extremely unlikely that Abadi was so stupid as to hand out his address to a cab driver."

"I know," I murmured.

I was clenching my stomach as if to hold myself upright. The urge to curl up into a ball and weep was strong. I looked around at the shuttered windows that faced the street. Any one of them could be hiding my daughter. Tied and gagged. Her captor waiting for the lockdown to lift.

"If the cab took them to this area then I only have to track down a few landlords to see who did a short term lease," I said desperately.

"Nobody can rent an apartment that quickly! In Paris? And in a lockdown? Your father must have safe houses or bolt holes all over Paris. How are you going to find those in time? They'll be impossible to trace to him."

I could do a scan of the entire neighborhood, but it would take me days to find which ones were owned by corporations or shell companies—which is probably what I was looking for.

"I need to go door to door," I said. "I need to ask the people living here if they remember seeing anybody new in the neighborhood. He'll have to grocery shop! Somebody must have seen something!"

"Come home. I'll go with you."

"We don't have the time."

And there's no way you can manage with your leg.

I looked at my watch.

Thirty-three hours left.

Newly infused with a blast of panic and pervasive desperation, I could literally feel the minutes ticking away and with it my chances of finding Catherine.

I called Adele and gave her the address of where to meet me. I knocked on doors until she arrived, and when she did I didn't waste time with conversation.

"She's here somewhere," I said, waving to the street. "Either this street or the next one. Go east. Knock on apartment doors. Go to shops, to cafés, *tabacs*, beauty salons."

There was no point in showing anyone a picture of Catherine. She will have been hidden away since the night she came. And I didn't have a photo of Abadi.

"Just ask if they've seen anybody new in the neighborhood,"

I said. "Middle Eastern."

Adele looked at me doubtfully. "Half the people in this neighborhood look like they're from the Middle East," she said.

In response I ran my hands through my hair. From the look on Adele's face I must have looked like a madwoman.

"Okay, well, I'd better get going," Adele said. And with that, she turned and strode down the sidewalk.

"Adele!" I called.

She turned around.

"Be sure and stop before curfew. Don't take a chance of getting caught."

She nodded and walked away.

I glanced at my watch. It was not yet lunch time. I had a full ten hours yet. And I had all day tomorrow. I took a breath and tried to calm myself. There was still time to do this.

The hours melded one into the other as I walked the streets, talking to people, oblivious to the ones who were offended by my questions or resentful about why I was in their neighborhood to begin with.

Nothing they could say could hurt me at this point. I was beyond caring. I knocked on doors and walked until my legs trembled. And when they did I rested until they could carry me again and I walked on. I bought a slice of pizza at a kiosk and a Coke for the caffeine and sugar to give me energy.

My daughter was somewhere in this neighborhood. I had to believe that. And believing it gave me strength. And comfort. If I lost her, never again would I be this close to her as I was right now. I took some bizarre solace in that, paltry though it was.

Adele checked in with me a couple of times but had had no hopeful interviews. When the light began to fade I realized I was out past curfew. Both Jean-Marc and Geneviève had texted me a couple of times to warn me but I'd ignored their words. It felt other worldly, caring about an arbitrary timeline when every minute was needed to search for Catherine.

Once I saw that all the shops were closed for the night, I had to slink into doorways to avoid the few police patrols I saw on the street. Because there were no Ubers available and the Metro had closed, I ended up walking the three miles back to my apartment.

Jean-Marc opened the door to my apartment. He was leaning on one crutch and I could already tell he'd gotten much better at moving around on it in just the single day we'd been apart.

Behind him I could see Noel and Bill in the living room with the children, and I could hear Geneviève and Haley in the kitchen. The fragrance of garlic and onions met me on the threshold.

If it hadn't been for the fact that this was one of the worst evenings of my life, I would have loved to have seen everyone in my apartment talking and taking care of each other. Noel and Bill were clearly helping to distract Cam and Robbie so that Haley could help Jean-Marc and Geneviève in the kitchen with dinner, allowing me to just come in and sit down and try to get my strength back from my long, frustrating day.

Dinner was sausage and peppers. I made a herculean effort to eat at least a portion of my plate but nobody seemed to mind that I wasn't eating.

When Geneviève and Bill got up to clear the table after dinner and Haley and the boys retired to the living room to play a game before bath time and bed, Noel sat down beside me.

"Bill and I are coming with you tomorrow," he said.

I nearly threw my arms around him, except I know how the French feel about that sort of over-the-top American demonstration of emotion.

"Thank you," I said, my eyes filling with unshed tears. I was so grateful that I felt the hand holding my wine glass begin to shake.

Bill and Noel helping me and Adele tomorrow would make a big difference. I'm not saying it hadn't occurred to me to ask them, but I'm glad I didn't have to. We still wouldn't cover the whole neighborhood, but we'd do so much more than just Adele and I could on our own. I stole a look at Jean-Marc. I knew he hated to stay behind at the apartment instead of joining us out on the street, but there was nothing to be done for it.

He'd already done a lot and paid a big price for it. I still wondered why Adorlee hadn't come up to see him in the hospital. I'd thought about suggesting that he invite her up from Nice but I didn't have an extra bed for her. Besides, if he wanted her here, he'd make his own arrangements without a permission slip from me.

When the children went to bed, I laid down with Cameron until he fell asleep. Then I came back to the living room where the adults were talking in low voices and sipping whiskey or wine. Again, if it hadn't had the distinct feel of a vigil, it would have been comforting to be surrounded by these loving, caring people. My friends.

I sat on the couch beside Jean-Marc, but was too weary and heartsick to join in the conversation. But I tried to take heart from being with them.

I felt a chill that shouldn't have been in the room and knew it was just my body dealing with the relentless disappointment and ever present dread.

I sipped a glass of wine as everyone talked softly, occasionally looking at me with trepidation or pity. Then I dozed for a moment with my head on Jean-Marc's shoulder.

Twenty-six hours left. Only twelve of them before curfew.

Twelve hours that stood between me and the worst pain a mother can endure.

49

I t was the morning light coming from above that woke Catherine. She blinked against the milky glow from the window and then froze.

Somehow she immediately knew she was still alone in the apartment. She sat up and felt the stiffness in her legs and arms. Her hands were still tied in front of her. Rashid must have forgotten. She peeled the tape from her mouth.

Her first thought upon opening her eyes had been the realization that she was still living the nightmare of her captivity. But it only took a split second before she remembered about Todd.

She remembered her last terrible words to him. Her stomach lurched violently. She stood up to stagger toward the bathroom but didn't make it in time. She heaved up the contents of her stomach onto the floor. Her bad ankle slipped out from under her and she fell to one knee.

The sobs erupted from a place inside her she never knew existed. Her head hung down, sweeping her hair into the vomit as she wept beyond all reason and hope, for Todd, for Cameron, for herself.

She eased herself down onto both knees on the slick tile and let herself cry it all out before attempting shakily to stand. Her ankle throbbed, but she could put her weight on it. She made her way to the bathroom where she used the toilet and held a hand towel under the faucet before using it to scrub away at her sodden slacks and face. Then she tossed the towel onto the pool of vomit and made her way to the kitchen.

The clock over the stove read ten o'clock. She looked around and saw their meals from last night. Hers was still draped down the wall where she'd thrown her plate. His was sitting in the sink.

That meant he hadn't come back since he left last night. He'd been gone all night.

She opened a kitchen drawer and found forks, spoons, and butter knives. She was about to pocket one of the forks when she saw a chef's knife in a block holder on the counter. She pulled it out and hobbled over to the mattress and tucked it under the mattress. Her hands shook when she did. She wondered if she had the guts to stick it into him.

To defend herself, yes, but up to now he'd not really assaulted her.

Could she just stab him? Maybe when he came to help her to the bathroom?

She felt a quivering in her stomach because she knew she couldn't do it. She sagged onto the mattress and was immediately awash with thoughts of Todd. The thickness in the back of her throat intensified when she remembered back to their fight and her words to him.

How could he be dead? Really gone? Yes, they'd been having trouble for a long time. She'd not acted very loving toward him but worse than that was the fact that Cameron had witnessed it all.

Cameron.

How heartbroken he must be! By now her mother had

surely told him that he'd lost his father. Catherine covered her face with her hands and cried again for the little boy she adored who was in so much pain right now.

And then she felt a flash of cold hard fury at being kept from him—from not being able to hold him and comfort him.

She pulled the knife out and looked at it. Could she stick this into the person who was keeping her from her boy? Could she?

Couldn't she?

At some point she must have slept. All the emotions in the world felt like they were crowded in her head and the exhaustion of experiencing them sapped her and left her limp and unsteady.

When she woke up this time, she could tell by the light through the window that it was afternoon. She craned her neck to look at the clock in the kitchen. It was four o'clock. She'd slept most of the day.

She eased out her legs. Between her sprained ankle and her grief and terror, it was no wonder she had slept so much.

He'd been gone all day. And all night.

Was he coming back?

She crossed and uncrossed her legs and sat back bouncing her knee and staring at the apartment door. She felt heart palpitations trembling in her chest as she stared at the door.

What if he didn't come back? Perhaps something had happened to him? Would she be able to find her way out of the apartment before she starved to death?

She looked at the zip ties on her hands. She hadn't bothered trying to cut them off before when she knew he would just come back and put them back on. But now she pulled the knife out, wedged it blade-side up between her knees and started to saw on the plastic.

She knew her screaming had done little to concern the residents of the apartment building. In fact, she'd heard a good deal of screaming coming from the building residents themselves. And calling out *Help I've been kidnapped!* would hardly help in a building that didn't speak English.

The zip ties broke suddenly against the blade

Just then she heard the key in the door.

Quickly, she hid the knife again, and cursed the fact that she hadn't waited. Now he would know she had something sharp to cut off her ties. She scooted back on the mattress, the knife hidden but an easy reach away.

He opened the door, his hands full of a cardboard box that he set on the dining room table. He glanced at her but didn't speak. He worked with his back to her as he pulled items out of the box. Milk, cheese blocks, a baguette, a bag of apples.

Catherine imagined racing over to him and planting the knife between his shoulder blades. She saw herself doing it, over and over again. Her hands trembled as she could almost feel the knife handle as she envisioned holding it.

He turned to face her and she saw the damage she'd done to his face last night. Red streaks were carved into both cheeks.

Good, she thought. *It's not much but it's at least something for the man who killed my son's father. And my husband.*

"Are you hungry?" he asked.

Catherine nodded. She hoped he would turn his back again to prepare the meal. Maybe she could do it after all. Maybe she could stab him when his back was turned.

He came over to her and knelt in front of her. He smelled of sweat, lemons and garlic. He hadn't shaved. He didn't look her in the eye as he spoke in hitching breaths.

"I won't apologize," he said.

"Good."

"But it doesn't mean I'm not very sad about what happened."

Now. She could stab him in the face right now. She could stab him for how *very sorry* he was for *what had happened.*

"You mean," she said, locking eyes with him, "you're very sad you killed my husband."

He sat back on his heels, his eyes wide at her words as if surprised.

"Yes. That's what I mean."

There was something soft that happened in his face when he said those words. Something honest and real and suddenly Catherine didn't think she could manage to stab him in the face after all.

"You owe me," she said.

He frowned.

"You owe me," she said. "You killed my husband. My child's father. You owe me the truth."

He looked at her, his eyes molten and soft and he nodded.

"Okay," he said.

"Who are you working for?"

He stared at her for a long moment. Catherine wasn't sure he would answer her question. But he got up and lifted a dining chair which he put beside the mattress and then sat.

He cleared his throat as if about to make a serious, important proclamation.

"Do you know anything about your grandfather?"

50

The Seventh and Final Day of the Lockdown

The next morning I was up early. Even Haley, usually the first one up, was still asleep on the living room couch. I crept quietly to the kitchen to make coffee. The aroma soon roused Haley, who picked up her pillow and blanket from the living room and slipped into my bedroom where Cam and Robbie were still sleeping.

I had just poured two cups of coffee when I heard Jean-Marc hobble into the dining room.

"You didn't wake me," he said. He still had on the jeans and t-shirt from yesterday. Since I knew what a production it was for him to dress with his cast, I realized he must have been up for a while.

"I figured the smell of the coffee would do that."

"I wish I could go with you, Claire," he said as he moved to a chair at the dining room table by the coffee mug I'd place there for him.

"I know."

"With the extra help, you should be able to cover a lot more territory."

I knew he was trying to sound encouraging. But it sounded pathetic even to my ears. The lockdown would lift at midnight tonight. What we were hoping to do wasn't impossible but it was a definite long shot. Plus, if I was wrong about my assumption that Abadi was holed up with Catherine in that section of Paris, then it was worse than a long shot. It was a doomed venture.

"Do you intend to stay out tonight if you don't find anyone who's seen him?" he asked.

"I'll come back before curfew for a quick meal and an hour's rest. Then I'll go back out until it's good and truly hopeless."

I didn't mean to say that. I'd been doing a pretty good job of pretending to hear everyone's comments of *have faith* and *don't give up*—even though it was so clear that everyone else had lost all faith in the enterprise of finding Catherine.

"*Chérie*," he said softly and reached out to touch my hand.

This was the first time he'd called me *chérie* since he broke things off with me a year ago and moved to Nice. Any other time I would've been thrilled to hear that word coming out of his mouth. But he was saying it now because of the pity and the sorrow with which he now regarded me.

He may have just ruined the word for me forever.

"I'm fine, Jean-Marc," I said abruptly, moving away from his reach and getting up to go to the kitchen to rinse out my mug.

A light tap at the door told me that Noel and Bill were here. I came back to the table, deliberately not catching Jean-Marc's eye. I patted my jacket pocket for the maps I'd printed out for Noel and Bill.

With the four of us hunting today, we might stand a chance of covering, if not the whole area, then most of it.

It might be enough.

It would have to be enough.

The second I reached the doorknob to let Noel and Bill in I realized I felt energized, as if something big was about to happen. It was the same feeling when as a child on Christmas morning I had to wait patiently at the top of the stairs for my mother to get up and put on her robe on.

I don't remember it as a blissful moment. I remember it as a slightly nauseating one.

That's what this morning felt like. Like something big was about to happen. But instead of a glittering Christmas tree with a pile of presents, it promised instead to be the precursor of the worst experience of my life.

But one way or the other, it was going to be big.

"Good morning, you two," I said as I opened the door. "Had coffee?"

Between the two of them I don't know which of them had come up with the idea to walk the streets with me. It could have been either. I thought again of how uncharitable I'd been in anticipation of meeting Noel.

"My mother made sure of that," Noel said. "We are ready to go if you are."

"Okay then," I said as I turned to Jean-Marc who had hobbled to the door as well. "We'll keep in touch and see you tonight just before curfew."

"With Mom?"

I turned to see Cameron standing in the door of my bedroom, still in his pajamas.

I felt as if I'd been hit in the stomach.

I went to him and kissed him.

"That's the plan, darling," I said and quickly turned away before my face gave away the truth.

～

Once downstairs, the three of us set out at a brisk pace for my neighborhood Metro station on boulevard St-Augustin. It was early but the sun was already hot. I could only imagine how it would feel midday.

"I can't thank you two enough," I said as we walked. In my eagerness, my legs matched their longer younger strides without effort.

"We're just glad we can help," Bill said.

"Especially me," Noel said earnestly. "You've been the friend to my mother that I am so glad she had after my father died."

I glanced at him and saw the guilt and shame in his face.

"I can't believe I stayed away so long," he said.

"I'm sure you had your reasons," I said.

"Does anyone have a good enough reason for turning their back on someone like her?" Noel said. "I guess it was just easier and I needed things to be easy."

"Don't be so hard on yourself," Bill chided him. "You talked about her all the time. And we're here now, aren't we?"

The two of them briefly held hands before breaking away.

"Did my mother tell you Bill and I are thinking of relocating to Paris?" Noel asked as we hurried down the steep stairs into the Metro.

I used my pass at the ticket stile while Bill got tickets from the ticket machine.

"She did," I said, finding myself grateful to be distracted if just for a moment by talk of people starting over in a new city.

The train was waiting for us on the platform when we reached it and we hurriedly boarded just before the doors closed.

"Will we have to change trains?" Bill asked.

I shook my head. "But it's a good fifteen-minute ride."

They sat across from me. The car wasn't crowded at this hour in the morning and I had a seat to myself. We'd been speaking French up to now, but now Noel switched to English.

"We were hoping," he said, glancing at Bill, "that when things calmed down, you could help us with something."

I nodded and tried to smile, but the euphemism *when things calmed down* rang in my ears, reminding me that one way or the other the resolution to this nightmare was going to happen today.

One way or the other.

"What do you need?" I asked.

"Noel has an ex-boyfriend in Paris," Bill said, putting his hand on Noel's knee. "He's been sending Noel emails for the last couple of months."

"Threatening emails," Noel said. "Telling me he's going to make certain letters of mine public."

"Blackmail?"

"I guess so."

"There exists a pretty straight-forward definition of blackmail," I said.

"Yes, okay then. Blackmail."

"Do you have these emails?"

"I do," Noel said, glancing again at Bill.

"And the nature of the thing he's blackmailing you for?" I prompted.

"I'd lose my teaching license over it," Noel said. "It was something I did a long time ago with a student when I was young and stupid. It wasn't sexual but it wasn't ethical either."

"Anyway," Bill said. "My idea is for us to confront the bastard head on."

"Such a cowboy," Noel said, smiling and shaking his head at Bill.

"Can you help us?" Bill said. "Can you find out what he wants to stop doing this?"

"Sure," I said. "I'll dig into it."

"Not right away," Noel said hurriedly.

When things calm down.

After that we talked about how amazing Geneviève is and how wonderful it was for Noel to have her back in his life. And how they intend to be a proper family as soon as they move to Paris.

It all sounded great and I was glad for Geneviève. I was tempted to ask Noel about his twin brother Noah, but I only had enough emotional energy for one crisis at a time. True, it might have distracted me for the rest of the train ride but I decided I'd rather focus on the mission than not think.

I handed out the maps I'd prepared for them. I'd shaded in the streets that Adele was canvassing today and the ones she and I'd done yesterday. I highlighted in yellow marker the ones I needed them to visit today.

"You'll have to split up," I said, looking at Bill. "Is your French okay?"

"I can manage," he assured me.

"Keep in touch by phone," I said. "Call me if anything—anything at all—sounds at all promising, okay?"

They both nodded and I felt a rush of, if not optimism then at least guarded hope that I wasn't totally alone in this. My phone vibrated and I looked at the screen.

"Adele says she's already on the street knocking on doors," I said.

The train screeched to a stop and both Noel and Bill stood up.

"Then let's get to it," Bill said with a sturdy conviction that made me love him even more.

In spite of the swarm of commuters pushing onto the train to take the seats we'd just abandoned, I stepped off the train first. As I moved onto the platform amid the crowd, I temporarily lost sight of Bill and Noel until suddenly I heard Noel shout.

I turned to see the mob had thinned and the train car doors were closing. Noel stood not fifteen feet from me, but he was crumpling to the station floor under the weight of Bill who sagged limply in his arms.

The world seemed to freeze as I turned to move back to them. Just then a man came from nowhere and slammed into me. I staggered at the impact but stayed on my feet as he raced down the platform and up the stairs. I watched him drop something metallic and shiny in the garbage bin as he went.

A knife.

The crowd of commuters seem to roar in agitation and a woman screamed. When I finally turned around again, Bill lay sprawled in Noel's lap on the ground, his arms outflung, his face turned to the ceiling.

A pool of blood grew slowly around him.

51

T he sidewalk in front of the Gare de Clichy-Levallois Metro entrance quickly transformed into a crime scene with police vans and a single ambulance clustered around the stairs that led up from the Metro station.

A half dozen policemen and several medical personnel stood near the ambulance conferring with one another. Several pedestrians and commuters complained about not being able to pass on the sidewalk where the police had cordoned off the area.

Noel stood beside the ambulance, his face white, his eyes wide with shock as the EMTs loaded Bill, already on a stretcher, into the back of the waiting ambulance. Noel climbed in the back with him and the doors closed.

I wrapped my arms around myself tightly as if to keep me from flying a part. As the ambulance moved away, its familiar two-tone siren piercing the air, the crowd began to dissipate.

The detective who'd arrived on the scene shortly after I'd called the emergency number walked over to me. She'd already spoken to Noel and a few other people who had witnessed the attack.

The detective was not anyone I'd ever seen before. I knew that, because she had a very prominent nose and buck teeth. Even with my face blindness, I would have remembered her.

I should have slipped away before now. Noel might forgive me. He might have understood. But I'm not sure I could forgive myself.

"Madame Baskerville?" the detective said.

"I told the other policewoman at the scene everything," I said, knowing it wouldn't matter.

"Would this be more comfortable downtown at the *Préfecture*?" she asked, her meaning very clear.

"I saw very little," I said wearily. "I'd already exited the train car so my back was turned." I took in a long breath. "Somebody bumped into me. He ran off. I saw him drop what looked like a knife in the bin by the stairs to the upper tracks."

I'd already told them all of this. I knew they'd recovered the knife. I knew mine wasn't the only description they had of the assailant.

"Medium build," I said. "But his face was turned away. Maybe facial hair but I couldn't swear to it."

"Would you be willing to look at photos?"

"Sure," I said.

That of course would be a total waste of time. I'd not seen his face but even if I had, it would have vanished from my memory seconds later. In my experience with this maddening disability I'd learned that trying to explain my anomaly was a waste of breath. Nobody believed it was real.

But if I did go through the charade of looking through police photos, I would very likely look right past the photo of the guilty party. And that action was not at all benign since *not* identifying him from the book would make the police think he wasn't in their book. When he very well might be.

It was just another example of how telling the truth was

always the best policy. Whereas *pretending* to tell the truth almost always ended badly.

I knew from the brief and terrible moments after the attack that Noel had seen nothing himself. Either that or he was too traumatized by Bill's attack to be able to recall anything about what happened. I just hoped that some of the other bystanders were more observant.

"Did Noel Rousseau see the man?" I asked, knowing very well he didn't.

"No," the detective said, putting her notepad away signaling the end of our interview. "But he mentioned someone had been recently threatening him."

I cringed when I heard that. Noel must have been in shock to have mentioned that. On the other hand, I could see how the fact that we'd just been talking about his problematic ex-boyfriend before the attack might make him mention it to the police.

"You're referring to his ex-boyfriend?" I asked.

But she'd clearly decided she'd said enough.

"You have given your contact information?" she asked as she started to turn away.

"I have," I said, watching her leave with relief.

I pulled out my phone, arranged for an Uber and then called Adele.

"Where are you?" she asked. "I thought we were supposed to meet at the Parc de la Planchette."

"I'll tell you when I see you," I said, hurrying to the curb to look for my ride. "Meanwhile, start canvassing. I'll text you when I can meet you."

I looked at my watch and felt my heart sink.

It was already midmorning.

The lockdown was to lift at midnight tonight.

This time there would be no more reprieves.

My phone vibrated and I looked down to see I'd received a text. It was an unknown number. Chills crawled up both arms as I opened the message.

< stop looking for her youve been warned>

52

"**M**y *grandfather*?" Catherine said, her body rigid.

She stared at him as if he'd lost his mind. The first thing that came to her mind was her grandmother's on again off again boyfriend ten years ago in the mobile home park where she'd lived in Jacksonville, Florida.

But then she remembered.

He means Phillippe Moreau.

"I see we are on the same pages," Rashid said with a sigh. "Your grandfather is my employer."

"That makes no sense! Why would Moreau hate me? He doesn't even know me!"

"Of course he does not hate you, *Habibti*," Rashid said, looking genuinely perplexed at the thought. "He wants...he wants to meet you."

A tightness gripped her features and she shook her head.

"No," she said, inching closer to where the knife was hidden under the mattress. "You're asking me to believe he would send a Pakistani terrorist to kidnap me and keep me tied up in a filthy slum so he can *meet me*?"

Rashid flushed.

"I am not Pakistani," he said.

"And that's not the point!" she shouted, pulling her knees into her chest in her agitation. "Quit lying to me! You owe me the truth!"

"I am telling you the truth!" Rashid said hotly.

"Why wouldn't he just call me up and ask to meet?"

"That's all I can tell you."

"Like hell it is!"

"It would be worth my life to tell you more."

"And is your life worth more than my husband's?"

Rashid blanched.

"It is not just my life," he said, looking away. "I have a younger sister. It is her life I cannot bargain with."

Catherine stared at him but she felt the stiffness in her shoulders soften.

"What's her name?"

"Malek."

"And your parents?"

He shook his head. "Both dead."

"Even your mother who taught you to cook?"

She couldn't help the bite in her voice. She reminded herself that he was a hired killer and a professional liar. He was probably lying right this minute.

"I'm sorry for telling you that," he said. "I am under strict orders not to...for you not to know the truth."

"Tell me why you are doing this," Catherine said.

He wiped a hand across his brow and took a quick breath as if to steel himself to speak. Catherine couldn't believe he was lying to her now. He couldn't be that good an actor. This had to be real.

"I was in med school in Dubai when my parents died. I was forced to leave school. My sister was only seven years old at the time."

"So this is your new career? Kidnapping people?"

"You think I enjoy this?" he said in frustration.

"Are you telling me that my grandfather is threatening your sister if you don't do his bidding?"

She made it sound as if only an idiot could believe something so outlandish.

Rashid looked at his hands and said nothing. Catherine took a breath.

"Why does my grandfather want to meet me?" she asked.

"I do not know."

"And you were doing so well, Rashid. And now you're lying again."

"Yes! I am lying!" he said, his eyes glistening with emotion. "I am lying because I cannot tell you what you want to know!"

They were both quiet for a moment.

"Did my grandfather instruct you not to hurt me?" she asked.

"Of course, yes," he said, his face relaxing somewhat. "He was very emphatic about that. You have nothing to worry about."

"Good," she said with a relieved smile. "I am aware that you and I don't speak the same language, Rashid, so I'll try to speak clearly."

He frowned in confusion.

"You will tell me what my grandfather's intentions are for me," Catherine said, "or when I meet him I'll tell him you raped me."

53

The Uber let me out deep in the center of the neighborhood of Levallois-Perret. I stood on the sidewalk for a moment unsure of which way to go while the words of the text message burned into my brain.

stop looking for her you've been warned

Shaking myself out of my self-destructive reverie, I started walking and put a call in to Geneviève. I was fairly sure that Noel had already talked to her so I wasn't surprised to discover she was in the back of a taxi rushing to the hospital.

"I am so sorry, Geneviève," I said, shaking with the horror of what had happened and my role in it.

"It was not your fault, *chérie*," Geneviève said firmly. "Do you know anything about Bill's condition?"

"No. I'm so sorry, Geneviève."

"Stop it, *chérie*," Geneviève said.

I stopped walking for a moment, and felt my body humming with energy, horror, and fear. And guilt.

"Are you back in Levallois-Perret?" she asked.

"I am," I said.

"Is it safe?"

"Do I care?"

"You must. There's Robbie," Geneviève reminded me sternly. "And Cameron."

I rubbed a hand across my face. She was right. No matter how this nightmare turned out, I had two children counting on me.

I looked around at my surroundings. I hadn't canvassed this street yet. It was part of the grid that Noel and Bill were to have done.

If I'd only listened to the first warning after Jean-Marc was attacked! Who else was going to get hurt?

Except. *How can I stop?*

I should never have allowed Noel and Bill to help me.

Except...I felt a wave of hopeless longing and defeat shudder through me.

Except, I am desperate. I am a desperate mother who is willing to sacrifice anyone and everyone for the chance—no matter how paltry—to try to recover her child.

"*Chérie?* I am at the hospital now," Geneviève said. "I will call you when I have news."

She hung up before I could uselessly apologize one more time.

I looked at my phone intending to call Adele...and I hesitated. I was calling her to tell her what? To stop? To go home?

I couldn't do that. I needed her. Now more than ever.

My phone rang and I saw it was Jean-Marc.

I answered. "Did you hear?" I asked him.

"Yes, *chérie*. He is in surgery. Where are you?"

"I'm about a block from where I was yesterday," I said looking around. I thought about telling him about the text message but decided to wait until tonight. What was the point of telling him since I was determined to carry on anyway?

"They think the assailant was an ex-boyfriend of Noel's," I

said. "I overheard the detective saying they were going to put security on Geneviève's apartment—"

"*Non,*" Jean-Marc said. "They have located the ex-boyfriend."

I felt a flinch of annoyance.

Clearly the police can move quickly when they're motivated.

"He was in Cyprus at the time," Jean-Marc said.

"Which means no security for Geneviève," I said feeling a wave of exhaustion.

"Unfortunately, not. Listen, I've been thinking," he said. "Abadi might have tried to replace the car he had to abandon."

"What are you suggesting?"

"Nothing really. I'm just thinking out loud."

"You think he might have bought another car? So he'll be ready to get out of Paris when the lockdown lifts?"

That made sense. I felt a flare of energy and hope at the thought. Any new idea helped.

Jean-Marc must have picked up on the excitement in my voice.

"Claire," he said in a strained voice, "is there any way you can stop?"

"What do you mean *stop*? How can you even ask me that? The lockdown lifts in just a few hours!"

"You must see how the warnings are ramping up, *non*? This was not a beating this time. Bill may not survive!"

"You think I don't know that?"

"Claire, listen to me," Jean-Marc said. "You cannot find Catherine. It is too late! But you *can* get yourself killed."

Or Adele.

He didn't say it because he didn't have to. Clearly even without my telling him about the ominous text message, he had figured out that the attack on Bill was connected to what we were doing.

What I was doing.

"I have to go, Jean-Marc," I said. I broke the connection and found Adele's number and as my eyes filled with tears, I pressed the number.

"Are you here?" she asked breathlessly. "I've already done a full block."

"Adele, You need to stop and go home."

"Why? Have you found her?"

"No, but Noel's husband has been attacked and I've been sent another message. It's too dangerous."

I heard Adele snort and I loved her for it even while my chest filled with terror at the danger I was putting her in.

"I'm not quitting," she said. "Did you want to meet up and grab a bite or just keep going?"

I was so overcome with emotion at her bravery and loyalty to me that at first I couldn't speak.

"Keep going," I said finally.

I walked through the next few hours with Jean-Marc's ominous words of warning reverberating in my skull.

You cannot find Catherine. It is too late.

That, combined with the new inclination to look over my shoulder every few seconds made me jumpy and on the verge of panic. But I couldn't help myself.

Without Noel and Bill's help—and I felt ashamed even thinking those words—I had an impossible area to cover. It had been largely impossible even with their help. How does one measure the limits of impossibility? How can you determine the scope of something to be even more impossible than it already was?

As I walked the hot sidewalk I felt like I was going through the motions of walking and knocking on doors because the alternative—either sitting with Geneviève and Noel at the hospital or watching cartoons back at my apartment with the children while I waited for the inevitable bad news to find me —was unthinkable.

An elderly woman operating a streetside *crêperie* told me she thought she remembered seeing someone "different" in the neighborhood. I nearly jumped across the counter when she said that. She even described this newcomer as a Middle Eastern man, good-looking, of medium height, but she had no idea which way he went. And he hadn't actually visited her *crêpe* stand. She'd simply noted him as he walked by.

Telling me he's here somewhere is not news. I know he's here.

"How did he walk?" I asked. "Did he stroll? Or walk quickly? Purposefully? Did he look tense?"

She gave me a look that said she clearly thought I was insane.

But it mattered. A man strolling by enjoying the day was not my man. Somebody who looked like he was just out for an espresso and a newspaper wasn't someone who was holding a woman hostage in a nearby apartment.

After that I decided to modify my questions to include affect but it didn't matter. Nobody except the woman at the *crêperie* remembered seeing anyone new or different on the street.

Amazingly, in spite of the heat and my mushrooming fear of an attack, I didn't feel the weariness and physical strain that I'd felt yesterday. It was as if my body wasn't going to recognize anything like blisters or leg cramps as the reason why I didn't search as far and wide and as long as humanly possible.

I resisted looking at my watch because, whenever I did, my brain automatically translated the time into how many hours I had left.

...how many hours Catherine had left.

My phone buzzed while I was leaning against a stone wall, resting. I was so involved in my desperate mental world of search and probable loss that I jumped in surprise and looked at my phone as if it were a foreign object

It was Adele.

"Hey," I said to her.

I appreciated that she didn't ask me if I'd had any luck. Obviously she'd have heard from me if I had.

"I've finished my streets," she said. "Do you want to give me Noel and Bill's?"

I'd been mulling that over and decided I had a different job for her that was at least as important.

"Jean-Marc thinks Abadi might have acquired another car in anticipation of the lockdown lifting," I said.

There was a pause on the line.

"Do you want me to try and find it?" Adele asked. Even on the phone I could hear the misgiving in her voice.

"I want you to look at the cars parked on the street where you are," I said, "and jot down the license plate numbers— unless you see somebody getting out of one who could not possibly be our man."

"Are you sure you don't want me to knock on doors instead?" she asked doubtfully.

I knew it sounded like a long shot. I knew I was asking her to finish her day with literally nothing to show for it.

"I'm sure," I said, knowing that the one thing I *was* sure of was that I was sure of nothing.

54

"Your grandfather would have me killed," Rashid said, his gaze darting around the room as if in a panic. "If you were to tell him I assaulted you he will kill me. And not quickly either."

"I figured as much," Catherine said. "Probably your sister too, don't you imagine?"

His face blanched.

"Why would you... Why would—?"

"Tell me what Moreau wants with me," Catherine said, interrupting him.

He licked his lips and softened his voice.

"You are a sweet woman," he said. "A good woman who loves her son. Surely you would not—"

"Yes, Rashid, I would," Catherine said firmly, her eyes glittering with ruthless purpose. "In a heartbeat."

"But to punish my sister for my crime is....is..."

"Not fair? Despicable? I totally agree. Maybe that's *her* punishment for being related to you, a heartless murderer."

He looked at her in horror.

"Tell me," she said.

She saw the moment in his face when he decided to tell her what she wanted to know. She'd have asked for her freedom but with his sister's life in the balance, she knew he could never do that.

"Where am I going?" she asked.

"Dubai."

She swallowed hard.

"Will I ever see my son again?"

"I'm sorry," he lifted his shoulders helplessly.

"Answer me!"

"No."

That single word hit her like a bullet to the heart. Lethal, fast, forever. She turned her head away because for a minute she thought she might vomit.

Just because he says it, doesn't make it true.

She turned back to him and saw that tears had welled up in his eyes.

"Does he intend to kill me?"

"What? No! Your grandfather...he wants...he wants a legacy."

Catherine gaped at him.

"What does that mean?" she said.

"Your grandfather had two sons. Both died tragically in the last four years. They were all he had."

"Except for my mother."

"Yes. He has your mother. And you. You are his chance to create a new dynasty."

She physically recoiled.

"A dynasty of incest?"

"No! Of course not! He has chosen your husband."

"My...?"

For a moment Catherine was speechless. That's what this was about? Her grandfather trying to create a new bloodline for his legacy?

"So he wants me to produce a child with this new husband?" she asked. "What about Cameron?"

"Your grandfather wants to control the purity of paternity."

Catherine stared at him for a moment, uncomprehending.

"You mean he doesn't like the fact that Cameron came from Todd?"

"You are young, *Habibti*," Rashid said, leaning forward earnestly. "You can have more sons."

"So that's the plan? Shanghai me to Dubai where I'll be impregnated with sons for my grandfather's legacy?"

"It is not as dire as you make it sound."

"How do I know he won't try to take Cameron?"

"He doesn't want your child by the American."

Her shoulders stiffened and she jutted her chin out sharply.

"*I'm* American."

"I am sorry," Rashid said, shaking his head sadly. "But you are whatever your grandfather says you are."

55

That evening I stood in front of the wrought-iron grill in front of my building's main door and my hands shook so badly with exhaustion that it took me three tries to put in my security code.

I'd kept in touch with Jean-Marc and Haley throughout the day and received a text from Noel saying that Bill was out of surgery. That did more than anything to restore my mood and flagging energy.

It was twenty minutes past curfew and the news alert I'd just received on my phone announced that the lockdown would definitely be lifted at midnight tonight. I tried to imagine all the Parisians who saw that alert and cheered. But for me, the words dug into my skin like razor blades.

There would be no more reprieves. The next four hours were the only time I had left.

The only time Catherine had left.

I moved slowly through the courtyard to my apartment building and then into the foyer like the old woman I was starting to feel like. Normally I never took the elevator unless I was exhausted or weighed down with shopping.

As I stood looking at the elevator tonight, so tired I couldn't concentrate long enough to make a decision, I heard Geneviève calling to me from the second floor.

"Claire? Is that you?"

"It is," I said. "I'll be right up."

I stepped into the elevator and sagged against the wall of the car until it arrived at Geneviève's floor. When the door opened, I saw her standing in the doorway of her apartment.

"How's Bill?" I asked as I stepped off the elevator, each foot feeling like it was wrapped in cement.

"He's stable," Geneviève said. "The doctors believe he will make it."

"Thank God," I breathed.

"Do you think it was him?" Geneviève asked. "Do you think it was your father who did this?"

I felt another wave of exhaustion.

"I got a text right after the attack telling me it was another warning," I said. "I guess my father felt he needed to up the ante after only breaking Jean-Marc's leg. I suppose the next warning will come in the form of hurting someone much closer to me to get me to stop."

"Cameron?"

"I was thinking you."

"Do not worry about me."

"Stay inside and I will try not to."

"Are you going back out tonight?"

I nodded.

"And Adele?"

"She has to work. Honestly I'm relieved."

"Of course you are."

Now the only person my father could opt to hurt is me.

After sharing a brief hug with Geneviève, I turned and walked the rest of the way upstairs to my apartment. At a quarter past eight I didn't expect Robbie to be up and he wasn't.

Jean-Marc met me at the door with a quick, awkward hug which surprised me. First, the French aren't a very huggy people, for all their double *bisouses*. And secondly, Jean-Marc had not even taken my phone calls in over a year. If I hadn't been so exhausted and heartbroken, I might have registered the significance of the moment.

Cameron and Izzy jumped up from the couch when I came in and I hugged them both before I even set my purse down.

Cam knew I hadn't found his mother yet and so he didn't ask. I don't know if that meant he'd given up. I don't know if he was aware that there were only three hours left on the clock between us and total devastation. I prayed not.

"Have you eaten?" I asked him as I sat on a dining room chair.

Haley came out of the kitchen with a plate for me and set it down on the table in front of me.

"We've all eaten," she said. "Come on, Cam. Let's let your grandma eat in peace."

I smiled my gratitude at Haley gave Cam a reassuring squeeze as she led him back to the couch and the omnipresent television. I looked at my plate. Chicken *Cordon Bleu*. Jean-Marc remembered it was a favorite of mine.

Jean-Marc struggled to sit down beside me, dropping his crutches to the floor by his chair.

"How do you feel?" I asked.

"Better than you look, I think."

I picked up my fork but knew I couldn't eat a single bite.

"You need to stay strong, Claire," he said.

Tears filled my eyes. He reached over and laid his hand on mine. Any other time I would have rejoiced at this overture. But now it only underscored to me how dire my situation was. If Jean-Marc was touching me, he wasn't worried about anything except the bottomless pit of despair he knew I was about to sink into come the morning.

"I just need to rest for an hour," I said.

"You're going back out?"

I wondered how he could ask me that and then remembered that he had no children himself.

He doesn't know.

"It's impossible, Claire. A thousand apartments, any one of which could be hers? And no time left? It's not possible."

"I have to keep trying," I said, forcing back my exhaustion and my tears.

"Someone will call the police to complain."

"I'm not knocking on apartment doors tonight. There are at least a dozen nightclubs that weren't open in the day for me to canvass."

"You think they'll be open with a curfew going on?"

"I overheard people talking on the street. It seems the proprietors think the cops won't bother enforcing the curfew this close to the end."

"I will come with you," he said.

I looked at him. He was barely able to hobble from the stove to the dining room table without falling over. I appreciated that he wanted to come, but he'd only hold me back.

"I'm going to lie down for an hour," I said as I pulled out my phone and set the alarm. "You can help me by talking to your cop buddies and checking the tag numbers I emailed to you."

I'd sent the car tag numbers to his phone that Adele had found. In the last couple of hours before curfew she had done a masterful job of recording no fewer than fifty cars parked in the surrounding area.

"The first car you find without the proper legal registration or that has been reported stolen or even has just been bought in the last day or so, let me know," I said.

It might be a wild goose chase, but at minus three hours and counting that was pretty much exactly where I was at right now.

~

It felt like less than a few minutes when my alarm went off.

I was on my feet and moving toward the door with Izzy by my side before I noticed that Jean-Marc was sitting at the dining room table.

"Did you sleep?" he asked.

"I did," I said. "Are the kids in bed?"

"They are."

I looked at what he was working on at the table and was surprised to see his gun.

"I thought they took that from you when you were assaulted," I said.

"No, they took the Taser, otherwise I'd be giving you that tonight."

"You want me to bring your gun?"

I was truly astounded. I did not have a permit to carry a gun. Heck, in France you needed one to carry a Taser. And I didn't have a permit for that either. It was testimony to how worried Jean-Marc was if he was asking me to illegally carry a firearm.

"I won't need it," I said.

"I know. Take it anyway."

It occurred to me that I would definitely be taken to jail if I was caught after curfew *with a weapon*. I held out my hand for the gun.

"I'll be fine, Jean-Marc," I said as I slipped it into my jacket pocket. "Don't worry."

"Of course not," he said dryly, before breaking our gaze. "I found the information you wanted. I've sent it to your phone."

"How many?"

"Three possibles."

I wanted to open my phone and find the three cars and

mark them on the map but I was already starting to feel anxious about the time.

"How did you find them?" I asked.

"One was unregistered, two were bought recently."

"This helps a lot, Jean-Marc."

I called for an Uber knowing that despite the curfew I'd probably get a few intrepid drivers willing to risk it.

Jean-Marc hobbled to the door and I turned and knelt by Izzy.

"Did she go out?" I asked.

"Haley took her earlier," he said.

I stood up and faced him.

"It's my last chance," I said.

He nodded. "It's not a safe neighborhood at night."

"I know," I said as I slipped my phone into my pocket. "That's what I remember whenever I imagine my darling girl is there somewhere."

56

An unnatural hush seemed to have descended on the streets leading to the river which cut through the edge of Levallois-Perret.

When my reluctant Uber driver turned the last corner heading toward the street where one of the parked cars was, I was heartened to see that I'd been right about the nightclubs and cafés. Everything appeared to be in full swing. I had to believe the police had their hands full tonight and wouldn't be trying to catch a few pedestrian curfew breakers.

It had taken longer than I imagined to get here tonight because my driver was nervous at the thought of being caught after curfew. He kept taking more circuitous routes in an effort to avoid possible police patrols. I hated the extra time it took and felt my anxiety and impatience build with every additional minute.

My driver finally dropped me off at the head of the street where one of the cars that Jean-Marc had identified was parked, then quickly sped away.

I was grateful that I'd asked Adele to indicate which street she'd gotten her tag numbers from. While I still had to creep down the darkened street with a flashlight to find the tags I was looking for, it could've been so much more time consuming.

I found the first car that Jean-Marc had indicated and felt a flush of annoyance when I saw that it was a tiny compact and simply unregistered. That was not likely to be Abadi's car. In any case, I used the flashlight to scan the backseat. There was a child's seat in it and little else. There was no way Abadi was using this midget mobile as his getaway car.

I looked Jean-Marc's list for the next car, which was on the next street over. I hurried to the corner, hearing the sounds of my sneakers thudding against the cobblestones as I ran.

I glanced at my watch. It was a quarter to eleven.

Beads of sweat appeared on my upper lip that had nothing to do with the heat of the day still trapped between the narrow streets. I gripped my purse tightly feeling my knuckles whiten and slowed my steps in spite of how keenly I felt the time slipping away.

A misplaced step now would only slow me down further— if it didn't stop me completely. When I reached the next street over, my heart sank to see how long it was.

It was all very well to know that the car was somewhere on this street, but where? And which side? As in many Paris neighborhoods, cars were parked on both sides.

Deciding it was faster to do one side and reverse back to do the other, I hurried down the street, shining my flashlight on each car tag looking for the letters and numbers I had memorized.

I refused to think about whether what I was doing was futile or hopeless—I just went through the motions of my task, single-mindedly, determinedly, doggedly.

Until I found it.

I didn't need to double check the numbers on Jean-Marc's list. They were burned into my memory as permanently as my own social security number.

With mounting excitement, I shined my light into the car's interior. There were three plastic jugs of water, a backpack and a folded blanket. I circled the car, and felt as though bubbles of lightness and effervescence were popping inside me.

This had to be his car. It had been purchased yesterday and was outfitted for a long trip.

I looked down the street and then up at the silent windows of the buildings on both sides. Catherine and Abadi were either on this street or nearby.

I glanced at my watch again.

One hour to midnight.

Should I stand by the car? Should I go looking for the third car? What if I'm wrong about that? What if this isn't his car? Short answer?

I'll have lost her for good.

But the clock was ticking. I had to make up my mind. Desperately, I decided I didn't have time to waste hunting down a third car. But neither did I have time to stand here and wait for someone who might never come.

I was seconds away from texting Jean-Marc to tell him to send reinforcements when it occurred to me that if he sent the police, it would certainly scare Abadi off. What if he heard the police sirens and panicked and killed his hostage?

I shivered and looked up again at the rows of shuttered windows. She probably wasn't on this street. There were dozens of possible apartments where she might be.

Finally, giving the car a last glance, I decided I had to eliminate the third car. It was surely a waste of time but I couldn't not check it out. I turned back to my map and Adele's notes about where she'd found the car that matched with Jean-Marc's data. The third car was also one that had also been bought recently. The street was nearly four blocks away, the furthest point of my search perimeter. I groaned. Should I skip it? Did I dare?

But I knew I couldn't live with myself if I didn't eliminate it if I could. I set out walking as quickly as I could, mindful of the irregularities in the sidewalk, the cobblestones, the debris on the pavement so as not to trip. Even so, I had to stop and rest twice, leaning against buildings, checking my phone for the time and giving myself a shot of panic each time as I watched the minutes tick down.

I found the vehicle twenty long minutes later. I approached it disbelieving and with mounting anger as I checked the tag number against both Adele's notes and Jean-Marc's. It was even smaller than the mini compact. Closer to the size of a roomy motorcycle. Furious at myself for the time I'd wasted, I turned to hurry back to the car I'd found that had fit the bill. When I saw where I was on my GPS I realized it would be faster to go back by way of the main drag.

Without thinking too much about it, I headed toward the lights and noise of the main street. When I reached the street I realized I'd have to walk down a full two blocks before I came to the street where I'd found the car. I started walking, keeping my head down so as not to attract attention when I realized that I still had time to canvass some of the places I hadn't gone to today.

Checking my phone I saw I had thirty minutes before midnight. I could canvas for twenty and have plenty of time to set up a surveillance by the car.

I went to the first nightclub that I'd passed earlier today when it was closed. Now music poured out its door. I went in, pushing past a few curious patrons. A bored woman stood at the bar polishing glasses as she watched me approach.

"I'm looking for someone," I said.

"He's not here," she said and signaled to someone unseen in the wings. Before I had the chance to ask her again, a large man appeared beside me.

"I'm not police," I said, although I would've thought that was obvious. The American accent for one thing.

He nodded at the door and I realized it wasn't worth trying to argue with him.

I walked back onto the street. It was dark and a few shadowy characters watched me from the corner of the building but I felt safe with the feel of the gun in my pocket.

Were my father's minions watching me? A part of me realized it didn't even matter now. Twenty minutes more and it was all over.

I went to one more nightclub. Everyone who responded to my questions each had the same answer: Nobody saw anyone new.

As I left the last nightclub, I wondered if Abadi would leave as soon as the curfew lifted or wait until morning. I tried to imagine my father allowing his man to get a full night's sleep before leaving in the morning. Even if it *wasn't* true that the police were actively looking for him—which they weren't—my father would have every reason to believe they were.

No. Abadi was going to bolt as soon as the lockdown lifted. At midnight. I knew that in my heart and in my gut.

It was eleven twenty.

I leaned against a stone wall and felt the bass of the nightclub's music pulsating through the wall, vibrating up and down my arm. I licked my lips and noticed that a nearby all-night *tabac* on the corner was doing a brisk business in cigarettes and beer.

It occurred to me that being thirsty was making my exhaustion worse, I walked to the *tabac* realizing that I'd already talked to the owner.

The bell chimed as I pushed open the door and walked to the counter. "Bonsoir, Monsieur," I said, pulling out my wallet. "A bottle of water, please."

He was a large man with a skimpy dark beard and beady black eyes.

"There's a curfew on or do you think the rules do not apply to Americans?" he said as he set a bottle of water on the counter.

I wasn't in the mood to argue with him.

"You were in here before," he said.

"I'm looking for someone. Remember? Someone new to the neighborhood?"

"This isn't a tourist spot."

"I'm pretty sure that's what you said when I asked you the first time."

"What does he look like?"

I'd already told him before whenever I'd been in here before. When was it? Two days ago? Yesterday?

The *tabac* owner was bored which was why he was bothering to talk to me. He had nothing better to do at nearly midnight but torture a hapless American tourist—and a woman at that—who happened to stumble into his shop.

"He's young," I said. "Maybe late twenties or mid-thirties. Middle Eastern."

I put down a euro coin and picked up the water bottle.

Behind him, a middle-aged woman stepped out from behind the curtain that divided the shopping area from a personal living space.

"What does she want?" she asked her husband, looking at me but not speaking to me.

"She's looking for someone. Pakistani."

"I don't know that he's Pakistani," I said. "Middle Eastern is all I said."

The woman looked at me, her face a mask of suspicion.

"Why?"

It wasn't a friendly question but I wasn't feeling all that friendly myself.

"My daughter is missing. She was last seen with this man," I said.

The woman snorted and curled her lip, giving me a disdainful look up and down. I was tired. I was discouraged. I was not in the mood to deal with this.

"You think because a white girl goes off with a Pakistani it has to be a kidnapping?" she said.

"She left her eight-year-old son behind," I said between gritted teeth.

The woman's face changed immediately. Still staring at me, she spoke again, but addressed her husband.

"Did you tell her about the one who was here yesterday?"

"They all look alike to me," her husband said with an ugly laugh. He turned to light a cigarette.

"This one was different," the woman said, talking to me now. "He had scratch marks down his face."

I felt the world go quiet at her words. As I stood there, it felt like this woman and I were the only ones in the whole world.

"When?" I asked softly. "Did you see which way he went?"

Neither of those answers would help me. But now that I'd found someone who'd seen Abadi my brain froze and I didn't know what else to ask. All I could think was:

Catherine's captor had been in this store. Recently.

And Catherine had attacked him.

My stomach heaved as I envisioned my daughter scratching the face of her assailant, fighting desperately as she attempted to...what? Escape? Prevent him from...from...?

"*Non*," the woman said, turning away to straighten a few cans on a shelf behind her. "Do you think we have time to watch where our customers go?"

I felt the wash of frenzied hope and desperation blanket me as I realized how close I was.

I couldn't leave. I couldn't move. I could only stare at the back of this woman who'd seen and interacted with my daughter's kidnapper—as if by somehow being close to her I was closer to Catherine.

"He bought groceries," she said over her shoulder. "Twice."

I turned to look at the entrance to the store, hoping beyond hope that there might be a camera in place. There wasn't.

When I turned back, the woman was facing me and holding out a small piece of paper.

"The last time," she said, "he had them delivered."

57

I t was late when Catherine opened her eyes. Discordant street sounds had awakened her. She lay on the mattress watching Rashid move about the kitchen, his back to her as he put food in a box.

Her heart began to thud in her chest.

He is getting ready to leave.

She sat up and fought down her mounting fear and agitation. He hadn't put new zip ties on her after she'd cut through her bonds, although he must have surely noticed she was no longer bound.

Or had he?

If he had, he'd be looking for the knife that had cut her ties.

It was possible—and Catherine prayed this was so—that he'd been so upset by their conversation earlier in the evening when he confessed her grandfather's involvement that he'd overlooked the zip ties.

Is that possible?

Maybe he couldn't bear adding insult to all the other grievous injuries he'd inflicted on her. Maybe he couldn't stand the idea of how she would look at him—after everything he'd done to her—if he were to tie her up again.

No. She was projecting a humanity and a sensitivity on him that he didn't have. He must not have noticed she was unbound. It was the only explanation.

Catherine watched him for a moment and realized she had only one possible course of action that she could clearly see.

She'd had seven days to escape from this apartment and had failed every time. Her only chance now was to somehow manage to escape once they left the apartment.

If they left by car she'd jump out of the car. If they took a train or bus, she'd start screaming once they were in a public arena.

But for either of those plans to work, she would have to get him to trust her, to believe she was on his side. Because otherwise, he would drug her again.

And there was no hope at all of escape if she ended up unconscious in the trunk of a car trunk.

"*Habibti*?" he said.

Catherine shook herself out of her thoughts, and realized he was watching her closely. She cursed the fact that he'd caught her unawares. Her face was usually an open book and even Rashid would have no trouble reading it.

"My foot hurts," she said.

Instantly, the expression on his face morphed into one of concern and he dug out a packet of Nurofen from his pocket and handed it to her with a bottle of water. Catherine knew she was taking a risk if she called attention to her unbound hands, so she made a point of capturing his eyes with her own.

"Thank you," she said earnestly, taking the pills. "This is something my husband never would have done for me."

He stared at her with a blatant desire to believe her in his eyes.

"No?" he said, begging for more.

"He didn't care about me," she said, still commanding his gaze. "He had other women."

The air in the apartment seemed to be suddenly electrified.

"I am sorry, *Habibti*," he said. A look of longing flashed in his eyes.

"What does that mean? *Habibti*?" she asked softly.

He lifted a tendril of hair from her face.

"It means *my darling*," he said.

"*Habibti*," she said. "Am I a bad person, Rashid, because I'm not sure I care that he's dead? Is that horrible? Is that wrong?"

He inched closer to her on the mattress, his face a visage of barely concealed joy.

"No, *Habibti*. Not at all. You are finally free. Your husband did not deserve you."

Catherine lowered her voice but kept her eyes on him, forcing him not to break their gaze.

"I think you are different, Rashid. I pray you are."

She reached out and touched his arm, again, risking the moment when he might see she was unbound but knowing that a touch—even a harmless one on the arm—meant something very different in his culture.

The touch detonated an explosion of desire in Rashid's eyes and he instantly pulled her close. Catherine could feel his arms tremble as he held her. She dropped her right hand to the side of the mattress where the handle of the knife barely protruded.

"I forgive you," she whispered, her face close to his.

Her fingers tugged the knife out from under the mattress and worked to position her grip on the handle as Rashid tilted her chin up, poising her mouth beneath his.

"I will always protect—" he started to say.

Quickly, Catherine jabbed the knife point into his side. She felt the instant resistance of a bone or a rib. The knife wouldn't go in.

She couldn't breathe as her panic began to overwhelm her.

She pushed harder. Rashid yelled and twisted away from the knife, grabbing Catherine's hand and squeezing hard. Pain rocketed up her arm and she dropped the knife.

Rashid held both her hands tightly in his, his face inches from hers. Her vision blurred in terror as she stared into his eyes.

And this time all she saw was a profound and maniacal fury.

58

I stood in front of the apartment building, no different from the one I'd visited earlier today. It was shabby on the outside, its windows darkened, its few balconies crumbling. This time I wouldn't need to count on the building having only one tenant. This time I had the apartment number too.

I stood across the street from the building and in spite of the late hour felt the day's heat settle on my face and neck. On my way here—no more than two blocks from the *tabac*—I'd decided and undecided nearly a dozen times about calling the police. If I called them before Abadi left the apartment building with Catherine, it would turn into a hostage standoff —with my daughter the innocent bystander whom no cop worried about accidentally killing.

But if I waited until Abadi got her in the car, and *then* called the police, there was the very real danger of a deadly high-speed chase. Or the police would just riddle the car with bullets, believing both car occupants to be murderers.

Again, in that case, only one person who mattered might yet die.

On the other hand if I waited until Abadi tried to take Catherine—probably drugged—to the car I could hold him at gunpoint—or heck, just shoot him—and worry about calling the police later.

The more I stood and stared at the building, the more I felt I had to wait for them to come out.

I glanced at my phone. It was eleven forty. A throb of fear erupted in my gut.

Could I be wrong about the car or the address? I tried to imagine who Abadi was and how desperate he must be feeling. For one irrational moment I wondered if perhaps he'd already moved Catherine to the getaway car.

Should I be waiting at the car?

I scanned the windows of the building, wondering which one belonged to the apartment that held Catherine. I'd been careful to keep to the shadows in case Abadi was watching the street. But the more the minutes ticked by, the more anxious I became.

Had I gotten it wrong? Or the woman at the *tabac*? Had she misremembered? Had she instead given me the address of some perfectly normal person who'd had his groceries delivered?

How insane would a kidnapper have to be to give his address out to have groceries delivered?

All of a sudden I knew I couldn't wait for Abadi to appear on the street. I had to know if I was wasting my time, wasting the last grains of sand in the hourglass of Catherine's time.

I took in a fortifying breath and walked across the street to the apartment building. Unlike the apartments in my arrondissement, few of these buildings had security codes or concierges to watch out for the residents. I'd brought my most used lock picks before leaving home and now I felt in my jacket for the tension wrench as I eyed the lock in front of me.

Normally I gained access into secured apartment buildings

by feigning old lady ineptitude. Inevitably someone from the building either coming or going would let me in. That wasn't likely to happen at nearly a quarter to midnight.

Before I started fiddling with the lock, I gave the door a push and felt it give under my hand. This was a neighborhood that needed extra security so of course its residents would consider that a luxury and skip it.

I walked into the small courtyard beyond the door that led to the residential section of the building. I stepped past weeds and trash and picked my way silently to the building door.

Like with the exterior door, there was no lock securing the front door to the building and I was able to enter without needing my lock picks.

I instantly saw several similarities to my own apartment building—a tiled foyer, a wide staircase and a narrow closet where an ancient post-war elevator was housed. But unlike my building, the foyer smelled of urine and rotten food, garbage bags sat in the corners for God knows how long, the staircase was missing most of its bannister, the floor tiles were chipped and missing and the elevator had an ancient yellow warning tape with the word *interdit* printed on it crisscrossed against its battered door.

I looked in the foyer for the mailboxes which in most normal residential settings would list the names of the residents.

I took a breath and walked to the mailboxes. I ran my finger down the list of names. There was a gap in the list of names. One apartment was left blank. But the apartment number matched the number on the slip of paper that the *tabac* owner had given me.

I stopped for a moment and listened but heard only the creaks and moans of a three-hundred-year-old building settling in the throes of a city's unnatural quiet.

I looked up the steps of the winding staircase and held my

breath against the stench. If I was wrong, if she was in another building or if Abadi had already moved her...I was seized with a sudden foreboding.

I should be waiting by the car.

My skin had grown clammy and I felt as if I'd run out of oxygen and I was having trouble breathing.

Had I consigned my daughter to a lifetime in some Arabian businessman's harem because I chose the wrong place to ambush her abductor? What if they've already gone to the car? What if they're already driving?

In a quickly mushrooming panic, I turned to walk out of the building, and back to the street, no longer sure of anything except the belief that I had to get back to the car.

As soon as I felt the cooler night air skitter across my skin I realized I was being irrational. I took in a deep breath and tried to steady my nerves. They wouldn't risk being out after curfew. Not this close to the whole thing being over.

I turned to go back inside the building when I became aware of the sounds of quickly approaching footsteps.

"Halt!" a strident voice called out.

I whirled around and saw with dismay the one thing I'd been praying all week long I wouldn't see.

Two uniformed police were striding toward me, one already freeing a pair of handcuffs from her belt.

59

C atherine's panic cascaded over her as she tried to twist away from him. She felt his fingers bit into her arms gripping her. His face had transformed into a mask of homicidal fury.

"You bitch," he said, his eyes racking back and forth as he stared at her—as if his mind was rocketing around too.

"R-Rashid, no," Catherine gasped, feeling as if she were seconds from hyperventilating. "It was a mistake."

"Liar!" he screamed into her face, his breath and spittle blowing her hair. He shook her violently. "You think I am a fool!"

"I didn't mean it," she whimpered and knew in that moment exactly how close she was to dying. "Please, Rashid."

"Stop saying my name! You deceitful woman! You lied to me!"

"I couldn't do it, Rashid!" she said desperately. "In the end I couldn't hurt you!"

He hesitated, his eyes searching her as if for the truth.

"Please," she whispered. "I thought I could but I couldn't. I swear I've come to care for you. Believe me. I tried to fight it but it's the truth."

"You tried to kill me!"

"No! I thought I wanted to but I couldn't." She searched his eyes. "Please. You have to believe me."

He let go of her then and sat back, staring at her, his eyes narrowed and calculating. And unsure.

"I saw you were packing to leave," she said, desperate to distract him. "I was afraid you were going to leave me again. I was worried sick yesterday when you didn't come back for so long."

He frowned but she could tell he wanted to believe her.

"And maybe I was angry at you too," she said, wondering what she could say that would help him believe her. "For leaving me."

"I would never leave you," he said, his face still closed and cold.

But at least he didn't look like he was going to snap her neck with his bare hands.

"So you're not going to hand me off to my grandfather?"

"That I must do."

"Even when you know you and I belong together?"

His face relaxed and Catherine marveled at how easy it had been in the end to make him believe her.

"That cannot be," he said sadly.

"It can if you want it to," she said. "In America, you can do anything you want."

"This is not America."

"Then come with me to America."

"That's impossible."

But she saw in his eyes that he wasn't thinking it was impossible. He was thinking it might be truly incredibly possible. He was seeing a life with her in America.

He stood up and massaged the point in his side where she'd pricked him and bent to pick up the knife.

"I will fix you something to eat," he said.

"Are we leaving so soon?"

"It will be many hours before you can eat again."

"Are you not coming too?"

"No more questions."

Catherine watched him go to the kitchen and put the knife back in the butcher block.

Had she made things worse? She no longer had a weapon but she was still unbound—for now. Had she convinced him? Or had the attempt to stab him ruined her chances of him trusting her?

She eased herself off the mattress and hobbled to the dining room. He watched her come with a frown.

"How are we getting there?" she asked.

"You don't need to worry about that."

"What would happen if you didn't bring me to him?"

He picked up a bag of oranges and settled them in the box.

"That's not an option."

"No, tell me. What would happen? Would he try to kill you?"

He snorted. "There would be no *trying*."

"So you believe he would kill you."

"And my sister, yes."

"So my grandfather is basically an Arabian El Chapo."

"He is not Arabian."

Immediately Catherine saw that Rashid had not meant to tell her that.

"He's European?"

"It doesn't matter what he is."

"It matters to me. If you're delivering me to a ruthless monster—"

"He is not a monster. He is a loving grandfather. You will

have a wonderful life of luxury and privilege. *That's* what you need to focus on."

"Will all the luxury take my mind off being repeatedly raped by a man I don't know?"

"It is a marriage," he said testily. "Your husband will not abuse you either."

"How do you know?"

"Your grandfather would not allow it."

"So if I complain about my husband, Granddad will have him thrown off a building? And get me a new one?"

"You are mocking me," Rashid said, his voice betraying anger and frustration.

He doesn't want to think of another man having me.

"Why can't I have you as my new husband? I know you."

The look on his face at that remark was a stricken one. In fact, Catherine was pretty sure it was the same question he'd been asking himself for the last several hours—if not days.

Suddenly the ding of a cellphone cut through the tense silence between them. Rashid pulled out his phone and looked at what was obviously a text message.

Rashid's face whitened and he put a hand to his forehead as he stared at the text.

"What is it, Rashid?"

He continued to stare at his phone. But now his mouth was open in shock. He looked away from the phone as if trying to digest what he'd read and his gaze settled on Catherine. His face was a stark portrait of indecision and agony.

Was there a change in plans? Was that his handler texting him? Her grandfather?

"Tell me, Rashid," she said urgently, taking a step closer to him. "Let me help you."

"Don't talk. I need to think!"

He covered his mouth and looked again at his phone before

rubbing his hand over his face. He shook his head and then staggered to one of the kitchen chairs and sat down heavily.

Catherine watched him in confusion and alarm.

What could possibly have happened?

The answer came to her in a sickening suddenness.

He's been given an order he doesn't want to carry out.

She swallowed hard and then opened her mouth to ask him again—to beg him to tell her what the text said. But before she could, there was a knock at the door.

60

Catherine turned to look at Rashid who was staring at the door in horror and confusion.

He's not expecting anyone.

Or is he afraid of who may be out there?

What had that text message said? Was it her grandfather sending someone to kill *Rashid* for not being able to leave in spite of the lockdown?

Or kill them both?

The knock came again more firmly this time.

"Aren't you going to—" Catherine said.

"Shut up! Let me think!"

Catherine looked at the door. Somebody was there. Somebody who had come to kill them? Or to help?

She didn't know but she had to decide. She had to do something!

"Help!" she screamed as she ran for the door.

Rashid snapped his head around to gape at her in horror and indecision.

"Help me!" Catherine screamed as she grappled with the

doorknob and tried to open it. It was locked. She fumbled with the latch but her fingers were clumsy and stiff.

"I'm American! I'm being held hostage! Help me!"

Rashid's shock and indecision cracked suddenly like a broken twig underfoot when he saw Catherine struggling to open the door. He ran to her and grabbed her arm, swinging her forcefully away from the door. She flew backward too fast

He watched in horror as she crashed into the dining table, her head snapping back as she hit it, before sliding to the floor.

He ran to her, his heart pounding in horror, and pulled her into his arms. There was a gash on her forehead. Blood trickled down from it to her cheek. Her eyes were closed.

"My dearest *Habibti*," he said searching her face for some sign of life. "Please, dearest one. Wake up!"

He cradled her body, his arms tightening with terror at how motionless she was.

The sound of my daughter's terrified screams sliced into me like a knife straight to my heart.

"Catherine?" I shouted. "Catherine, answer me!"

I pounded on the door with both hands, my terror ratcheting up higher and higher.

"Open this door!" I screamed. "Open it! Hello! Fire! The building is on fire! Everyone save yourself!"

I waited breathlessly as I heard a few sounds from above me as doors opened in curiosity. But there were no more sounds from inside the apartment where I'd heard Catherine's voice Panic welled up in my chest as I stood there, my hands stinging from pounding on the door.

In desperation, I pulled out the gun from my jacket pocket, fully intending to shoot the lock off as I'd seen in every action movie I'd ever watched when suddenly the door swung open.

A hand shot out and grabbed me by the front of my jacket and yanked me inside.

61

I flew into the apartment from the sheer force of his powerful swing and knocked over a chair before landing on my knees.

I twisted around, unmindful of anything else but finding her. There were no lights on in the apartment but a sliver of moon through a high window gave a muted eerie light to the interior.

I saw her ten feet away from me on the floor. The scream that erupted from me as I stared at her body was involuntary and feral. I scrambled across the floor to her. My hands went first to her beautiful face, still and inanimate, her eyes closed. The blood on the side of her head made my heart seize but I knew head injuries often bled out of proportion to their severity. I felt for her pulse.

Steady and strong. Thank God.

I didn't know what he'd done to her, whether she was drugged or...but no, she'd been screaming just a few seconds before!

I looked up at him as he walked over to where I sat with her on the floor.

My gun was in his hand.

I must have dropped it when he grabbed me. He stood before me, shorter than I'd imagined, his eyes were dark and desperate. I pulled Catherine further into my lap and held her tightly.

The wound on her head seemed to have stopped bleeding but it had bled down her throat to her blouse. My mind couldn't think, I felt frozen.

"You are the mother?" he asked in a guttural voice.

I looked at him and felt the ferocity in my voice.

"What did you do to her?" I said.

"Are you alone?" he asked, licking his lips.

"No! I'm not alone," I said. "The place is surrounded by police."

I didn't know I was going to say that and I was immediately sorry I did. For one thing, it wasn't true. The two police who'd briefly attempted to detain me outside the building had been suddenly called away to a robbery happening two streets away. After instructing me to contact my nearest police station in the morning in order to be fined for breaking curfew they'd hurried away.

Now, as I stared at Rashid Abadi I realized that it was possible that while the average American criminal might react to information that the cops were outside by deciding to negotiate or give up this man probably saw arrest by the French police as not the worst thing that could happen to him. Especially if he was here on the orders of someone who had the power to hurt him.

Abadi stared at me as if the information about the police hadn't even penetrated. I would've expected him to at least glance at the window where I'd told him the police were gathered. But he did nothing.

"They know the car you intend to take," I said. "You can't

leave here with her. But you might be able to get away yourself if you take the stairs to the roof."

I had no idea if there were stairs to the roof.

"I won't leave her," he said.

Right then she moaned and I turned to focus on her.

"Catherine?" I said.

"M-m-mom?"

"Stop! Stop!" Abadi said, pointing the gun at me. "Stop talking! Catherine, I am sorry. I didn't mean to hurt you."

"It's over, Abadi," I said. "You won't get away unless you leave right now. The police know about your car. If you try to take it, they'll intercept you. You'll be apprehended at the train station or however you're thinking of getting out of Paris."

He hunched his shoulders as if expecting to be stoned at any minute. His eyes appeared feral and hunted as they darted around the small dark room.

"You're lying. They are not looking for me."

"Are you serious? You kidnapped an American tourist! Your face is plastered everywhere on the news!"

"Why couldn't you just let us go?" he said angrily, waving the gun at me. "Why did you have to make everything so difficult?"

He was alternately looking at Catherine in my arms and looking at the door out of the apartment. I could see he was getting more agitated.

I had no idea how to effectively reason with a desperate killer from Dubai. I had no idea what mattered to him, if anything did beyond completing his mission. But I had to at least try.

"My father sent you, didn't he?" I said, impulsively. "Give me your phone. Let me talk to him. I can tell him—"

"Talking is no use!"

Catherine moved to sit up which I was glad about except I

could see that Abadi would view it as her being able to walk out of here on her own. With him. *Now.*

"He'll listen to me!" I said. "I'm his daughter. He doesn't want me hurt or Catherine. I don't care what he told you—"

"Stop!" Abadi shouted, grimacing as if in terrible pain. "Your father died of a massive heart attack two hours ago!"

62

I stared at him. I hadn't slept well in over a week. My exhausted brain couldn't process what he was saying.

"I don't believe you," I said.

He picked up his phone from the dining table and waved it at me.

"I got the text ten minutes ago."

He looked at Catherine as if talking only to her.

"I no longer work for him," he said.

I didn't have time to process that Moreau might really be dead. All I knew was that if Abadi *wasn't* working for my father any longer, then he was doing this for himself. And if that was the case then things could start to go seriously sideways.

"He wouldn't want you to do this," I said.

He spat. "I care nothing for what he wants now. I'm glad he's dead."

Okay. Wrong approach.

"Then why are you not running? Why not save yourself?"

"Mom," Catherine said weakly. "It's not his fault."

I looked at her. Her eyes didn't appear dilated but she still looked groggy. If she had a head injury, she wouldn't be thinking straight.

"She's telling the truth," Abadi said. "I was forced to take her. Your father threatened my sister unless I did as he said."

"How about Catherine's husband?" I asked. "Did he force you to do that? Or did you come up with that on your own?"

I saw him glance at Catherine as if hesitant to answer in front of her.

"He didn't mean to hurt Todd," Catherine said, her eyes on Abadi's face. "He didn't want to do it."

Could she really be under his spell? In just a week?

"But now I'm free," Abadi said. "And so is Catherine."

"So I guess we can all just leave," I said.

He shook his head as if negating that idea, or maybe trying to clear his mind. He pointed the gun at me.

"I cannot allow anyone to stop what was meant to be," he said.

"Rashid," Catherine said piercingly. "My darling, help me up, please."

He looked at her in surprise, but never lowered the gun he had aimed at me. He took a hesitant step toward her and she held out her arms to him.

"My head hurts," she said to him. "Help me."

"I will, my love," he said, uncertainly.

He seemed confused, as though he was not sure how to work out the logistics of pulling Catherine into his arms and also keeping the gun aimed at me.

"I will not stand in your way," I said to him, scooting away from Catherine. "If this is what my daughter has chosen, I only want her to be happy."

He shook his head in apparent disbelief. But his gun arm sagged to his side as he stooped to embrace Catherine and pull her to her feet.

I wished I was standing but I knew that now was not the

moment to try to move in any definitive way. Anything could trigger him. The gun was briefly not pointed at me. But it was still in the hands of a madman.

"You have forgiven me, my love," he murmured to Catherine, his voice muffled by her long hair.

"I have," she said softly.

"But I cannot let her live, *Habibti*."

"I know, my love. It's all right. I forgive you for that too."

He turned to look into her eyes, to get the full effect of her love and forgiveness and when he did I glanced frantically about. There was no cover, nowhere to hide. He must have reacted to my head movement because I heard Catherine's voice, forceful and seductive.

"Kiss me, Rashid," she said.

I looked wildly around the darkened room for anything to shield me or to throw at him. But there was nothing.

Expecting any minute to feel a bullet drill into my back, I turned and looked frantically at the window over the bed—at the very instant I heard the gun shot.

63

T he shot sounded like a cannon in that small enclosed space. The noise reverberated around the room, gaining volume as it ricocheted around me.

I instinctively covered my head with my arms until I heard something heavy clattering to the floor.

I turned and saw the gun on the floor. I lunged for it, snatching it up from the floor. I backed up and held the gun on him as Catherine embraced him until I realized that Rashid was slowly sliding to the floor.

His hands reached impotently for her but she shoved him away and staggered backwards. Her eyes were round with horror as she watched him collapse to the floor.

"Don't look at him," I said to her.

She stared at me as if she didn't know me, her expression contorting into that same one I'd seen so many times when she was little—about to cry her heart out because she felt her whole world had been destroyed.

Only this time it very nearly had.

"Mom," she whimpered and ran to me.

I caught her in my arms and let the euphoria of the moment flood through me.

"I've got you, sweetheart," I said, feeling a joyous lightheadedness that made me feel like I would faint.

I held her for a few seconds before both our legs threatened to give way. Looking over her shoulder, I could see there was no way Rashid Abadi was going to ever get up again.

"I wasn't sure I could do it," she said, sniffing back her tears. "I tried to stab him earlier and couldn't."

She was shaking as if she were about to go into shock. With her head injury I wasn't sure that that wasn't the next step. I tucked the gun into the back of my waist band and began to rub her arms to warm her up.

"You had to do it," I said, guessing that at least part of her shock had to do with the fact that she'd just killed a man in the middle of a kiss. "He'd have killed me."

"I know."

"Try not to think about it, darling."

That had to qualify as the most useless advice I'd ever given anyone. But it was all I had for now. I took her firmly by the hand, leading her past Abadi's body to the door and down the stairs. She followed as if in a trance, yet twice she stopped to look behind her to make sure he was not coming after her.

"He killed Todd, Mom," she said, her voice flat.

"I know, baby. I'm so sorry."

In moments we were outside and the stultifying heat of the July night never felt so rejuvenating to me. I led her through the main double doors onto the street and both of us sagged to the curb, our legs jelly and unable to hold us a moment longer.

I pulled out my phone and called Jean-Marc and told him where we were, but to hold off calling the police. I spoke quietly, aware once I hung up that Catherine wasn't even listening.

She sat next to me trembling violently. I put my arms

around her again to warm her up, although the night air around us was at least eighty degrees.

I listened to the night sounds, hearing a siren in the distance and hoping that Jean-Marc had not called the police after all.

I was suddenly aware of noise from the nearby cafés and nightclubs. A crowd was chanting and singing. I imagined people were celebrating the fact that they'd done a full week with an eight o'clock curfew.

The Paris lockdown had lifted at midnight as promised.

"He said your father wanted me to mate with a man of his choosing," Catherine said, trembling a little less now.

I stared at her.

"What?"

"Rashid told me your father wanted to leave a legacy. He said Moreau once had two sons but they both died with no kids. And you were too old to produce more heirs."

I always knew Moreau was venal. But until tonight I'd only suspected he was crazy.

"Well, it's all over now," I said. "Sweetheart, do you think you can handle sitting out here for less than sixty seconds by yourself?"

She looked at me and I was gratified to see the look wasn't one of fear.

"Why?"

"There's just something I want to confirm."

"I'll be okay, Mom."

I stood up, hesitant to leave her after finally finding her, but the urge was too strong to resist.

I turned and hurried back through the double doors, the foyer and up the stairs. Careful not to touch anything in the apartment and keeping my eye on the body on the floor to make sure it really wasn't going to move, I pulled a tissue out of my pocket and stepped gingerly to the dining room table where Abadi had set down his phone.

Careful not to touch it with my bare fingers and praying the passcode had a longer lockout time than fifteen minutes, I picked it up with the tissue.

The phone opened up immediately. I felt a rush of relief. At the same time I saw a flash outside like the sweep of headlights on the street. I hesitated and nearly turned to leave but I knew I couldn't take the phone with me. And I had to see for myself.

I went to Abadi's messages, my heart thumping in my chest, and scrolled to the last text received.

<Moreau had massive heart attack. Kill the girl and return to Dubai ASAP>

My mouth was dry as I set the phone back where I'd found it. I retraced my steps to where Catherine was now standing, waiting for me.

"What did you do?" she asked.

"Nothing," I said. "I just needed to check on something."

"You needed to see if he was really dead, didn't you?"

I nodded, knowing she meant Abadi. I looked up and saw a car creeping down the street toward us.

"It's them," I said.

Catherine turned to watch as the car came to a stop at the curb. The passenger door swung open and Cameron jumped out.

"Mom!" he shouted. "Mom!"

Catherine clapped a hand to her mouth to stop the moan as she dropped to one knee and her son flung himself into her arms.

My eyes stung with tears as I watched Cameron now completely enveloped by his mother, both of them sobbing in relief and gratitude.

Jean-Marc got out of the taxi more slowly, his crutches

leading the way. I waved to him before turning back to the sight of Catherine and Cameron.

Things may not be okay for a long time; in fact they may never be okay.

But someday they would be better.

And that someday starts tonight.

64

I always love that moment when you can taste the first hint of fall in the air.

It can be hot as blazes—as it still is in mid-August in Paris—but there is something that teases the senses to tell you that cooler weather—roasted chestnut stands, mulled wine and falling leaves is on its way.

I was thinking that as I sat on the park bench in Parc Monceau with Geneviève. We were watching Haley and Robbie throw a ball on the lawn beside Robbie's favorite duck pond. I'd been taking him here since he was six months old, and it was deeply satisfying for me to know he had a favorite anything related to something I'd introduced to him.

I listened to his laughter and watched him run against the dark green background of the perfectly manicured grass. I found it impossible to believe that just two weeks ago the city had been in lockdown and both Geneviève and I had had our apartments full of our loved ones.

Now everyone had gone—most of them with terrible injuries, physical or emotional or both—and the city was going about its business as if nothing had happened.

I glanced at Geneviève as she folded up one of Robbie's bibs to tuck away in his stroller while he and Haley tossed a whiffle ball back and forth.

"I'm sorry about Bill and Noel," I said.

As soon as Bill was stable enough to be moved he had transferred back to the States where both he and Noel believed he would get better care. Or maybe that was just the excuse they felt they needed to go home. Noel had intimated to his mother that their plans to move to Paris were on hold.

Ever since she learned that her son would not after all be moving back to Paris, I'd been watching Geneviève closely to see how it was affecting her. But she seemed the same as ever, good-spirited and ready to go out with me and the baby at the drop of a hat.

"Are you okay with Noel staying in the US?" I asked.

"We French are philosophical. It is what it is. At least Noel and I are in touch again."

"Why don't you go over for Christmas?" I asked. On one of my visits to the hospital to see Bill, he and Noel were very hopeful that Geneviève might visit them over the holidays.

"It is a thought," she said, watching Robbie as he chased the ball along the rim of the pond.

She doesn't want to miss Christmas with Robbie, I realized. Because yes, she loves her son. But we're her family too.

Catherine had gone home with Cameron a week after the shooting.

As it turned out, Jean-Marc insisted on calling the police that same night. When his gun was found at the scene—he had me put it back inside the apartment while we waited for the police to show up—it was assumed that Abadi was connected to Jean-Marc's earlier assault. Jean-Marc told Bonnet that the gun had been taken from him along with the Taser.

In the end, Bonnet let Catherine go. He had no concrete evidence to link her to Todd's murder. Plus the Australian

Matthew Butterworth would say in deposition that he saw Todd and Abadi quarreling seconds before Todd was killed.

And while there may be a couple thousand Rashid Abadi's in the world, there was only one with *this* Abadi's fingerprints and dental work. He was quickly identified and connected to a murky underworld criminal web.

This left Bonnet with a dead body for a prime suspect, something—Jean-Marc pointed out—was just about the most ideal way for any detective to wrap up a murder case. No trial to worry about. Without apologizing for any overt insinuations, Bonnet had cleared Catherine of any wrong-doing and allowed her to return to the States with Todd's body.

I still found it hard to believe that my father had hired all these people with the single nutcase intention of creating a dynasty using Catherine as his broodmare. And while Todd's death underscored how mad my father was, I honestly wasn't sure if Todd's murder had been Abadi's idea or Moreau's. And I guess now I'll never know.

"I still find it hard to believe that your father could have attempted something so mad," Geneviève said.

"I know," I said as I watched Robbie now playing with Haley on a nearby swing. "He wanted a descendent of his own design, with his blood." I turned to her. "Did Catherine tell you that Rashid told her that my father had already selected her new husband?"

Geneviève shook her head. I wasn't surprised Catherine hadn't told her. After that night Catherine had not wanted to rehash any of the details of her ordeal.

"The irony is that Catherine and Todd had been trying to get pregnant for six years," I said as I watched Robbie swing. "She and Todd had essentially given up."

"What do you think would have happened when your father found out she may be infertile?"

"My guess is they'd move her to somebody's harem until she went mad or died of a drug overdose."

"*Mon Dieu*." Geneviève crossed herself and shook her head. "But he is dead now, your father, yes?"

"At least that's what the text said that I saw on Abadi's phone."

I didn't mention to her that the text also said *Kill the girl and return to Dubai*. Geneviève was doing fine processing everything that had happened—including the assault on her son-in-law— but some of the goriest bits just didn't need to be shared.

"Do you really believe he's dead?" she asked.

"It has crossed my mind that he might not be," I admitted, thinking back to the text message. It hadn't really specified that Moreau had *died* just that he'd had a massive heart attack. "I wouldn't put it past him to play dead," I said.

Although if he were alive why had the edict been given to *kill the girl*?

"For what possible reason?" Geneviève asked.

"Who knows? It's unpleasant trying to get inside the mind of a sociopath."

"Until proven otherwise, can we at least try to believe it's true?" Geneviève said.

I grinned at her. "Absolutely. It's over. Hallelujah."

Except I couldn't help but wonder *who* had sent the text to Rashid telling him of Moreau's death. Was there a network? Surely with Moreau dead there was nobody else who wanted Catherine?

"What are Catherine's plans now? I thought she might decide to stay in Paris."

"I think Paris has blotted its copybook with her. What with her father and now Todd dying violently here."

"Yes, I can see that."

"She has a big support group of friends back home. I think she'll be okay."

"She is free to take Robbie now," Geneviève pointed out.

"We talked about that. She has her hands full right now. And Robbie's happy here."

"And you are happy."

"I am."

"Speaking of that, what about Jean-Marc? It was wonderful seeing him again. Is he still getting married?"

Jean-Marc had gone back to Nice and to his fiancé. There had been a few moments—more than a few if I'm honest—that led me to believe that he'd forgiven me. But this had not been the time for me to focus on sizzling looks and uninterpreted gazes. And now that I was free once more to look at my life and imagine how a future with him might look, he'd gone back to Nice. And Adorlee.

"We didn't talk about it."

"But surely you talked of her? The other woman?"

I laughed.

"Nobody's married now, Geneviève. There is no *other woman*. He did talk of her a little. She's helped him a lot this last year and he's very grateful to her."

"Hardly a basis for a marriage."

"Men have married for dumber reasons."

She raised an eyebrow at me that spoke loudly without a single word uttered.

"The *point*," I said firmly, drawing a line under the end of this topic of conversation, "is that Jean-Marc is very close to her and I'm glad he has someone."

"I believe you, *chérie*," Geneviève said with a knowing smile. "Millions, I think, would not."

～

That night, like most nights where Robbie has spent the afternoon frolicking like a three-month-old Labrador puppy, he was falling asleep in his mac and cheese. Haley had plans for the night—and thank God for that. I was starting to worry she didn't have a life outside of us. Geneviève, also, was meeting friends for the evening.

As I went through the motions of cleaning the kitchen, then putting Robbie in his bath and his pj's, it occurred to me that this might be the first time since the lockdown that I'd been on my own. It was nice.

I was half tempted to go to bed as soon as Robbie fell asleep. But like most parents, I wasn't willing to give up the gift of an evening to myself, regardless of whether it meant I'd be exhausted and sleep-deprived the next day. As expected after his day in the park, Robbie was out halfway through *Goodnight Moon*. I kissed his sweet face, seeing as I always did my husband's features in it, and turned the light out.

Before Cam's visit, Robbie called me *Maman* but he'd lately switched to calling me Grammy like Cam does. I thought about it and decided the new name felt right to me.

I went back to the kitchen to spoon up my dinner—a premade ratatouille that I'd picked up at Monoprix with fresh pasta—and poured myself a glass of Cabernet Sauvignon. I drank it with a couple of ibuprofen as I had on and off since that night where I'd lunged for the dropped gun on the floor of the apartment after Catherine shot Abadi.

I was always amazed how long a minor injury could continue to plague me now that I'm in my sixties. There was a time I wouldn't even bruise.

I'd been so jacked up on adrenalin at the time that I barely remembered hurting my knee when I hit one of the table legs. It wasn't until several hours later that I realized I'd also strained a muscle in my thigh.

Izzy curled up next to me on the couch where I was eating my dinner in front of the TV. I felt positively luxuriant as I sat on the couch in preparation for enjoying my solo meal and glass of Cab when my eye fell on the Braves baseball cap on the hook by the foyer.

I stared at that cap, stunned that I hadn't seen it until just now. It was of course Todd's.

Because of everything that had gone on surrounding Catherine's return to the States, there had been very little said about Todd's death, especially around Cameron. I think Catherine's feeling was that she wanted to focus on her and Cameron's blessings and that there was plenty of time later for unpacking and dealing with the grief.

But it also meant that I never really got a chance to tell her how truly sorry I was for her loss. She knew I didn't like Todd, which was all the more reason why I should have made sure she knew I felt terrible about what had happened to him—and to her and Cameron as a family.

Just looking at his cap now gave me a punch of sadness. Sadness, and of course guilt. As I looked at that cap I couldn't help but wonder if I'd really given Todd a chance. Once I decided I disliked him did I ever try to reevaluate and try again?

Could I have liked him if I'd tried harder?

I looked at Izzy who was watching me with that worried expression she gets when she can tell I'm preoccupied with something.

A few steps forward, but so many steps backward.

I heard my phone signaling with a melodic ding that I'd received a text. I glanced at the clock in the kitchen as I got up to get my phone. It was not quite eight o'clock so the text was probably not from Catherine or Cameron back in the States.

I went and brought the phone back to the couch with me and took a long sip of the wine—a very good red that Jean-Marc had recommended to me—and saw that the text message was in fact from him.

<*just wondering how you are doing. Am on med leave for*

another month and thinking of coming back to Paris. Get together? A
gallery opening in Le Marais might be fun to hobble around?>

I grinned at his message and felt a very pleasant breathlessness. I didn't know what this meant as far as he and Adorlee were concerned, but I found myself daring to hope. I quickly texted him back.

<sounds great! How's the leg?>

I took a bite of my ratatouille and turned on my Netflix show but muted the sound.

<Pretty good. Have you heard from C?>

I loved that Jean-Marc asked about Catherine and that he knew the things that mattered most to me. I was just about to text him back when I got another text message from a number I didn't recognize. I switched to that number and read the message.

Shock slowly rippled through me as I re-read the text.

<Thank you for saving me the trouble of killing Abadi>

I stared at the screen and my mind struggled to make sense of what I was seeing. I read it again and again and began to slowly shake my head in denial as another text formed on the screen.

<Did you think we were finished, mon chère?>

To follow more of Claire's sleuthing and adventures, order *Murder Flambé, Book 7 of An American in Paris Mysteries!*

ABOUT THE AUTHOR

USA TODAY Bestselling Author Susan Kiernan-Lewis is the author of *The Maggie Newberry Mysteries,* the post-apocalyptic thriller series *The Irish End Games, The Mia Kazmaroff Mysteries, The Stranded in Provence Mysteries,* and *An American in Paris Mysteries.*

Visit www.susankiernanlewis.com or follow Author Susan Kiernan-Lewis on Facebook.

Printed in Great Britain
by Amazon

62500744R00180